INFLUENCED TO DEATH

LILY ROCK MYSTERY BOOK TWO

BONNIE HARDY

eBook ISBN: 978-1-954995-02-4

Paperback ISBN: 978-1-954995-03-1

1

I LONG TO HEAR YOU

"Come on, ladies, you're up next!" The scruffy-looking stage manager gave Sage a wink. Olivia held her autoharp in her arms, glancing out at the inattentive crowd. One man in the front row had his eyes closed.

Sage turned to her. "I don't know, Olivia. I mean, this may not be a good idea. We may get booed right off the stage."

"You mean right out of the tent?" Olivia teased her friend. "Don't worry. Most of the loud talkers will leave before we begin. A few will stay. Keep in mind that when we signed up and sent the festival committee our recording, they accepted us, so we must fit in here someplace. I have the feeling the crowd won't shut up long enough to hear us anyway. Just two girls with a fiddle and the world's least recognized folk instrument," Olivia held up her case with a grin, "the autoharp!"

Sage shrugged. "No one wants to hear that thing. Why didn't you learn to play guitar when you were a girl instead? Our only chance for survival is for you to start singing as soon as possible." The din of the crowd made it hard for Sage to continue talking.

The manager gestured with both hands. "Come on," he

hollered. "We have to get you on and off quick. The big band is right behind you."

As Olivia predicted, the audience had thinned out by the time she and Sage stood on the stage. Several people had their backs turned, talking to each other. Even as Olivia reached for a wooden stool to get ready for the set, no one sat down. Perched on the edge of the seat, she held the autoharp upright on her lap. She ran her fingers over the strings to check the tuning.

"Come on, sugar pie," the guy who had been previously asleep jeered from the front row. "What you gonna do with that old thing anyway? Give it to me, and I'll give it to my grandma." His friends laughed while the guy assessed Olivia more closely. "You are pretty cute. Maybe we could get together later?"

Olivia sighed, nestling the old Appalachian tricornered instrument further into her belly. She took a deep breath, appreciating the protection the instrument offered her. No one expected anything good to come from her or her autoharp, Olivia held it even closer. *Why didn't Mom make me practice the fiddle? At least people wouldn't prejudge my instrument as often.*

Even her old boyfriend had asked, "Why didn't you take up the guitar?" Don had grown tired of crowds jeering at Olivia, feeling they judged him too. *If only Don had supported me, I wouldn't have given up.* She'd put away her music in favor of Don and *his* feelings for the past eight years, pushing away how much she missed expressing herself creatively.

And then last year in Lily Rock, Sage changed all of that. She'd plucked an old autoharp from her wall when Olivia showed an interest. *I knew then my life would change for the better.*

The jeering stranger at the World Music Festival thought he was original? *Nothing I haven't heard before.*

Olivia closed her eyes, still aimlessly strumming the strings with her thumb and forefinger. Fitting perfectly into her arms, the instrument felt a part of her, smelling of new varnish and sentimentality.

Michael. He brought it back to life and sent it to me even though I left with no explanation that day in Lily Rock. Michael kept his promise. I don't suppose he knows how much that meant to me.

Olivia inhaled deeply, picturing Michael's dark blue-gray eyes the first time they met. He'd looked at her that way from the beginning. First her face, then the casual shift of his glance down her body and back again to her mouth. Her heart fluttered thinking of him even a year later.

She felt herself flush and then looked up at her audience. They had stopped talking. Most everyone sat facing the stage, some on chairs, most in the grass. They waited for the two women to begin.

"Olivia," hissed Sage. "Introduce the song!"

Standing to her full height just over five feet, Olivia fluffed the hair on the back of her neck with one hand. "Sure is hot in here," she commented into the microphone.

"Not as hot as you, baby," jeered the drunk man. "Wanna put that thing down and step over here to sit in my lap?"

"Oh, I don't think so, stranger." Olivia put on her flirty voice, the one she used when she performed on stage. "But I'll sing you a song instead."

With that promise, she nodded to Sage, who held her fiddle to her shoulder. Olivia bowed her head, listening to the vibrato and mournful notes from her partner's instrument.

Stepping back from the microphone, Olivia leaned against the stool, planting her feet so as not to slip. She began to strum a few chords to accompany Sage's melody. The words forming on her lips, she sang, the sound vibrating deep in her chest, "Oh Shenandoah . . ." Olivia drew out the last note.

"I long to hear you," she continued, "away, you rollin' river . . ." By the time she finished the entire first verse all eyes watched her from the silent audience. One man reached to grasp the hand of the woman next to him. Several couples moved closer together, their shoulders touching as Olivia continued to the second verse, now with Sage dropping back, accompanying.

Her pure, lilting voice filled the tent. Olivia's chest expanded as her voice soared. She closed her eyes remembering Michael and that first penetrating look he'd given her as she stood trembling in the road, having crashed her car on the way to Lily Rock. Then a person's cell phone accosted her ear.

Someone from the crowd hissed, "Shut that thing off. I'm trying to hear the angel's song."

Working with her memories of Michael, Olivia closed her eyes, sharing her intimate feelings with the audience in the words of the old folk melody. That was how she reached people in her songs: combining skill with emotion and sheer instinct.

"It's a gift," her mother told her when she was small. "Use it wisely."

Olivia held each note briefly before leaning into the next. With tears in her eyes she told the timeless story of the river called Shenandoah, about a man who longed to see the woman he'd lost. Michael's hand felt warm as he touched her arm that day. "Before you dart out, just let me have my say." *But I didn't let him have his say. I just ran away because he frightened me . . . his feelings frightened me.*

More people in the audience leaned forward, anticipating

each note. One woman held her hands over her heart. She sat next to a man who stared down at his lap, seemingly overcome by the old tune. He reached over to pat the knee of his companion as if he wanted to tell her something, something important. Something he'd kept hidden, which now needed to be revealed.

With a deep sigh, Olivia sang the last note. The moment she finished, in one motion she rose to her feet, shoving the stool away. At the same time the audience stood, clapping and shouting as she bowed. Sage stood next to Olivia, holding her fiddle next to her side. Both bowed together. The women turned in unison and exited the small stage, disappearing into the night sky.

When the clapping continued, Sage and Olivia returned. After three encores they waved for the final time and left.

"Wow, you two were much better than I ever thought you'd be," the stage manager confessed. "I mean, I really figured you'd be booed off the stage. And why am I admitting this exactly?" Shaking his head he mumbled, "You bring out the truth in me." He shook his head again and then turned to walk away.

Olivia smiled, dodging past the crowd with her autoharp tucked under her arm.

"Why does everybody end up confessing to you?" Sage laughed, taking Olivia's free hand. "Your singing makes people say the most outrageous things."

"I know," Olivia admitted. "But now we're done, and I have to drive to Playa for my job tomorrow morning. Do you want to stay with me, or are you heading up to Lily Rock this evening?"

Dropping Olivia's hand, Sage turned to face her. "Don't you think it's time for you to come back? You've been gone a year. Surely you've come to terms with Marla's murder. Plus you have to look in on your property, right?"

"I'm not ready to return to Lily Rock," Olivia told Sage firmly. "I may never get back there. I can manage the house from Playa. I have a solid renter who signed a two-year lease. And your mother would let me know if anything went wrong with the house, I'm sure."

Sage laughed. "You are right on that account. Meadow has her eye on everyone in Lily Rock. She'd be on the phone to you in a heartbeat if something looked amiss."

"I also know your mother doesn't want me to come back nearly as much as you do. She's pretty certain I bring trouble wherever I go—at least that's what happened the last time."

"You mean the only time, don't you? Two murders in two weeks. You didn't even give us a chance to return to normal." Sage gave Olivia a fake pout and then added, "You know Michael wants you to come back. And Mayor Maguire . . . he's still pining."

Unwilling to admit, even to Sage, that her feelings had only deepened for Michael, Olivia quickly said, "I do miss M&M. He gets me."

"I get you too. We're in a band, right?" Sage said.

"Oh, you so get me. I didn't mean to imply you don't." Olivia patted Sage's shoulder.

"Hey ladies, want a drink now that your set is finished?" The jeering guy from the front row stood in front of them. He no longer looked contemptuous. "I can carry the autoharp. If you want me to, that is."

"Oh, so you no longer want to hand it over to your granny?" Sage said, sarcasm dripping from her voice.

"Oh no, ma'am," he shook his head. "I would love to hear you two sisters sing again, though, maybe later tonight at my campfire?"

Olivia's gut clenched. This wasn't the first time someone had caught the similarity between Sage and Olivia. Their eyes were the same shade of blue-green, and their hair had a similar light brown color, though Olivia wore hers shorter. Usually, Sage or Olivia would brush off the sister comparisons, but on this particular occasion, Olivia felt reluctant to be the one.

Every time she said, "Oh, we're not sisters," she lied, and the lies were stacking up on each other like a pile of soggy pancakes. She'd avoided telling Sage the truth, the same way she'd run away from Michael. Even when the women reconnected in Playa six months later, there was never a right time to explain.

"Sage is not my sister," Olivia boldly lied to the man. "And we have to get back to our day jobs, but thanks for the offer, maybe another time."

The man walked away dejectedly, as Olivia strode past the crowd toward her small car. This time she did not stop when she heard her name called.

She'd already packed her tent and clothing, so now she and Sage could move forward in two different directions, one more music success under their belt.

On the way to their campsite, Sage greeted people while Olivia kept her eyes cast to the dirt pathway. Consumed with her own thoughts, she heard Sage yell from behind, "Olivia, your cell!"

Reaching into her back pocket, Olivia looked at her screen. Meadow McCloud. *Why didn't she ping her daughter instead?* Olivia tapped redial, and Meadow's voice filled her ear.

"Olivia, I'm glad you called me back. I have some difficult news."

Olivia froze in her spot, the toe of her boot digging into

the dirt. Since the sun had gone down, her cell phone was the only light to illuminate her stricken face. "What is it, Meadow?" She struggled to keep the panic from her voice. *What if something happened to Michael or M&M?*

"It's your house, dear," answered Meadow.

Olivia took in one quick breath. Frequent fires made all Lily Rock residents anxious. *Has the house burned down?* Olivia had hefty fire insurance. Michael had advised her to get a reliable policy as soon as she inherited the property.

"You will feel a lot more secure," he'd said, pushing a stray piece of hair from her face before quickly removing his hand.

Michael did not insist. She had to give him that.

"What's wrong with the house?" she asked Meadow, doing her best to sound calm.

"Oh my, I am so sorry to have to tell you this." Meadow's voice got slower, her words coming out one by one with a small pause in between.

I bet this is the voice she uses to tell children stories at the library, all soft and calm. Olivia's impatience got the better of her.

"Is the house on fire, Meadow?" she insisted. "Just tell me right out, okay?"

"Oh, no. Your house is not on fire. It's intact. I called about your renter. What was her name again?"

Olivia searched her brain. The renter paid on time, with an automatic deduction. Olivia arranged the lease over the phone in a hurry nearly a year ago, and so far she'd had no trouble. *What's her name again?*

"I think her name was Lana something. Let me think. I know! Her name is Lana de Carlos. Sorry, I forgot for a second. She pays with an automatic deposit."

"I understand a brief lapse in memory. In fact, I have an herb blend with Ginkgo—"

Olivia interrupted, "I'll talk to you about that later, Meadow. What happened to Lana?"

"Oh, right. Lana. That's why I called. Well, Olivia, it seems that one of our Lily Rock residents found her dead, right on the doorstep of your house, just a couple of hours ago."

Olivia squeezed the phone in her hand as her legs began to tremble. Another dead body at Marla's old house?

She felt Sage's arm around her shoulder. "What's the matter?" Glancing down at the screen, Sage asked, "What does my mother want?" She took the phone from Olivia's shaking hand, holding it to her cheek.

"Mom, it's me. What's going on?" Sage listened and then said, "Olivia looks like she's seen a ghost. Tell me what I should do."

By the time Sage clicked the phone off, Olivia had sat in the dirt, her knees pulled to her chest. "It's happened again. Another dead body. What is wrong with me? Am I attracting all of this death for some reason?"

Sage leaned over to sit in the dirt next to Olivia. "Of course not. You weren't even in town when it happened. Not like last time." Both young women huddled together for a few minutes, letting the news sink in.

Swallowing down her emotions, Olivia stood on wobbly legs and dusted off the seat of her pants. She considered her next words carefully. "Does this mean I have to return to Lily Rock?"

Sage nodded, her chin ducking into her chest to cover a small smile. "Yes, it does. You have to go back just to check on the house. You can stay with me and Meadow until things are settled."

"Just like last time?"

"Just like last time." Sage smiled openly. "Only I won't let

Mom drug your tea with her herb supplements like she did that first morning. I'll keep an eye on her for you."

Olivia felt a giggle begin in her throat. She stifled a grin. "I'm beginning to think that I have some kind of destiny with Lily Rock, no matter how hard I try to keep away."

2

UP THE HILL

It took some time to finish packing up the music cables and amplifiers. "I'll follow you to Lily Rock," Olivia called over her shoulder as she slid into the driver's seat of her old Ford.

Sage waited beside her truck, hollering, "Good idea. I've driven that road more times than I can count. Plus I don't want you falling over the edge like last time."

Olivia tried the ignition. With her cell phone on the passenger seat, she attached the seat belt, watching for Sage to back up from the other side of the parking lot. Then she put the car into reverse before shifting to drive to follow.

Good thing I had the car tuned up last week. I won't have to visit Brad this time. Arrive late, leave early. That's my motto.

After driving for over an hour, Olivia stifled a yawn. *How will I keep my Lily Rock arrival under the radar?* Her cell phone lit up. Sage's name appeared on the screen, so Olivia put it on speaker.

"How are you?" asked Sage.

Olivia chuckled. "As good as I can be with a dead tenant, on my way back to the place I swore I'd never return. And you?"

Olivia smiled. *I love our small talk.*

Sage interrupted her thoughts. "So here's the plan. It will take us six hours to get to Temecula, so we can stop for coffee along the way. When we get to Temecula, we can drive through town and get some refills. After that, we head up the hill. With a few stops and some smooth driving, we'll be in town for breakfast. I called Mom back and she said she'd have a meal for us when we arrive. I can taste her homemade toast with strawberry jam already."

"And you're sure she's not planning on dosing my tea with one of her concoctions like last time?"

"I already told her you were not interested in any of her most recent cures, especially without being fully informed."

"She is pretty peculiar, you have to admit."

"She adopted me, a premature infant only a week old. She went to a lot of trouble to take care of me properly. I can handle some peculiar in my most important family member."

Olivia took a deep breath. *I wish I could tell Sage that we had the same birth mother.*

"My situation feels really clear, but your mom died so young, it must have been hard for you," Sage continued.

Olivia looked into her rearview mirror. Headlights from a tailgater briefly blinded her vision. The car passed and then slid between Sage's truck and her car, barely missing the truck's back bumper.

"Wow, crazy driver," Sage commented. "Everyone is in such a hurry on this road."

Olivia's hands tightened on the steering wheel. What's the hurry? That's what she figured a year ago. *I don't have to tell Sage about Mona being her birth mom. I can keep that quiet. It's for Sage's sake. She's been through enough.*

Her grip tightened even more. *What a bunch of nonsense. I keep this to myself because I don't want any more attach-*

ments to Lily Rock. That's the full truth. A sister, a new relationship, and a small town do not fit into my plans.

"I'm going to speed up a bit when the road splits to two lanes. Follow me," Sage said.

After a couple of deft maneuvers, Olivia drove behind Sage's truck again. She tentatively braked to slow her car, creating plenty of space just in case Sage needed to stop suddenly. The silence grew between them over the cell phone. "Are you still there?" asked Olivia.

"I am. And I think I'd better tell you something. I didn't mention it before because it didn't seem relevant, but I actually knew your renter, or at least met her a few times."

"You did?"

"Since you made it clear you did not intend to return to Lily Rock, I didn't say anything. But I did meet Lana."

"So tell me more. What was Lana like?"

"She seemed okay at first. Michael introduced me when I ran into him at the Village Pie Shoppe right after she moved in." She sounded tentative when she said Michael's name.

Of course Michael would be the one to connect the two. Hadn't he done the same thing her first day in town? He'd used his easy charm and slow drawl to draw her into the Lily Rock community. It only took Michael a couple of days to become indispensable, at least in his opinion.

"You can talk about Michael. It's okay," Olivia told Sage. Actually, that was a lie. Every time his name came into the conversation, Olivia wondered who Michael was dating and what he was up to. *I don't want to care.* But the quick beat of her heart at the mention of his name said otherwise.

Sage continued. "I liked Lana a lot, at least at first. She got a job at the pie shop, but then things went really wrong."

"What do you mean?"

"She got sick, I mean *really* sick. Cancer."

"That's awful!" *None of the details of my renter's personal life showed up in an automatic deposit. Should I have gotten to know her beyond her eligibility to rent from me and pay on time?*

"It was terrible. For the first couple of months, we waited for her test results. After that, Lana documented all of her chemo and radiation online. She even had a cameraman follow her to every medical appointment."

"A cameraman?"

"That's the part I left out. Lana was an influencer on Instagram."

Olivia tapped her fingers on the steering wheel. "Can we stop for some coffee? My head is feeling muddled."

"I know an all-night diner coming up in two exits. Let's hang up, and we can talk more while we wait for our food."

* * *

Standing next to each other at the counter, Sage and Olivia checked their cell phones before continuing their conversation in person.

"Here's your coffee and cookies," a young woman said, shoving the half-filled to-go cup across the counter.

"Could I have a little more? I don't take cream," commented Olivia. She turned toward Sage while she waited.

"So Lana was an influencer. Did she have lots of followers?"

Adjusting the lid of the hot to-go coffee cup, Sage continued to speak. "Oh yeah, Lana had over a million people following her cancer journey online. Once they reached a million, they celebrated on social media with a cake and an enormous new wig. It was right after her surgery."

Sage sipped her coffee, wincing from the heat. "Lana had both breasts removed and rebuilt."

"And you know this because?"

"Like I said, everything she did was documented by her new boyfriend, who was also her cameraman, and posted on her account."

Olivia nodded toward the diner exit. "Let's get going and keep talking. I'll put you on speaker in the car."

"Do you want me to follow you from here?"

"I'm good at following you. Let's not break what's working."

Sage hoisted herself up into the cab of her truck. She held her coffee cup with one hand and slammed the driver's side door with the other.

"I have to stop for gas before we go much farther," Olivia told Sage through the open window of her truck.

"Me too. Wouldn't hurt anyway. We can pull over across the street."

Olivia walked the few steps to her Ford and got behind the steering wheel, then leaned over to settle the coffee cup into the holder. Glancing into her rearview mirror, she put the keys into the ignition, pleased that the engine rolled over on the first try.

Pulling out of the parking lot, Olivia noted the gas station Sage had mentioned, maneuvering her car into the center lane to make a left turn.

After they both filled up their tanks and paid, Sage pulled forward first onto the highway. Before following right behind, Olivia reached for her phone to access the recent caller list, pressing Sage's name.

"Hey, I'll be right behind you," she said, shifting out of park to follow Sage again. "Okay, so Lana had cancer and a boyfriend who was also her cameraman. Tell me more about him, the guy. Did Michael also introduce you to him?"

It was Sage's turn to sigh. "Not Michael. I met the soon-to-be cameraman on my own. Remember when you first left Lily Rock, how we didn't talk right away?"

"I remember we didn't reconnect for the first six months or so. I had a new temp job. It was after the holidays, around January some time?"

"That's right," Sage agreed. "After you left, I had some thinking to do. I mean, my world had been turned upside down. I thought Meadow was my bio mother. The whole adoption and the lying kind of threw me for a bit. It really shocked me when I learned my father was not dead as I'd always been told. My family house of cards collapsed all at once, you've got to admit."

Sage continued, "During that time I was dying for a distraction. Then a guy called me at work. He wanted to interview me for a local paper down the hill, you know, all about the Lily Rock Music Academy and our boarding students. Of course I said yes."

"Of course you did. How did he sound on the phone?"

"He sounded just my type, if you must know. Kind of a good listener, calm, insightful. Every time we talked, he'd sum up our conversation before he hung up."

"I have no idea what you're talking about."

"Oh, you know. I'd try to get off the phone, and he'd keep me on, and then an hour later he'd say, 'Sage, the way you run your school really intrigues me, the delight you take in your students, along with your rehearsals in town.'"

"Sounds like he really wanted to get to know you better," Olivia said, the sarcasm dripping from her voice.

"I know. I wanted to know him better too. By the time he

arrived to do the interview and photoshoot, we could hardly keep our hands off each other."

"And you dated for how long?"

"Only a couple of weeks, and then one day, my mom called."

"Ah, Meadow the meddling mama strikes again. Can't wait to hear." Sage's mom rarely approved of any of the people Sage dated. She kept her daughter to herself. *Is that for Sage's protection or to sustain the lies about her birth parents?*

"So Meadow calls me."

"Give me the setup. Were you at work?"

"No, I wasn't. I was in bed with Wilson."

"That's his name, Wilson?"

"Yep. Not Will either. He insisted that I call him Wilson. So Meadow starts jabbering about seeing Wilson at the movie theater in town, right as I'm curled up next to him.

"It seems Wilson had a woman with him at the movies. At first, Meadow didn't recognize her, but my mother, ever resourceful when gathering gossip, pretended to drop her cell phone to edge closer as she walked down the aisle. And then she recognized the woman as Lana. She wore a blond wig. An interesting detail that only Meadow would relate."

"Must have been post-chemo if Lana covered her head with a wig."

"Right."

"So, what did you do?"

"At first, I got out of bed to take a shower, just to think. I decided to give Wilson the benefit of the doubt. He may have taken her out to be nice, you know? Until I realized—"

"What movie were they watching?" interrupted Olivia.

"That's it, Olivia. How do you always do that, read my mind? They were watching *A Star Is Born* with Bradley Cooper and Lady Gaga."

Olivia and Sage sighed simultaneously. They both knew what that meant. "A date movie, right?"

"Right. So I broke up with him that day. I also stopped talking to Lana. She wasn't working as many hours at the Village Pie Shoppe, so that wasn't a big shunning or anything. Her chemo treatments kept her home most of the time after the diagnosis. I guess she didn't need the cash or was too sick to work."

"Am I to assume Wilson stayed in Lily Rock?"

"He didn't just stay, he moved into your house to be with Lana. The next time we ran into each other, he apologized for his behavior. You won't believe what he said."

"Try me."

Sage's voice dropped as she mumbled, "I am so sorry, Sage. I really like how we talked on the phone, hung out on your campus, got to know the people in Lily Rock. But I felt sorry for Lana and the cancer thing, so I offered to be her photographer through her journey."

"It's the list thing again."

"Right! He read a book on how to seduce women by listing points in the conversation and followed the suggestions one by one, checking each box as he went along. Compliment her job. Check. Compliment where she lives. Check. Compliment her friends. Done."

Sage continued, "Before I could lick my wounds, Wilson became the big savior in Lily Rock, helping out a woman with breast cancer."

Olivia paused, wondering what to tell Sage. She seemed over the Wilson guy. "Have you talked to Michael since you broke up with Wilson?"

"Back to Michael again?" Sage commented dryly. "For a guy you supposedly couldn't care less about, it's interesting how our conversations mostly turn back to him."

A blush made its way up Olivia's neck. Sage had caught her in the act. She thought she'd been more subtle, but apparently not. Instead of denying Sage's accusation, Olivia pretended she didn't hear by changing the subject back to her tenant. "Do you think Lana killed herself? I mean, maybe the treatment and the mastectomy got to be too much for her. Even a million followers can't be a substitute for good health."

Olivia waited for Sage to respond, navigating the road, which had narrowed to one lane as the sun came up over the distant mountain range. "Are you still there?" she asked Sage.

"I was thinking about what you said. Lana made such a big deal about her illness. She had new photos up every day, documenting her journey. Some of them were pretty risqué— just ask Meadow when we get home—but I don't think Lana was the type to kill herself. What she wanted was attention and she got lots of that from her followers and Lily Rock. I think Lana considered our little community her new home, unlike some people." Sage's sarcasm did not escape Olivia.

It was the word *home* that made her inhale deeply. *Lana's home, not mine. I wish it could be different. Playa is my home. I'm a beach person. I was raised there. My mom feels present to me so long as I stay in Playa.*

"I was just thinking about our mother," Olivia said, then her stomach dropped. Would Sage notice that she'd said "our" instead of "my"?

"Our what?" Sage asked as they turned the steep corner, driving steadily up the mountain. For a moment the phone reception dropped off. Olivia could no longer hear Sage's voice.

When her phone reconnected, she said, "I thought we might need some more gas before we go any farther."

"Oh, I thought you were saying something about Meadow. Sorry. You're probably right. Plus, I could use a bite to eat. Let's stop soon. We can clean up a bit in the restroom, get a breakfast burrito and more coffee, then get going."

* * *

After the twenty-minute stop, both women walked toward their vehicles. Olivia waited for Sage to back out before she followed. Taking a deep breath, she blinked her tired eyes several times. *The last part of the drive is the most treacherous. Stay focused, not like the last time when I spun out and nearly died.*

As they climbed in altitude, Olivia felt her ears pop. She noted the casino on the right-hand side, along with the change in vegetation. Fresh pine scent filled her car from the open window. *Just like the other time. That was when I first met Michael.*

"Are you okay?" he'd asked that day.

It took her months in Playa to finally admit that as soon as her eyes looked into his, she knew. Michael Bellemare was no ordinary man, and their meeting was not by chance. She'd felt their connection immediately. *I thought he was just like my ex, only he wasn't. I wanted to believe he was because if I admitted my feelings, I'd get attached again. I wasn't ready then.*

One more sharp turn and we'll be there. Olivia looked through the top of her windshield, squinting to block the early morning glare of the sun. The *Welcome to Lily Rock* sign, printed on a banner in bold letters, made her smile.

The village is quaint . . . a certain bygone charm. By the afternoon a lot of tourists would be licking ice cream cones, sauntering along the boardwalk. Then they could always shop for mugs and t-shirts to take home. *Good ol' Lily Rock.*

I wonder if the Old Rockers are still complaining about

"those tourist people" who eat at restaurants without tipping . . . Do they still resent the weekenders who spend hours in rented cabins?

"They clog up the streets with their fluffy dogs and children." That's what the town council president used to say.

Then another Old Rocker would add, "Those kids walk in the middle of the road as if they were spending the day in Adventureland with Mickey Mouse. They realize that real people live here, right?"

Olivia chuckled under her breath. *I do love Lily Rock . . . and even the Old Rocker complaints.*

Looking over to the left, Olivia passed the Lily Rock Brew Pub. *I wonder how Cayenne and Arlo are doing . . . Did Cay thrive after her last operation?*

Olivia swallowed to moisten her dry throat. Her thumb pressed the recent calls button and then Sage's name. "Sage?" she asked tentatively.

"What's up? We're almost to Mom's house."

"Just so you know . . . you're right about Michael. I do. Still have feelings for him." Olivia's voice trembled.

Sage spoke softly. "I was just teasing you. Don't worry. I'll be your wingwoman and keep you out of his path. You'll be in and out of Lily Rock in no time. Michael won't even know you've come home."

3

SO MANY LILIES

Stepping inside Meadow's house brought back instant memories for Olivia. *It's the smell of lavender. I wonder what kind of medicinal cure she's concocting right now.* The correct dose of a pinch of this and a pinch of that and everyone would be cured.

Or the incorrect dose.

Olivia tugged her carry-on behind her through the doorway.

"Welcome back to Lily Rock!" Meadow greeted Olivia, taking the suitcase handle from her grasp. Then she turned to hug Sage. "It's good to see you both safe and sound. I'm so relieved the road trip is over."

"Not a road trip," Olivia corrected her, lest she jump to the wrong conclusions. "It was one festival. That's all."

Pausing to run her hand over her forehead, Meadow put on a smile. "Sweet Four O'Clock, such a good name for your band. *Mirabilis longiflora*, native to the southwest, but we have some here in Lily Rock during the dry months. You can eat them, did you know?"

A feeling of dread came over Olivia. "I didn't know. You

aren't making them for breakfast, I hope?" She smiled, hoping to coax a laugh from the older woman.

"Would you like some soothing tea?" Meadow suggested, ignoring Olivia's attempt at humor. Meadow's face shifted as if contemplating what she'd brew in her tea.

I know that look. "I'd prefer water," she said quietly.

Sage intervened. "I told Olivia you would not be interfering and adding drops to her tea this time. You won't be doing that, right?"

Meadow flung her shoulders back as she gave her daughter an indignant glare. "Don't be silly. I learned my lesson the last time. I'm just concerned." Meadow put one hand on Sage's shoulder and the other on Olivia's. "You both look exhausted; you haven't slept in days. Driving from Northern California straight to Lily Rock may shock your immune system and bring on any number of symptoms. Now you both need hydration and rest. That is my prescription . . . I mean suggestion."

Olivia nodded. Meadow wasn't all wrong. When she wasn't dosing unsuspecting people with CBD oil and other substances, she would make an excellent wellness coach.

Sage merely shrugged, nodding toward the hallway. "After a hot shower, it would be wonderful to sleep for a few hours."

"That would be amazing," agreed Olivia.

Taking the hint, Meadow turned toward the kitchen. She came back with tumblers of clear water. "Here you go. Start the hydrating, and I'll pull the curtains in the front room so that no one knocks on the door to disturb your sleep. Now go along, you two."

I miss being mothered. The sensitive touches and support remind me of Mona. Olivia smiled. "Thank you. I appreciate the water and bed."

She locked eyes with Meadow, feeling a warmth over her heart. *Can I trust Meadow after the other time, when she gave me a sleeping potion without my knowing?*

Meadow smiled at Olivia. "You look so much like Sage at times I would think you were sisters," she said casually before turning to pull the living room curtains closed.

Olivia clamped her jaw tight. *Does she know about Sage and me?* It wouldn't be out of the question. How would she know without having access to Marla's DNA research account? *Now that Marla is gone, I'm the only one with the password.*

I'm just being paranoid. If Meadow knew, she'd say something.

Olivia shook her head to clear her thoughts as she followed Sage down the hallway. Dragging her suitcase along the carpet, she glanced into the guest bedroom where she had stayed before, then headed inside. "Does Mayor Maguire still live here?" she asked Sage.

Sage poked her head into the room, looking at the bed where the dog used to rest. "He's hanging out with Michael these days. Mom still takes him to all of the town council meetings. Sometimes he shows up at the pub, and I see him there. But otherwise, the mayor has become, for all intents and purposes, Michael's dog."

That's what he told me in the last letter, Olivia admitted to herself. Mayor Maguire used to travel from house to house picking his people as he went along. *I guess he's changed.*

Sighing with fatigue, Olivia lifted her suitcase to rest on the small table under the window. "I suppose that's to be expected. Is it wrong to say that I miss you and Mayor Maguire the most since I left Lily Rock?"

"I thought you missed Michael the most."

"I do miss him, but not the same as you two. Michael is something that could have happened but didn't."

Looking unconvinced, Sage's gaze lingered on Olivia. "You get a shower first. I'll start a load of laundry," Sage said.

Olivia hefted her bag to the bed, unzipping the flap. She pulled out underwear, sweats, and a T-shirt, the last clean clothing from a long week of festival camping. Placing them on the bed, she called through the open door, "Could I add some clothes to the wash?"

Meadow answered from the hallway. "Of course. I'll gather everything into this basket, and I'll add it to the load."

Meadow stood in the doorway as Olivia dug into her suitcase again, this time selecting her dirty clothes and shoving them into a pillowcase. She handed the bundle to Meadow, who dropped the contents into her basket. "Give me what you're wearing for the laundry. You can use a towel to get to the shower. Then I can wash everything you'll need."

Taking the towel from Meadow's hand, Olivia gently closed the door. She took off her clothing and bundled it together. Wrapping the towel around her thin frame, she held it closed with one hand to open the door. Meadow stood waiting. She took the rest of the dirty laundry from Olivia's hand, placing it on top of the filled pillowcase. "Is this it?" she asked.

"That's everything," Olivia admitted, clutching the towel closer. She watched Meadow disappear down the hall, past Sage's closed door, to the laundry room located behind the garage door.

After a hot shower, Olivia dressed in her wrinkled but clean clothes before she returned to her room, where she combed her hair in front of the mirror. Her once short style had lengthened past her chin, nearly reaching her shoulders. She ran her fingers through the wet curls.

Puffy eyes met her gaze. *I look like I feel. Tired and appre-*

hensive. I don't know what I need to do about a dead tenant or if I need to do anything. As soon as I figure this out, I'll slip out of town. But now some sleep.

With a turn, Olivia pulled down the comforter, sinking beneath the sheets. Her hand reached over to her side. *No M&M. I thought he'd know I was here and just show up. I am persona non grata in Lily Rock, even with the mayor.*

* * *

Olivia awakened to a quiet house. She rose immediately to stand next to the bed, reaching her arms to the ceiling in a stretch. *My muscles feel tight.* She rolled her neck from side to side. *I'd better get dressed.*

Reaching into the bottom of her suitcase, Olivia found a toothbrush and moisturizer. She walked down the hall toward the bathroom. After brushing her teeth, she applied the skin cream, making faces at herself in the mirror.

Her ritual complete, she glanced down the hallway; Sage's door remained closed. *I'll make myself a sandwich*, Olivia thought, padding over the wood floors toward the kitchen. Sure enough, a loaf of homemade bread stood on a well-used cutting board with a note: *Help yourself. I'm at the library. Call my cell if you need anything. XO, Mom.*

As Olivia munched her peanut butter toast, she looked around the familiar kitchen. The worn kitchen table stood in the center of the room. The walk-in pantry door on the other end of the kitchen had been closed. Olivia stood in front of the sink admiring the pine tree right outside the window. A squirrel looked at her briefly and then scurried away.

She opened a cupboard to the left. Sure enough, all the standard vials of herbs with the black labels still clearly marked with chalk filled the shelves. Apparently, the admonition from the local constabulary all those months ago had not put Meadow off from her unofficial passion for herbal remedies.

She sat back down at the table, dunking a diffuser filled with mint tea leaves into a mug filled with boiling water. Both of her hands encircled the mug. *The heat makes my fingers feel more limber.*

Late summer in Lily Rock. Really hot. I wonder when the cooler breezes will come. Maybe after Labor Day. Olivia took a long sip from her mint tea.

Crows squawked outside, calling to each other from the pine trees. She smiled. *You brazen birds. Are you friend or foe . . . I can't figure out if I love or hate you.* She heard two crows caw to each other. *You're kind of like nature's cleanup crew.* She looked at the top of the kitchen window from her chair as the bird perched on the topmost pine tree branch.

As she rinsed her cup by the sink, Olivia heard someone clear their throat from behind her. She turned to see Sage's sleepy face, her hand stretched out. "Is there any more of that?"

"You mean tea?"

Sage stared into Olivia's tea mug, her nose wrinkling. "Oh, heavens, no! I mean coffee. Where's the coffee?"

"I looked for some earlier but came up empty. How 'bout I brew you a nice mug of—" Olivia swung open Meadow's apothecary cupboard. "Anything you want."

"She ran out of coffee," mumbled Sage. "Meadow doesn't drink it, so she probably doesn't buy any when I'm not around. Funny though. I left her five pounds of Lily Rock special beans for my return. Did you check the freezer?"

"I did. Maybe she's been drinking your brew with a stranger?" suggested Olivia.

"Hopefully not!" groaned Sage. "I can't keep her out of trouble for one second. Where is she, by the way?"

Olivia shoved the handwritten note toward Sage.

"This may work out to our advantage. Since Meadow isn't here, we can head right over to your house to check things out."

Olivia's gut clenched. *Now I'm trapped and can't avoid the scene of the crime.* The sight of Marla's dead body from her first visit still haunted her dreams. And now there was another body on top of that.

"Don't you think the body has already been removed from the house?" she asked Sage.

"I suppose so. It's been at least twenty-four hours. Why don't we head over and check things out?" Sage looked unfazed by the prospect of approaching the scene of another death.

Yet the knot persisted in Olivia's stomach. *Maybe I'm not admitting what's really bothering me. Michael Bellemare might show up. Since he lives right behind my house. I wonder how much he knows about Lana's death or if they were friends.*

Even if Olivia didn't leave Michael the official job as caretaker, she knew he had a special interest in what the *Chicago Tribune* called his "architectural triumph." He'd designed and served as the head contractor for her house and the beautifully appointed cabin nestled into the grove of pine trees in the back.

"I'll get my shoes on," she mumbled to Sage, ducking her face to hide her anxiety.

Ten minutes later, Olivia and Sage made their way toward the gravel driveway outside Meadow's house. Sage climbed into the driver's seat while Olivia pulled herself into the passenger side. She glanced over to her small car parked a few feet away.

"It's good to drive together this time," she said to Sage.

Olivia clicked her seat belt as Sage backed up the truck, shifting gears to pull onto the highway toward Olivia's house.

Maybe now is the time to tell her, Olivia thought. *The longer I wait, the worse this feeling gets.* Reaching over, Olivia touched Sage's elbow. "Could we pull over for a minute? I want to tell you something before we go any farther."

With some surprise, Sage slowed down her truck, parking by the side of the road. She glanced over at Olivia, her eyes wide with expectation.

"It's about Marla's house and something I've been wanting to tell you for a while," Olivia explained. She took a deep breath. Before the next words came out, a loud thump came from outside the passenger door. Startled, Olivia ducked her head, the noise breaking her concentration.

Sage peered over her shoulder, a big smile on her face. "Looks like you have a visitor," Sage said, poking Olivia in the shoulder to get her to look up.

Olivia brought her eyes from her lap and turned to face the window. Two large brown paws and a black licorice nose pressed against the glass.

"Grrr," commented the dog.

Olivia rolled down her window. "Well, look who's here," she said, reaching out to scratch the neck of the furry beast.

Sage scooted out from behind the wheel to dart around the back of the truck. She opened the door behind the passenger seat for Mayor Maguire. "Get in, you big mutt," she ordered the dog.

Mayor Maguire instantly obliged. Sage slammed the door shut as he rubbed himself against the upholstered seat. His eyes darted forward as he leaned over to sniff Olivia's neck. His big pink tongue rolled out of his mouth, and Olivia felt the wetness on her cheek.

"Stop it, you crazy dog!" Olivia exclaimed, loving every minute of the tongue bath. She reached over and wrapped her arms around his furry neck. "I thought you were mad at me," she mumbled into his fur.

When Olivia pulled her arms back, she stared into M&M's bright eyes. "No grudges?" she asked to make sure.

In response, Mayor Maguire turned once, twice, then three times on the seat. He curled up in a ball, tucking his nose in between his paws.

Sage commented dryly, "I guess he holds no grudges. Very zen of the mayor, if I do say so myself. I'm not sure the rest of Lily Rock will feel the same when they find out you're back."

"I really don't care. As long as M&M and you are on my side, I can face anything, even another dead body."

Rethinking her initial intention of talking to Sage about her birth mother, Olivia changed her mind. "Drive on," she said in a happy voice.

I have a dead body to see right now. That's the priority—there will be a better time to tell Sage we share a mother.

The first thing Olivia noticed when they pulled onto the gravel road to her house were the mounds of flowers and candles along the driveway. She pointed at them. "What's up with the mess?"

Sage nodded. "People must have laid flowers as a memorial. I told you Lana had lots of followers. They must have found out where she lived and made pilgrimages to the house."

By the time Sage drove to the end of the long driveway, Olivia saw a group of people lingering near the entrance of the house. Some held bouquets of yellow lilies. Others held up candles in glass votives that sputtered in the late afternoon sun.

Tears threatened as the back of Olivia's throat constricted.

Mayor Maguire rose from his slumber to look out the window at the crowd. Swinging the truck around, Sage parked out of sight in the grove, under the pine trees off the gravel path. "Looks like the mourners are still here," Sage said.

Olivia looked back over her shoulder. "Are these people from Lily Rock?"

"Her followers are from all over. Lana had a million people, remember? They found her in Lily Rock and they made journeys to meet her personally. Some said Lana had healing powers, especially after she beat the cancer. All of those lilies?" Sage pointed to the heap of dead flowers near the front door. "The yellow lily was Lana's favorite flower, so everyone picked them from the meadow to bring to her."

"That's just crazy," Olivia replied. "So many people honoring a social media personality."

"Everyone nowadays is more than willing to open their heart to another faith healing, even if they tell you right up front they don't believe in God. At least that's what Mom tells me."

"Was Meadow also a follower of Lana's?"

"Oh, no! Now that's the odd part. Meadow hated Lana. Despised her. Did everything she could to open the eyes of the Old Rockers and get the town council to push her out."

"The Old Rockers still rule," Olivia agreed. "They don't like newcomers, that's for sure, especially if they bring changes."

Sage added, "The Old Rockers hate any kind of entrepreneur, especially the ones who open upscale restaurants and design fancy architectural buildings."

Olivia shook her head. "Old Rockers don't like the entrepreneurs, and they don't like the curiosity seekers either, especially ones who pick their town's flower, the yellow lily. That's a big no-no, even I remember that."

Before Sage could say more, Olivia focused carefully on the group of people assembled around her front door. In the back she noticed a tall thin woman who looked familiar. Her head of raven-black hair rose higher than the rest of the crowd, making her literally stand above.

"Is that Cayenne?" Olivia asked, pointing.

"Looks like her," agreed Sage.

"If I hide in the car, do you think you could get her attention? I'd love to talk to her."

"I can try." Sage opened the door and slipped from the front seat. Olivia watched as she sauntered toward the crowd, stepping next to the tall woman with the long dark hair. Words were exchanged. Sage got up on her tiptoes as the woman stooped down. Then Sage walked away, leaving the woman behind.

"What did Cayenne say?" asked Olivia.

"She said she'd see you later . . . maybe at the pub."

Olivia suspected that Sage held back some of Cayenne's actual words.

"Okay, I guess I deserve that," she admitted to Sage.

"I guess you do," agreed Sage before changing the subject. "Do you want to walk around back and look around?"

Olivia observed the police tape stretched around the side of her front entrance. "I don't think so. It looks like a crime scene has been established and the body has been removed. I don't want to interfere."

"That would be the first time ever," said a voice near the open back window. "Move over, Mayor, I have a few words to say to the one in the front seat."

Mayor Maguire sniffed Janis Jets and then curled up on the other side, leaving room for her to sit down.

"Hello, Janis," Olivia said, anticipating another shunning.

"That would be Officer Jets to you," snapped the woman, slamming the car door shut.

Olivia gulped. *Okay, so that's how it's gonna be.*

"Sage," commanded Officer Jets. "Drive this buggy downtown. I want to interview Olivia Greer about her tenant and the house. This is the second time we've found a dead body at her place and I want some answers."

Without argument, Sage backed the truck over the gravel and then reversed gears to drive down the road toward town. She glanced over to Olivia, who slumped with her head against the passenger door.

I really have no choice. It looks like the police can order me into the town of Lily Rock whether I want to go or not. If only I had one of those invisibility cloaks.

4

"ON THE ONE HAND . . ."

With Mayor Maguire leading the way, Olivia opened the door to the constabulary. The dog stepped in front of her, so she followed. Sage closed the door behind the three of them. Olivia stood in the center of the room looking around in amazement.

Where the old desk and computer once stood, double glass doors had been installed, separating the waiting area from the office interior behind the scenes.

This place feels more like a bank. "Where's the cash station?" Olivia asked sarcastically. "Do they still have cells behind those closing doors?"

When Sage did not answer, Olivia sniffed. The aroma of citrus and pine filled the room. She looked toward the reception desk and saw a diffuser spewing mist into the room. Okay, so not a bank but at least a spa. *Where's my fluffy white bathrobe?*

And boy, do I know who designed this new renovation. His stamp is everywhere . . . in the use of glass, how the place feels stark in furnishings but the textures, the wood planking on the floors, add warmth. Even that huge ficus in the corner looks like a tree from outside.

The glass walls and outside-to-inside design smacked of Michael Bellemare. Looking around one more time, Olivia commented aloud. "Pretty nice setup. Clean and functional."

The glass doors swooshed open, revealing Janis Jets, who had come around from the back entrance. Olivia pretended not to notice the police officer's grimace as she looked past Janis's shoulder to the interior beyond.

Janis observed Olivia looking the place over. She spoke first. "Yep, well, Mike did a good job, don't you think?"

Olivia nodded.

"On the one hand," Janis held up her square palm, "the old place was good enough."

Olivia smiled at Janis, waiting for the familiar next remark.

"But on the other hand, Mike needed a project. So he turned to me, and the town collected the funds, and here you go. A new jailhouse, all for the likes of Lily Rock!"

Mike needed a project. He and Janis were good friends, with the kind of friendship where they could lean on each other in a crisis. *That could have been Janis and me, if I'd not run away without saying goodbye.*

Janis stepped closer to the reception desk. Shuffling a few papers, she looked up. "Why don't you wait right here while I look in the back. It seems my receptionist has disappeared."

Janis doesn't trust me or she would have invited me to go with her. And why would she? I left without saying goodbye.

Olivia shrugged as Janis disappeared through the glass doors. *What a big mistake I've made returning to Lily Rock. People are still angry at me for leaving, and I don't want to feel the guilt. I did what I had to do to protect myself. That's all I can say.*

She glanced toward the doors again. *I wish I was still part of the team . . . like last time. It felt important, and I liked having people like Janis and Michael around. I'll get this over with as quickly as possible, get back into my house to make sure everything is okay, then I'll leave as smoothly as I arrived.*

When Janis returned to the room, she was accompanied by a young woman, probably early twenties, with straight dark hair swinging from a ponytail high on the back of her head. Thick eyelashes emphasized her violet-blue eyes, which she blinked several times. "My name is Antonia," she said, her voice edged with importance.

"Olivia Greer," she said, reaching for the young woman's hand.

Janis Jets interrupted with an official introduction. "Ms. Greer, this is my new assistant. She will be watching the front while we talk in the back. If you have any information you want to share with the constabulary, you should feel free to contact Antonia."

Don't call me. I'm not interested in reconnecting with you. Well okay, Janis, if that's how you want it.

"You may follow me," Jets insisted in her formal voice. The glass doors swished open at her command.

There must be a sensor somewhere near the desk. So Bellemare.

"I'm going to head to work, Olivia. See you later," Sage said.

Olivia nodded, then followed Janis, looking to the side where the cells had once been located. The steel bars no longer kept prisoners separated from the rest of the population. Each cell had glass doors and an ID pad for official entrance. Even the interior of the cells looked more like a doctor's waiting room with a wooden bench and some sporting magazines. A Bible had been tossed into the reading pile, along with a *Lily Rock Gazette.*

"Wow, state-of-the-art cells," Olivia commented under her breath.

"Nothing but the best for our Lily Rock residents," added Jets.

Olivia followed Janis farther down the hall, entering a larger room at the end. Where a kitchen once stood, now a conference area had been arranged with chairs surrounding an oak table. Beyond the table a stack of folding chairs was propped against the wall, providing more seating. On the side of the conference table four smaller rooms with doors ajar caught Olivia's attention. Each separate door had glass panels so that a person from the outside could look in. Those were probably the offices and interview rooms.

"Sit in room two," Janis suggested. "I'll get us some coffee. You still take yours black?"

"Black is perfect."

Minutes later, the two sat across from each other, a narrow pine table between them. Janis opened her laptop. "This feels familiar," she said, wiping a smudge off the screen.

Olivia caught a micro expression on Janis's face; a small lift of her eyebrows. *Do I detect a bit of emotional vulnerability in Officer Jets?* Her cheeks flushed.

Olivia hesitated. *I have hurt Janis Jets. I meant something to her and I hurt her.* Olivia gulped. *I knew we got along, but I never expected Janis to be so vulnerable.*

Willing herself to sit quietly, Olivia considered her options. *I can apologize. I can pretend nothing happened. I can push back. I can accept the shunning until Janis feels better.* Olivia chose the last option.

She smiled gently at the police officer, her defensiveness

giving way to a softer feeling in her chest. *I'm not going to get offended by your hostility; like it or not, I care about you too.*

When Olivia didn't speak, Janis shrugged and continued her questions.

"Did you know your tenant well?" asked Janis, her hands poised, ready to type Olivia's answer into her computer.

"I never met Lana. We made all the arrangements over email and phone. She sent her paperwork to my office down the hill. Since she paid on time, I had no reason to think there was anything unusual going on."

Janis nodded. She typed quick notes and then looked up. "Did you know about her roommate?"

Olivia didn't know what to tell Janis without divulging Sage's ill-fated dating experience with the man called Wilson. Sidestepping all the details she said, "According to Lana's rental agreement, she was supposed to let me know if anyone else moved in with her."

"Well, I guess she forgot that part. A guy named Wilson Jones moved in with Lana. He was a photographer."

Olivia thought for a moment. *Since Janis brought Wilson up first, I might as well tell her.* "Sage mentioned him to me."

"It's my understanding that Sage and Wilson were an item for a couple of months before he moved in with Lana." Janis chuckled and then added, "You could say I knew your tenants to their very core. Meadow and a couple of the other Old Rockers caught Lana and Wilson buck naked in the forest, taking all kinds of photos for her social media account."

"Naked? That must have really upset Meadow." Olivia grinned.

"Oh, yes, it did. No one is allowed to run naked in Lily Rock without Meadow's permission. She has the lease on primal activity, or at least she thinks so. On the one hand, I don't mind. Her surveillance keeps things quieter here, for the most part. On the other hand, Meadow is a big pain in my behind. She calls at least five times a day to complain about someone."

As if on cue, a woman's voice said, "Excuse me, Officer Jets?" Antonia poked her head in the door. "Meadow McCloud would like to have a word."

Olivia and Janis both grinned. "See what I mean?" commented Jets. "Tell her I'll call back later," she informed Antonia. "And you don't have to interrupt anymore, just text me on the cell."

When the door slid closed, Janis Jets leaned closer to Olivia. "Antonia is a little too nosy for my comfort. I didn't need an assistant really, but the town council insisted. Ever since a year ago . . ." Janis looked sharply into Olivia's face. "Ever since a year ago when things got so dicey."

"I know," sighed Olivia. "You were a one-woman police department the last time I was here. No wonder the council wanted you to have more paid help."

Twirling a pencil on the table, Janis appeared to be thinking. "I was mad at you, Olivia. I thought you'd stay a while and become part of our crazy little town. Instead, poof, you disappear like a plate of hot nachos and a craft beer on Friday night. We felt like dust beneath your feet."

Caught off guard, Olivia flushed but said nothing.

Janis immediately changed the subject. "Did you know the doc passed away?" she asked in a quieter voice.

Olivia's head jerked up. "No." Her mouth quivered. "I didn't know. Can't say I'm surprised. He was older, and the shock of everything that happened must have hit him hard."

Shifting in the chair, Olivia closed her eyes for a moment as Janis continued to type her notes. She opened her eyes when Janis asked, "So, will you look over your house now that the dead woman's body has been removed? I mean, you want to inspect everything and rent again, I assume."

Olivia hesitated before speaking. "I suppose that would be the responsible thing to do. I should look it over. Do some cleaning up and painting. Will I have to disclose the death to potential tenants?"

"I don't know about that; you'll have to ask a realtor. I heard Cayenne got her license just a couple of months ago. You can ask her, and she'll advise you. I must warn you, though. Cay isn't happy with how you left us."

"Oh, you don't have to tell me," Olivia said, remembering Cay's snub from earlier.

Closing her laptop, Janis Jets stood behind the table. "Your house is still taped off while we look for evidence. After we get all we need, I'll have Antonia give you a call. You can go in to look around at that point."

A feeling of dread came over Olivia. She took a deep breath. "No hurry," she told Janis.

"I thought you'd be in a big rush. Don't you want to get out of town before anyone else sees you?"

"I do," Olivia admitted. "But I'm staying with Sage and Meadow for another night so I can figure out my next step. I may just hire some people to clean and paint. I probably also need new photographs afterward for the website advertising, and then I'll return to Playa."

Janis Jets cocked her head to the side. "I'm not stupid, Olivia. You're afraid of that house, aren't you? Can't say that I blame you. Two dead bodies in one year. It's not your fault, you know. Things happen."

"I only wish I could believe that was true." Olivia stood abruptly, pushing her chair under the table. Time to change the subject.

She pointed to the light over the door. "Is this one of those interview rooms with the two-way mirror?" she asked with a forced laugh.

"Yep. Just like on TV."

"I kind of liked the old living room with a kitchen setup."

"I kind of did too, but as I said, Mike needed a project." And then Jets waved dismissively. "See you later, Olivia Greer. Take care."

The use of her first and last name felt familiar, like using a nickname. *Maybe she's not so angry*, Olivia hoped. Finding her way back down the hall, the doors swished open to reveal the waiting area.

Olivia stood in front of the door pulling out her cell to call Sage. She dreaded walking through town, but she'd left her car at Sage's house. Maybe she could get away from work and pick her up at the constabulary and give her a ride.

"I'm taking you to the pub for dinner," Sage announced as Olivia swung herself into the passenger side of the truck. "They don't need me in the office, and I need a beer even if you don't. I can't drink at home because of Meadow."

Olivia remembered that Meadow was one of the many people on the hill recovering from alcoholism. *I get it. I've been sober for nearly two years. Meadow must be more vulnerable. I don't mind when other people drink.*

"I can sit with you at the pub, but I don't want to see anyone I have to talk to."

"No worries," laughed Sage. "No one is speaking to you anyway. I'll get a seat so you can have your back to the bar, and you won't even see people giving you the finger as they pass by. All will be well."

Driving to the pub took a short five minutes. Nestled into

the pines, the recently constructed brewery had become the focal point for visitors and residents alike. As Sage and Olivia walked up the stairway to the outdoor seating area, Olivia's eyes lingered over the table close to the fireplace. No one sat in Doc's old place, where he'd held court every evening, greeting people as they paused to talk.

"You can sit over there," said a young man. He looked familiar.

Olivia grinned. "Hello, Brad. You working here now?"

Maybe Brad didn't hold a grudge like the rest, or perhaps he'd smoked enough weed not to care; either way, he wrapped his arms around Olivia for a hug. "Hey, Olivia. Good to see you." He hugged even harder, almost clinging to her for warmth. "Missed you."

Sage interrupted. "Okay, enough of the welcome home hugging. Let's grab a table before someone else does—away from the crowd, please." She looked at Brad to make sure he was paying attention. "In case you didn't notice, Olivia attracts attention, and we want some privacy."

Brad nodded, walking toward the back of the pub. A newly constructed stage

caught Olivia's attention. *Live performances?*

Next to the stage, one high-top table with two chairs stood unoccupied. "I can seat you out of sight over there," Brad said, gesturing.

Olivia's eyebrows raised. "Looks like you have a live music setup here since I left."

They walked toward the table as Brad explained. "Yep, we do. Friday, Saturday, and Sunday, we get small local bands to play." Brad looked from Olivia to Sage and back to Olivia. "Why don't I put you two on the schedule? Sweet Four O'Clock is the band name, right?"

"Wrong," said Olivia without considering his offer. "I

don't want to advertise my return. You may even be in danger of losing money if I show up. I'm not exactly everyone's favorite right now."

"Don't worry, Olivia. People will ignore you," Brad assured her. "They like Sage. They'll show up for her."

Ouch. She stared at Brad, who seemed unaware that he'd insulted her. He wore his innocence accessorized by the distinct smell of weed. *I can't blame him for speaking the truth.*

As Sage suggested, Olivia sat with her back to the bar. By the time Brad arrived with her seltzer and Sage's beer of the day, she felt calmer and more accepting of her circumstance.

"Here you go," offered Brad. He looked over his shoulder and then pulled over a chair to sit with them.

"So, the dead woman was your tenant," Brad commented, leaning in to polish the tabletop with his shirt sleeve.

"She was," admitted Olivia.

"Do you know what happened, I mean how she died?"

"I do not."

"I found her," Brad said in a hushed voice.

Olivia looked up with startled eyes. "I didn't know, and Brad, I'm so sorry. I remember how it felt, you know, to find Marla. It was awful; I still have dreams."

Brad's mouth drooped. "Lana and I weren't really good friends like you and Marla, but she was someone I knew pretty well. She had cancer, and she'd talk to me when I came by." Brad looked over his shoulder again as if he thought someone would be eavesdropping.

Olivia leaped to a conclusion. "You were her weed dealer?"

Brad nodded, affirming her suspicion. "I was. Delivered every Wednesday. She'd text, and I'd show up. When she didn't text at the usual time, I got worried. I went to the house and there she was. Poor old Lana. Sprawled out by the front door, her neck all red and her eyes wide open."

Olivia felt shock move through her body. Up until now, she'd not asked how Lana died. She didn't want to add to her already wakeful nights with any more images of dead people.

Instead of asking more specific questions about the body, Olivia said, "Did she smoke a lot?"

"She vaped and did edibles. I think it helped with her pain from the chemo and everything. I got lots of referrals from her. She'd talk about my company on her social media account and then folks would call me."

Sage interrupted. "So you were one of her sponsors?"

"I guess so." Brad looked back and forth at the two women. "She needed the weed, you know. She was in awful pain."

Olivia, Sage, and Brad sat in silence for a moment. Then Brad said, "I gotta get back to work. You can find me over there." He stood up, putting his chair back under the closest empty table.

By the time Brad returned to the bar, Sage had finished her drink. She reached into her pocket to pull out some money when her hand froze. "Don't look around," Sage warned Olivia. "But the last person you want to run into is sitting in Doc's old place."

Olivia felt her heart pound. "Michael?"

"In the flesh. Mayor Maguire is with him. It almost looks like the mutt is his date. He's sitting on a chair with his paws up, drooling on the table." Sage wrestled with the exact change for her beer, keeping her head ducked low.

Before Olivia could make a dash for the restroom, a man stood next to their table. He was tall with a lean face and a familiar smile. "Well hello, Olivia. To what do we owe your presence?" Before she could answer, a woman came up next to him. She didn't speak, but she stared at Olivia, dark eyes filled with resentment.

Olivia sat back in her chair.

Arlo and Cayenne continued to stare, but Cay's eyes were the ones drilling into Olivia's as if to say, *Why did you leave without saying goodbye?*

"Hi, Arlo. Hi, Cay. Good to see you both." Olivia smiled tentatively, then she turned her face away to inhale deeply. *Did Cayenne just search my soul in an instant, finding me empty and wanting inside?*

With eyes cast downward, Olivia felt a nudge under the table. She glanced to her lap, watching her napkin inch away, moving of its own accord. Olivia ducked her head to stare under the table. Mayor Maguire held the cloth in his mouth. His tongue slipped past his jowls as the napkin dropped onto the floor.

Olivia reached over to bury her fingers in the ruff behind his neck. Mayor Maguire licked her knee.

With her head under the table, Olivia made an instant decision. She put a smile on her face. "Found it," she said, holding the retrieved napkin in her hand over her head.

Cay, Arlo, and Sage shook their heads at the same time. "You were looking for your napkin?" Arlo asked in disbelief.

"The napkin and Mayor Maguire." Olivia grabbed the dog by the collar to lead him out from under the table.

"You and that dog." Cay's face softened.

Olivia looked from one to the next, her eyes stopping at Cayenne's. "I know I left without saying goodbye, and I am so sorry. It wasn't about you. It was all about me. I was scared."

Arlo's eyes held the same blank stare, but Cayenne's searched her face as if for more answers. "I don't know you well enough to assume why you left," she admitted.

Olivia sighed, reaching out to touch Cay's arm. "I know. I

feel our connection, but I was afraid you'd talk me out of leaving and I had to go."

Before Cay could say more, Arlo interrupted. "Have you been back to your house?"

"Not exactly, at least not inside," Olivia admitted, ducking her head.

"Still running away?" asked Cayenne quietly. Her black eyes now gleamed with a fierceness as she waited for Olivia to respond.

"Yes, still running away," Olivia admitted. "Seems to be what I do best."

Olivia rested her palm on the tabletop. She watched the sharp angles of Cayenne's face soften as the woman reached into her pocket and then slipped a business card underneath Olivia's hand.

Flipping it over, Olivia read Cay's cell phone and email.

"I got my real estate license since you were last here. If you need any help with the property, let me know."

"Thanks, Cay. I'll be in touch." Olivia's voice sounded unsure.

Cayenne nodded before taking a step backward. Arlo leaned over to pick up the utensils and plates from the table. As Cay made her way back to the bar, he added, "Your tenant was an odd one. She'd come here to eat during the week. As soon as the weekend hit, she just disappeared in the middle of the night.

"We thought she was going down the hill for medical appointments, but I found myself behind her one night driving kinda close, and she turned toward the hot springs. No hospitals there, just meth dealers and people living off the grid mostly." Arlo's face softened as he added, "There is that one famous spa with the palms and natural hot springs where she may have been headed."

"Interesting," Olivia said, unsure what to add.

As Arlo slid away, Olivia felt the back of her neck tingle. What was Lana up to? Running naked through Lily Rock for photoshoots. Using Brad as her dealer and then giving him referrals? And now she learned that Lana left the hill for weekends. Olivia found herself imitating Janis Jets.

On the one hand, if I go right back to Playa, I'll be free from this town. On the other hand, if I stay and help figure out what happened to Lana de Carlos, I can get ready for the new tenant. Then I could leave and not look back.

5

LOOK WHO THE DOG DRAGGED IN

After Cay and Arlo left, Sage leaned over the cleared table-top. "Want another drink?" asked Sage. "We could have another one while we figure out how to get out of here without being seen by you know who." Sage pointed her finger under her hand so that Olivia could see her pointing toward Michael.

"He's still there?" asked Olivia, not wanting to look over her shoulder. When she asked, she felt a shove at her knee. Reaching under the table she said, "Okay, M&M. One more head scratch and then I have to go."

"Stop moving around so much," hissed Sage. "You don't want to draw Michael's attention, do you?"

Olivia brought her hand back to her lap. "I'll be quiet, but M&M came in with Michael. Will he look for him and find me?"

"Would that be a problem?" Sage held a sly look in her eye as she pretended indifference to Olivia's answer.

Her heart skipped a beat. It would be good to get the first sighting over with. *I may be in town for longer than I thought, especially if he isn't holding any grudges. We could still be friends. We don't have to take it to the next level.* A flush crept up her neck.

"Why are you blushing? Thinking about Michael or the dog?" Sage grinned fully at Olivia, appearing to know the answer to her own question. "Oh, oh, wait a minute." Sage's voice dropped off as she looked furtively over Olivia's right shoulder. "Looks like Michael has human company."

"Who is it?" Olivia asked, willing her voice not to sound too interested.

"I'm not sure. A tall thin blond. I think she has extensions, nobody's hair looks that great naturally. Not sure I've seen her around Lily Rock before."

Olivia's mouth drew into a straight line. "Probably Michael's new girlfriend," she muttered.

"Could be. Do you want to stay and spy on them or slip out while he's ordering her a drink?"

Change of plans.

Before Sage finished her sentence, Olivia was on her feet, heading toward the red exit sign, which led to the restrooms and the back door. Sage followed. Mayor Maguire trotted close behind. Sage turned to the dog. "Shoo. Go away. Get back to Michael," she told the mayor.

He sat down on his haunches, stubbornly refusing to follow her directions.

"Are you trying to give us up? Get going," Sage hissed at Mayor Maguire.

The fluffy dog looked past Sage toward Olivia. With a sigh, M&M's head drooped.

"Michael," Sage reminded him.

The dog turned and headed toward the table by the fireplace.

"Where's M&M?" Olivia asked when Sage reached her by the exit.

"I sent him back to Michael. We don't need any confrontations right now." Sage glanced at her cell phone. "It's getting kind of late. I have a pony to exercise at the shelter, and Meadow wants to have a word with you before you leave."

Olivia shrugged. *I wish meeting Michael and his new girlfriend didn't bother me as much.*

Once out of the pub and into the truck, Olivia buckled her seat belt while Sage texted the Paws and Pines Animal Shelter. As she backed out of the parking space, Olivia looked out the passenger window. *I do miss everyone here in Lily Rock. If only I could figure out a way to live here and still not get too attached. If only . . .*

After they drove the short distance from the pub back to Sage's house, they found Meadow waiting for them on the porch. "I had a feeling you'd be arriving now," the woman said in her lilting voice. "Come on in, Olivia. I have someone I want you to meet. We can chat while Sage is exercising her horse."

Meadow and her intuition. Sage left the engine running as Olivia stepped out of the truck, slamming the door behind her.

"See you soon," Sage called through the open passenger window, driving back toward the main road.

Olivia walked toward the front porch, where Meadow had left the door open. Stepping lightly, she pushed against the door and then walked inside, closing the door behind her.

In the living room, her eyes found a visitor sitting on the overstuffed sofa, a middle-aged man with thinning gray hair. He rested his arms along the back, appearing comfortable. With one knee crossed over the other, Meadow's visitor looked the picture of respectability, even though he'd spread himself over cushions meant for three people, not just one.

Meadow is a magnet for iffy men. Now a manspreader who, if I'm right, drinks lots of morning coffee.

"Hello," Olivia greeted, seating herself in a single over-stuffed chair across the room.

Meadow stood between them to make formal introductions. "Olivia, this is Thomas Seeker. He moved to Lily Rock just after you left, and we've become . . ." Meadow blushed as she shoved her hands into the pockets of her denim jumper. "Well, we've become quite close."

Now Meadow turned to Thomas. "This is Olivia Greer, the woman I told you about who inherited that beautiful home across from yours."

Olivia felt her ears burn. *He lives close to my rental property. I wonder what he knows about my old tenant?*

Seeker's eyes darted back and forth in nervous anticipation.

Olivia repeated, "Hello."

Lifting his crossed knee back to rest against the other, Thomas smiled and nodded. "So you're the owner. I knew Lana, but I didn't realize that she was renting. She never mentioned it."

"You knew Lana," Olivia stated.

"I did. We shared the same . . ." Thomas looked to Meadow for approval. She responded immediately by adding, "Weed dealer."

Meadow sat down on the sofa, shoving Thomas Seeker's body to one side. She patted his knee. "Don't worry, sweetie. Olivia understands our proclivities here in Lily Rock. She knows we consider ourselves the weed and CBD capital of the West Coast."

Thomas nodded his approval and continued to speak in

his low-pitched voice. "I knew Lana because we shared the same weed dealer." Now he smiled at Meadow. "He'd drop off for both of us on his midweek route."

"You mean Brad," added Olivia.

"I see you've already heard," Thomas grumbled under his breath.

He's not gonna out-Lily Rock me. I own property here. What about you, buster? Have you invested financially in the town and helped solve not one but two murders? Look at me getting possessive about Lily Rock.

"You're the one who has lived here a year, so you must know how news travels in this small town," Olivia baited the man. *Take that, Thomas Seeker. I may not want to live in Lily Rock, but I know my town.*

To smooth the immediate friction between Olivia and Thomas, Meadow interceded. "Thomas does know. That's why I wanted you to meet him. You see . . ." Now Meadow looked to Thomas for encouragement. He nodded, and she continued, "Thomas is a naturalist, like John Muir."

Oh sure, just like Muir. A bit inflated even for Meadow. Olivia put on her amused face, wondering why the man triggered her so strongly.

"Thomas takes lots of photographs of the flora and fauna here in Lily Rock. He's also a bit of a preservationist. So kind and lovely of him, don't you think?"

As Meadow complimented her new boyfriend, Olivia registered disinterest. *What do I care about an old guy who takes photos of . . .*

"Did you happen to take any photos of Lana across the street?" she asked quietly, feeling a familiar tingle in her gut.

"I do have a few pictures—well, a few folders filled with pictures, probably five hundred photos of Lana total."

Thomas looked so proud of himself, as if photos of women were his specialty.

"Prints?"

"Some prints, some digital . . . there's a range."

Meadow rested her hand on his knee again. "We don't want you to get the wrong idea, but Thomas even has nude photos of Lana, along with her partner, of course."

Thomas patted Meadow's hand. "I took some photos for the Lily Rock town council. They didn't like the way Lana and her friend kept prancing around, attracting people to our beautiful mountain sanctuary with their influencer photographs of Lana's breasts."

"Specifically her breasts?" Olivia asked.

"She showed them to everyone." Meadow's forehead wrinkled. "Quite distressing. At first, the breasts were huge, you know, with implants, and then—"

"Well, I can just show her," interrupted Thomas. "I have a few snaps right here on my phone."

To Olivia's surprise, Thomas bumped into the edge of the coffee table in his eagerness to pull his cell phone out of his back pocket. He poked at his screen and then handed the phone to Olivia before sitting down.

Sure enough, there was a photo of Lana standing at the base of Lily Rock, her shirt lifted so that everyone could see her perfectly augmented breasts. They rose against her chest like two smaller lily rocks, prominent and fully formed.

Olivia glanced away. She felt embarrassed, not so much because Thomas showed her the photo, but because Lana needed to pose for the image. "Did she post these on her social media feed?" asked Olivia.

"She sure did. That photo is her 'before' the surgery image," replied Thomas. "She had a series of shots that she'd post in sequential order with a running commentary. Of course, none of them were my pictures. She didn't know I was documenting for the town council. Lana worked exclusively with her boyfriend when it came to her social media cancer journey."

Meadow took up the story. "This one was one of the first pictures, showing how she used to look. Then the ones that came after documented her therapy and surgery. Finally, she posted photos of her amputated breasts and the reconstruction with nipples. They were tattooed."

Olivia resisted the urge to put her fingers in her ears and make noises. Even "la la la" with her tongue on the roof of her mouth could not detract from the idea of tattooed nipples. So painful.

Olivia cringed. *I am such a prude.* She handed the phone back to Thomas.

Olivia sat down, folding her arms in front of her body. Thomas Seeker had the habit of some men; he kept staring at her chest. When no one else spoke, Olivia asked, "So why are you showing me these photos anyway?"

Meadow smoothly explained. "I was afraid that Janis Jets would find out about Thomas and his collection and maybe think he had something to do with Lana's death."

To Meadow's credit, she did not put quotes around the word collection. Still, Olivia could tell that Meadow was slightly uncomfortable about her boyfriend's prominent peeping Tom pursuits. *Naturalist, my sweet bippy. John Muir is probably rolling in his grave, that old Scottish Presbyterian.*

Meadow continued, "So I was hoping you would put a good word in for Thomas to Janis Jets, since you two are such good friends and all." Meadow turned to Thomas. "Janis and Olivia solved Marla Osbourne's murder."

Olivia sighed. "Janis and I aren't good friends, and by the

way, I am out of the detective business. These photos must be given to Janis as soon as possible so that she can pursue leads."

Thomas shuffled his feet. "The problem is, Meadow paid me for more photos, even after the town council had enough. She was very upset about Lana and the people who followed her around here in Lily Rock. She thought Lana brought the wrong element to the town, so she kind of wanted me to catch Lana doing something illegal so that she could be arrested."

"Are you a private detective?" inquired Olivia.

"Oh, no. I'm not one of those. I took Meadow's money, but I only did it as an excuse to get to know her better. I planned to give it back."

"But we're afraid that Janis won't believe Thomas," Meadow added. "And that she might think we're both suspects in Lana's death. Now we can't have that, can we? So improper and not true!" Tears formed in Meadow's eyes.

"So we were thinking," said Thomas, glancing at Meadow. "When you get into your house, could you do a little investigating and find my photos and just hide the ones I took? Just to keep me out of the police's investigation. I'm innocent." Seeker looked so sad, as if he really believed he could manipulate Olivia into tampering with evidence to help him out.

"How did Lana get hold of your photos? I thought she hired Wilson as her photographer, not you."

Thomas's leg began to bounce. He wiped a hand across his forehead. "I gave her examples of my work, hoping she'd hire me so that I could observe her more closely. I want those photos back."

Bingo. Thomas Seeker may be my first suspect. He had motive and he's got a certain vibe. No wonder I felt triggered.

Olivia calmly folded her hands in her lap. *Don't want him to think I suspect anything.* "I think the police have already come and gone. They probably picked up the entire stash of photos, yours included. I may not get into the house this trip . . ." Olivia's voice trailed off as if seriously considering the possibility.

"Without looking at your house?" Meadow's eyes grew wide with surprise. "It *is* your house, and you must want to check it out before you go."

Memories of Marla pushed aside, Olivia felt her interest in who killed Lana assert itself. So unfair. A woman dead who recovered from cancer. *I have to help get to the bottom of this.*

"Like I was saying, I'm on my way down the hill. I'll stop in town to put in a good word for Thomas with Janis Jets. That's the best I can do for now. I hope it helps. But the police have not released the crime scene yet, not even for me, the owner."

After two brief hugs and a quick goodbye, Olivia left and swung her suitcase into the trunk of her car. *One more trip to the constabulary,* she thought to herself. *Then I'll get going. Janis needs to know about Thomas Seeker, assuming she hasn't figured it out already.*

With a deep breath, Olivia sat behind the wheel, putting her key into the ignition. After backing out she glanced ahead, keeping her eye out for oncoming traffic before pulling into the lane of the main road.

If Mayor Maguire were with me, he'd hang his head out the open window to greet the squirrel scurrying across the road. M&M is such good company, almost like a companion and protector.

As Olivia approached the town, she found an empty parking space in front of the constabulary. Taking her key out of the ignition, she slipped out of the seat. With a click she locked the closed car door, moving around the front to the boardwalk. No one sat on the bench outside the constabulary, so Olivia quickly turned the handle to step inside, leaving one hand on the open door behind her.

Standing in the reception area, she looked around the room for Antonia. Before she could reach for her cell phone to text Janis, Olivia heard a familiar voice from outside.

"Well, if it isn't Olivia Greer. Back in Lily Rock."

Michael Bellemare stood near her in the doorway, sending an involuntary shiver down her spine.

Olivia stepped away, turning to face him. He smiled, that lazy kind of grin he reserved for friends. Shoving the door closed with his foot, his eyes did not leave her face.

"Oh," she said. "How are you, Michael?" Olivia didn't need to ask. She could see for herself that Michael was just fine. He was still six feet tall and his strong shoulders still filled out a soft flannel shirt. *He's got more gray hair. Looks good on him.*

Michael broke the silence. "I thought I saw you last night at the pub. But then I said to myself, 'Surely Olivia Greer would let me know if she were coming to Lily Rock.' But I see now I was wrong. Checking in with Janis about your tenant?" he asked, his eyes daring her for an explanation.

He's not gonna let me off the hook that easy. His eyes say one thing but his words, another thing entirely. She felt the wariness creep over her. *I'm so tired of being on the defense all the time.*

The glass doors swept open and Janis Jets appeared. She held her laptop in one arm and a look of surprise on her face. "Well, well, well. Two times in two days. To what do I owe the pleasure?"

Olivia looked down at the tiled floor and then back up at Janis. *These two don't need me. Should I just leave?*

Her glance shifted back to Michael. The telltale clench of

his jaw told his real feelings. *Will he call me out in front of Janis?*

As Olivia assessed Michael's expressions, Janis watched. Michael glanced casually toward the desk and then back to Olivia. *He doesn't seem to mind my scrutiny. In fact, I think he likes it.* Her heart fluttered rapidly in her chest. *I better say something. He's enjoying his own anger way too much.*

"I planned to make a quick turnaround and head back to Playa," she told them. *Sound more confident.* "As soon as possible," she added.

Michael was the first to look puzzled. "Of course. Why would you stay?"

"Of course Officer Jets doesn't need me. But Lana was my tenant, I rented to her, and I feel responsible. Plus what about the cleanup before the next renter? I have to advertise and interview."

"Your house? That's the only reason you're here?" Michael's low voice challenged her.

Jets stepped in between Michael and Olivia. "On the one hand, you'll most likely just get in the way of my investigation, but on the other hand, you have information about Lana that would take me days to figure out even with the internet."

Olivia ignored Michael, who glowered at Jets.

"I have some information for you already," Olivia said hastily.

"Good, you can explain on the way over to your house. I want you to look inside. Lana left some of her stuff, but I'm not exactly sure what was hers and what was yours."

"Lana was a pretty good egg," Michael offered.

"Did you know Lana well?" inquired Olivia. *Don't be too nosy. He might think I care.*

"She kept to herself. Even though I lived so close, I just met her the once."

Janis pivoted to face Michael, drilling him with her own question. "Did you ever help her with the security system at the big house? I thought you had access to all the codes from when Marla lived there."

"I did have access. I planned to hand over codes and keys before Olivia left town. We all know how that turned out."

"That's why you wanted to talk to me?" Olivia couldn't keep the surprise from her voice.

"What else did you think I wanted to talk about?"

Oh really? I've played that scene from a year ago over and over in my head. I thought he implied that he wanted to talk about his feelings and our relationship, and now he covers up his original intent with an excuse about the security codes.

Maybe I imagined Michael's feelings for me. That may have happened. I'd just survived a car accident and a head wound. Maybe I misinterpreted his intentions.

Olivia glanced into Michael's eyes; his expression had relaxed into a pleasant grin, his eyes turning gray-blue, like a deep lake. *He's inscrutable.* Instead of arguing with him, she smiled back.

"I apologize for not stopping that time. I was in a hurry to get back to my new job. Why didn't you just send me the codes?"

Michael shoved his hands into his pockets. He stood rocking back and forth on his worn cowboy boots. *Gotcha there, buddy. Lie some more or admit the truth. You were into me, at least then.*

Michael shrugged. "I didn't want to send you the codes. You never know how secure the internet can be with that kind of information."

I guess that might be true, how disappointing.

"Why don't we all pile into my truck and go see your house?"

Janis reached for her jacket, which hung on the chair by the desk. "I feel like you two are having a private conversation that I'm not privy to. Just so you know, we have a murder to solve. So let's get moving." She pointed to Olivia. "I don't want Olivia going through the house by herself. She may disrupt the crime scene. I'll lock up. Antonia isn't coming in until later."

"Don't worry." Michael grinned. "Olivia won't disrupt the house. She's very tidy. She will upset your entire life without a care though. She does this just by being Olivia." He held the door as the two women exited the constabulary, then pointed to where he'd parked.

Olivia felt his words in her body as her neck tingled, her cheeks turning red. *He sees me so clearly.*

He held the passenger-side door while Janis jumped in.

"I can get my own door," Olivia told him, ducking her head to hide her reactions to his words.

"Nothing has changed in that regard," Michael commented, walking to the driver's side.

To her surprise, Olivia was not alone in the back seat. The slap of a wagging dog tail greeted her. Mayor Maguire stood up, poking his head on the far side to watch Michael lurch into his seat.

"Hello, M&M. Have you been here all along?" Olivia asked.

The dog turned to face her, his tongue darting from his mouth. He sniffed her face and then gave her a quick lick.

Olivia slid next to him as his tail swept her face. He hung his head outside the open window. She patted his haunch while Michael reversed out of the parking space.

So how did this happen? I didn't plan on seeing Janis or Michael on my visit here. Still, somehow we're all together in this truck heading toward a new investigation. Are we a team again, uncovering bad guys with our noble dog at our side?

She tapped Mayor Maguire on the haunch. He pulled his head away from the window to look at her. When she scratched behind his ears, he finally sat down on the seat.

Are you psychic or my guardian angel? Olivia wondered, leaning over to hug the dog.

6

THE DARK ROOM

When they reached Olivia's house, Michael parked the truck in the shade under the pine trees. Janis was out of the truck before the engine stopped. Olivia followed her, urging Mayor Maguire to come along. "I'll get the mail and meet you in front," she shouted.

Michael had already found his way to the front door while Olivia reached into the mailbox, tugging on the contents. Piles of magazines and a few letters tumbled into her arms.

"Hurry up," commanded Janis Jets, shifting from one foot to the next.

Holding the stack of mail against her chest, Olivia made her way down the driveway. She nodded to Janis, swallowing down her anxiety. *I don't want her to know how nervous I am.*

When she took a quick look at Michael, she caught him staring at her. She felt her cheeks blush. *I wonder if he remembers the time we both stood on this doorstep. I told him that he couldn't spend the night. He took the news with good humor.* "Just so long as you're safe," he'd said at the time.

She let her gaze drop.

Janis removed the police tape from the front door as Michael and Olivia stood back to watch. After she balled up the tape, she flung it to the side near the dead flowers, which had most likely been left by Lana's followers.

Reaching into her pocket, Janis removed a key, holding it up to Olivia. "I suppose you ought to unlock it, since you're the owner of the property. I got this key from the dead body."

Olivia held the key in her hand as Janis added, "I suppose he also has a house key?" She looked toward Michael.

"I never used them!" protested Michael, casting a quick glance at Olivia. "Not once after you left did I go into your house. I just held them for emergencies, you know, in case of fire."

Like the animal shelter last year.

He kept the keys to be helpful. So he's not like Don.

"I'm taking the car keys," Don would say.

"But I need them today," she would protest.

"You don't have anything you need to do. Just stay home and clean the house. I'll be back later."

"But you don't always come back," she would object to his back as he walked away.

Pushing the memory aside, Olivia placed the stack of mail behind a planter next to the front door. With a deep breath, she said, "Here goes," trying the lock. The door opened easily, revealing the house much as she remembered. *Welcome home* said the beautiful wood flooring and expansive high ceiling with the exposed timber beams.

Olivia looked toward the doorway for the numbered keypad.

"Remember, I told you," commented Michael, "I turned off the alarm after you left Lily Rock. Did Lana activate it when she moved in?"

"I never heard from the company, so I suspect she didn't," admitted Olivia.

Lana must have felt safe in her home if she didn't use the alarm. *I wonder if more surveillance could have prevented her death? My fault.*

From the center of the great room, the rest of the house looked much the same as when she'd last seen it. The floor-to-ceiling glass windows left the impression of merging the inner space with the forest beyond.

"I forgot how beautiful this looks. It's hard to tell where the inside ends and the outside begins."

Michael grinned. "I think the architect had that in mind." He smiled shyly at her, clearly pleased that she noticed his signature statement.

On the other side of the wall of windows, the redwood deck extended into the forest, supported by steel and wood. Instead of cutting down the pine trees, the deck had been designed to work around the tree trunks, leaving spaces large enough for the trees to age and expand.

The wall of windows and the expanse of deck opened to an observation point at the farthest distance, specifically constructed out of redwood. Two chairs with a small table in between invited one or two people to sit and appreciate a view of the town's namesake: Lily Rock.

"I don't suppose we can spend time outside," Olivia sighed.

"Do you think this is a vacation?" snapped Janis. "Stay here and let's figure out our next move."

Reluctant to begin a search, Olivia looked over the great room seating area. The stone fireplace stood empty, all of the ashes removed. Even the side bin stood empty. No wood neatly stacked.

Michael used to keep the wood ready for a fire. He did that for Marla and he did it for me too. A fire was so easy to start on an early morning or a cool evening when the sun made its descent behind the forest of trees. *I guess my tenant wasn't a cozy evening and morning fire kind of person.*

"Looks pretty much the same here, if I'm not mistaken," commented Janis, still glancing around the room.

"It's the same," Michael and Olivia said in unison. Olivia smirked as Michael looked to the ceiling to cover his embarrassment.

Olivia inhaled deeply. *This isn't as bad as I thought it would be. I feel like I'm home, not like I'm intruding.*

"Maybe Lana spent a lot of time in bed," Olivia suggested. "I bet she left her personal belongings there. Have the cops already taken fingerprints from the large suite?"

"We have not," Janis said definitively. "We did not have a warrant or permission to do so. Getting a warrant takes forever on the hill, as you might remember from last time."

"I thought you could easily email and ask for a warrant."

"It doesn't work that way," Janis said. "We have to wait quite a while for most requests in Lily Rock. We aren't, as you might think, a priority in San Bernardino or Los Angeles counties. So let's take a look, shall we?" Janis walked toward the door to the large suite. "But don't touch anything until we get that court order." She tried the handle, shaking it a few times to try again. "I can't get in here."

"Let me give it a try," offered Michael. Janis moved aside to give him room. After twisting the knob himself, he ran his hand over the heavy wood door and then stopped to inspect the hinges. Reaching into his back pocket, he pulled out a Swiss Army knife. One pointy blade met his approval. He gingerly slid it into the small hole in the handle. "I may be able to get the lock to release with this," he told the women.

Olivia heard the pop of the lock.

Taking a cautious approach, Michael said, "Let me have a look at these hinges before you go in there. It feels like this door has taken some hard use in the past year." With outstretched fingers he touched each hinge.

"Come on, Bellemare," Jets said dryly. "We don't have all day to admire your door. Just push it aside and let us in. You can fix the doodads later."

"I can come over tomorrow and repair the door," Michael offered. He smiled at Olivia. "If it's okay with the landlord, that is."

Olivia felt her cheeks burn. *Is he deliberately slowing down the process to give me more time? He must know that entering a bedroom once occupied by my friend Marla may be hard for me.*

Jets stepped into the room first.

Michael swept his arm in front of his body. "After you."

Olivia inhaled as she followed Janis, instantly aware of a thick familiar smell. *A mix of patchouli and marijuana.* She waved her hand in front of her face to push away the heavy odor.

"I smell it too," said Michael.

Jets's mouth hung open. "What have we got here?" she asked, her face registering shock. She pointed to the far corner of the room.

"Looks like an entire film studio," Michael said, disbelief in his voice.

He walked across the expansive room to inspect a series of cameras on tripods set to various heights. Ring lights and soft boxes were sprinkled around generously. Cords circled the flooring, causing Olivia to lift her feet to keep from tripping. "This is no amateur operation. Lots of money in the equipment."

The cameras pointed to a large king-sized bed with an

array of pillows and comforters. Olivia shuddered. An indentation of a human body remained on the comforter. A large area rug kept the bed anchored in place.

A nightstand had been shoved next to one side of the bed where a person could easily reach for one of the several bottles of medicine. A filmy glass, half-filled with water, stood nearby. Michael cleared his throat. "Looks like Lana slept on that side so she could get to her pills late at night."

"Here's another camera," said Jets, pointing a few feet away to another bed. The second area held a standard-variety hospital bed. The mattress, adjusted to a flat position, displayed sheets and a white coverlet carefully tucked. The planked floor looked scuffed.

The stark contrast between the large bed with the luxurious bedding and the sterile bed with the hospital-style setting drew a sharp intake of breath from Olivia. She turned her head and noticed a functional chair placed next to the hospital bed. *Just like a hospital, a place for a visitor to sit.*

Curious about the different scenes, Olivia turned to look at the opposite side of the bedroom. Yet another area had been arranged, this one staged to look like a living space. A large rug designed in a swirling pattern of gray and white delineated the space even further.

Olivia pointed to a large recliner dominating the camera-ready living space. "That looks like one of those expensive recovery chairs they advertise for post-surgery patients. I wanted to get one for my mom when she was sick, but we couldn't afford it."

Jets nodded.

Stepping up to the chair, Olivia noted the assortment of cushions that must have been used to support Lana and relieve her discomfort after the mastectomy. She noted the small occasional chair, which faced a loveseat-sized sofa. A quilt hung over the back with embroidery saying "You got this, Lana."

Looking to the center of the room, Olivia observed an antique wardrobe. Next to the wardrobe was a full-length mirror with scarves flung over the top, reminding her of a stage dressing room in an old play she'd seen in high school. Both the mirror and the wardrobe served to partition the two bed scenes.

Olivia opened the wardrobe door slowly. Inside, an array of T-shirts with cancer slogans caught her attention. One shirt had been hung on the inside of the wardrobe. "Cancer is my bitch!" Olivia read. She quickly closed the door.

"If I may offer an observation," Michael said. "This entire room has been arranged to look like a movie set. You have the living area over here, the bedroom, the dressing room, and then a hospital setting."

Michael continued, "With all of these cameras, we can conclude that Lana did most of her filming work from here. The cameraman could fluidly move from each of the settings, depending on the day and her story."

"So then Lana pretended to be in the hospital when they filmed her medical journey?" asked Olivia.

"It might have been more convenient that way," commented Jets.

Michael added, "Hospitals rarely give permission to film, due to the privacy of all of their patients."

Michael turned around to look at the paneled wall behind him. "Remember the hidden closet?" he said to Olivia with a slight grin. "Another one of my signature touches," he added, his eyebrows raised. "I wonder if they used it too."

As the architectural designer and builder, Michael had created a hidden closet for the large suite, which Marla used to dress and to get away from the builders who frequently worked on her home. By the time construction drew to a close, Marla spent much of her down time in the uniquely designed hidden space. She would nap and read and shut out the world.

Michael ran his hand across the paneling. Resting on the exact right spot, he pushed against the wood as the door slid open with ease. "There we go," he said, his eyes filled with satisfaction. "Sure do know how to make a great private closet, if I say so myself."

Michael walked in first, with Olivia following. "Why is it so dark in here?" She reached out her hand, touching the back of Michael's shirt. He turned and held it for a moment before letting it go.

"I think they blocked the window for some reason. Stay put and I'll figure this out." After a few seconds, he said, "Here's the reason," and pointed toward the wall in front of them. "The window's been covered with butcher paper."

With one sweep of his arm, his fingers clutched the paper and tore it away. The sun had gone down, but a sensor light from outside the house blinked on, providing enough illumination for Olivia to see Michael as he found the light switch on the far side of the room.

Once the room was illuminated, she gasped. "I don't remember any of this."

"You're right. This is not how Marla left the space. It used to have a seating area, a small refrigerator, and plenty of closet extras, you know, for her fancy wardrobe. Not this!" He spread his arms wide.

Olivia looked around the room. Cheaply designed metal and plastic tables had been pushed together, and photographs lay in piles across their surfaces. Behind the tables, along the back wall, more photos hung. Some were black and white and some sepia toned. Stepping closer, Olivia felt herself blush.

"Is this Lana?" she asked, pointing to the topless woman in the photo.

Michael came closer, yanking the picture from where it hung. "Look at this," he said, motioning to Janis. The officer sidled up to Michael. She focused on the one photo as Michael watched.

Lana de Carlos stood on a rock, her shirt held above her chest. The photo revealed two prominent scars where her breasts had once been.

"Is this the post-surgery photo?" asked Olivia. *Poor Lana.*

"Must be," muttered Jets. "Look here." She pointed to another row of pictures. "These must be the pictures from before the surgery."

Sure enough, Lana stood at the entrance of the Lily Rock trail. She held her shirt up, revealing large perky breasts.

"I've seen that one before." Olivia pointed to the picture. "Or maybe a similar photo?"

"What do you mean?" asked Jets.

I never got to tell her about Thomas Seeker.

Then Michael interrupted. "Were you one of Lana's followers on the internet? Is that why the photo looks familiar?"

"Oh, no!" Olivia protested. "I had no idea Lana was an influencer until just yesterday, let alone that she had over a million followers. Believe me. Let me explain. A guy named Thomas Seeker has a bunch of photos of Lana on his phone. He showed them to me. He's a friend of Meadow's. That's why I came to see Janis this morning—to tell her. And then I saw you and things got complicated, and I forgot what I'd originally come for."

"Yeah, yeah, yeah . . . I don't care," Jets said. "I want to know how did two guys take the same photos of one topless woman. Did they know each other? Were they rivals? Could one of them have killed her?"

Olivia explained some more. "I don't know if Wilson and Thomas knew each other. I don't even know Thomas very well, but I'm under the impression most of his photos were taken from behind bushes and trees, as if he was paparazzi."

"The other camera guy who took this picture," Michael pointed to Lana's image post-surgery, "must have been Wilson Jones. He was most likely Lana's official photographer."

"Wilson Jones," mused Janis, turning to Michael. "And how do you know about him, might I ask?"

Michael shrugged. "I saw Jones a few times. I met him at the pie shop."

Jets glared at Olivia. "You knew Jones as well?"

"Sage told me about Wilson Jones," Olivia answered hastily. "They dated for a couple of weeks before he hooked up with Lana."

Jets held her hands in the air. "You are here for less than two days and you already met the local paparazzi and know who Sage was dating? You didn't waste any time."

"I thought you had no contact with Lily Rock." Michael glared at her. "It seems you kept connected with Sage."

"We play music together," Olivia explained. "She called me a few months after I left Lily Rock. I told her about my music dreams and we decided to play together to see if we jelled. Our band, Sweet Four O'Clock, came from those conversations. I never came back to Lily Rock. We rehearsed in Playa."

"Just you and Sage play together?" Michael asked.

"Sometimes we hire a bass player or a drummer."

For a moment, Olivia felt guilty. Then she shrugged it off. *None of Michael Bellemare's business what I do with my time or who I stay connected to.*

Janis Jets had already lost interest in their conversation and moved across the room. "Look here." She held a piece of paper in her hand. "This is addressed to Wilson Jones at this address. It seems he had some equipment delivered up here just two weeks ago." Jets stepped back with the paper still in her hand. "I will get my team on this right away. From what I can tell, this Jones guy is our most likely suspect," concluded Jets.

"Maybe Wilson got in an argument with Lana," added Michael.

"They had it out on the front doorstep and whammy," said Jets.

"He strangled her with his own two hands," finished Michael.

Now we're getting someplace. Janis thinks Wilson is the guy.

"So what I want to know is, how will you find Wilson Jones?" Olivia asked. "It's been nearly three days since the murder and you haven't seen him since."

"Oh, don't you worry, little mind-your-own-business. My team will find Jones and bring him down. We will get justice for Lana de Carlos. No cancer victim, no matter how indiscreet, is gonna get murdered on my watch without someone paying the price. It just seems even more wrong. Plenty of my friends have gone through chemo and it is no picnic. I'm furious!"

"What bothers me," added Michael, "is that Lana got through all the radiation and chemo treatments and she received a clean bill of health, and then she most likely got killed by her cameraman. It feels personal, this death."

"It's so unfair," Olivia agreed.

* * *

Back at the constabulary, Olivia sat in the corner while Michael and Janis Jets plotted the next step of the investigation. "We need to get some information on this Wilson character," Jets commented. "On the one hand, I need to interview Sage. She has first-hand experience with him, even if it was brief."

Olivia smiled, waiting for Janis to finish her predictable second idea.

"On the other hand, I want to talk to Meadow. She kept tabs on Wilson and Lana—at least that's what Olivia said."

"I bet you'll get two birds with one knock if you just go to their house. That's where I left Meadow with that Thomas guy." Olivia resisted looking smug.

"Good idea." Jets nodded.

At least she didn't call me Miss Runaway this time.

"What about the peeping Tom guy? What's his name?" asked Michael.

"His name is Thomas," reminded Olivia.

"A guy who takes sneaky photos is actually named Thomas like a peeping Tom?" Michael groaned.

"Well, his name is Thomas, and he does have a creepy vibe."

"Let's reel him in as well. You never know what more information he can offer us," said Jets.

From the corner of the room, Olivia enjoyed watching Janis and Michael immerse themselves in a new investigation. For a moment she longed for the purposefulness she'd felt when tracking down Marla's killer with Janis and Michael. They'd been a team.

I'm not as frightened to see the house as I was. I want to claim my space again. Hopefully Janis will let me know.

Then I can get up early and start cleaning. Now I have more energy. Solving a problem beats ruminating about

Michael Bellemare and who he's dating or if he has feelings for me.

Michael will always be full of himself and I will never know what's going on in his head. So I'll pay attention to me. That's how I'll move on, by helping to solve this murder instead.

As soon as she made her new commitment, she looked over at Michael and he stared right back. A half smile lifted the corner of his generous mouth as if to say, *Just try to ignore me. I dare you.*

Olivia sat up abruptly in her chair. *Oh no. This is not happening—no endearing Michael for me. We gotta find this Wilson guy, put him in jail, and then I'm down this hill and back to my music.*

Olivia spoke up. "Give me someplace to look and I'll get on the search for that Jones guy."

"What makes you think you're on this investigation team?" asked Jets with a sniff.

"You need me, and frankly, Wilson Jones won't suspect me because he doesn't know me."

A slow smile came to Michael's face. "Olivia has another thing going in her favor. As the property owner, she can ask any number of invasive questions, and Jones wouldn't necessarily suspect that she'd be reporting to the police."

Janis's eyes narrowed as if not quite convinced.

So Olivia added, "The sooner we find Wilson Jones, the sooner I'm out of your hair."

Now Janis stared down at her shoes, stubbornly refusing to agree.

Michael's jaw tightened. "If you still want to leave. I hope your car is in better shape than last time."

Olivia laughed. "My mode of transportation is just fine.

The brakes are hardly worn. You won't be trying that trick on me again."

"You two are on the same page about this joint investigation," Janis observed. "You both agree that Olivia should look for Wilson Jones. I don't like it much when you agree. It makes me uncomfortable."

I'm going to assume I'm in on the investigation whether Janis likes it or not.

"How will I begin to search for this character anyway? Do the police have any leads?"

"Oh, don't you worry. We have plenty of leads," commented Janis dryly. "We can talk later and I'll get you up to speed."

7

EVERY HAIR IN PLACE

As the sun began to set, the newly formed investigative team stepped out the front door of Olivia's house and into a crowd of mourners. A group had gathered on the driveway. One woman held a lit candle to her chest with both hands, her tear-stained cheeks glistening in the light.

Fresh bouquets of flowers lay by the front doorstep. Some glass candle containers, placed along the path, flickered by the side of the darkened driveway.

Olivia looked into the crowd for anyone she knew. "She looks familiar." A tall woman with a swinging ponytail stood at the back of the crowd.

"That's Antonia. You just met her at the constabulary." Janis gave Olivia the side-eye.

"Right. Did Antonia know Lana?"

"I didn't think so. Not sure why my assistant is here. Let's ask her."

Leaving Michael on the doorstep, Janis and Olivia moved through the center of the crowd toward Antonia. The young woman ducked her head, kicking her toe in the dirt as they approached. "I didn't think you'd see me," she explained as Janis and Olivia walked up.

"Let's talk over there," suggested Janis, pointing and ushering them to where Michael had parked his truck. "What are you doing here?" asked Janis. "Personal or police business?"

"I was just curious, you know?" Again Antonia rubbed her toe in the dirt. "I followed Lana online, and I felt kind of sad when she passed."

"You mean when she was murdered," corrected Janis. "You must know Lana was murdered—you work in the constabulary, and you forwarded my emails from the coroner."

Antonia lifted her eyes. "I don't read everything I forward." A tear trickled down her cheek. "I know Lana was murdered, but I just can't wrap my mind around it. I mean, who would do such a thing? After all of Lana's suffering with the cancer and the operations . . . I mean, she was just getting back to her old self, trying to walk more and not sleep so much. The last time she posted, she sounded so happy and hopeful." Antonia's bright eyes shined in the darkening night.

Olivia felt confused. *I have no clue about the life of influencers. I've underestimated the importance of the whole thing.*

Glancing back over the crowd of mourners, Olivia stared at them. *How do these people feel so connected with each other? None of them even knew Lana de Carlos personally. Yet here they are together, mourning her death.*

"So you post as yourself or as your band?" a fan had asked Olivia only a few months ago after a Sweet Four O'Clock gig.

"I don't post at all," she'd admitted.

"Baby, you really should. You'd get lots of followers," he'd told her in a concerned voice.

At the time Olivia had dismissed the idea immediately.

Our fans don't need to know us up close and personal. But Antonia is different. She wanted to know Lana, every aspect of her life and cancer journey. And Lana encouraged her followers by leading them to think they did know her.

Now she looked back at Janis and Antonia. Neither woman spoke.

Janis's face softened as the wrinkles disappeared on her forehead. She reached out to give Antonia's shoulder a squeeze. "I know. It's a tough world out there. Lots of murder and mayhem come our way even in a place like Lily Rock. Working for the police isn't for everyone. Are you sure you want to continue on as my assistant?"

"Oh, I do," insisted Antonia immediately. "I love the job and working with you. Please don't worry about me. I just wanted to pay my respects to Lana before news of her death got picked up by the media. The crowds will grow, you know; she had over a million followers."

"How do her followers know where she lived?" asked Olivia, stepping closer to the two women.

Even in the dark, Antonia's beauty caused Olivia to inhale quickly. The way the girl held herself and her wide-eyed innocence made her heart soften.

Antonia raised her eyebrows. "I'm afraid news of her whereabouts got out a couple of weeks ago. One of her ardent fans recognized the Lily Rock photos and leaked the location online to the rest of us."

"Is that so," Janis said, inhaling deeply. "Did they leak Lana's cell phone, for example?" She could not disguise the edge in her voice.

"I have all the information!" Antonia's ponytail bounced with her excitement.

Janis grinned at her assistant.

Beauty and the beast; Janis and Antonia make a good team.

* * *

As Antonia walked toward her car, Janis waved over her head at Michael. She shouted, "I think we can ask this crowd to disperse. Want to help?"

Her loud voice brought moans from the mourners. Janis ignored the resistance. She and Michael walked into the middle of the largest group. "It's time for you to leave," they each repeated, as if they'd done it together a million times.

Olivia walked to the side of the house and pulled out the business card Cayenne had handed over earlier. As soon as she stepped closer, the sensor light lit up, and she could see the card better. She tapped in Cayenne's number.

"Hello," a throaty voice answered.

"Cay, it's me, Olivia."

"Hello," Cay said. "Glad you called."

"Any chance we could get together tomorrow for breakfast?"

"Sure, come to the pub. I'll whip you up something from the kitchen."

"Why don't you come to my house? I'll get some eggs and bacon, and we can eat over here. It's been a while."

"You mean at the scene of the crime?" asked Cay.

"The very place," affirmed Olivia. "I'll be up early. Does seven work for you, or is that too early?"

"I get up at four to send my cleaning team out on their assignments. I may be ready for lunch by seven."

"I'll make you a very hearty breakfast or brunch. Just no mimosas."

Cayenne laughed. "I remember. I don't drink that early, and you don't drink at all. Just lots of strong coffee works for me. See you tomorrow."

"See you then." Olivia smiled, clicking off the phone.

It was nearly nine o'clock by the time Michael, Janis, and Olivia returned to the constabulary. "I'll see you both tomorrow," Olivia told Janis and Michael before walking to her car.

Out of town and heading toward Meadow and Sage's house, her headlights led the way on the darkened road. After she parked and slammed the car door closed, she walked to the lit porch to knock on the door.

No one answered. *"We keep a spare key under the dog rock,"* Sage had told her some time back. So Olivia looked around the porch and sure enough, tucked behind a potted plant she found the rock with a painting of Mayor Maguire's acrylic likeness.

She unlocked the door and returned the key under the rock.

"Hello," she called. When no one responded, she closed the door and walked into the kitchen. Leaving a note on the kitchen table for Meadow and Sage, she made her way to her room where she tossed into her suitcase the clean clothes Meadow had left in a heap on her bed.

Time to face my fears in my own house. I'm so tired, it won't be that hard to fall asleep. Probably for the best my first night back. She rolled her suitcase to the front door and set the lock. The doorknob stayed in place, assuring Olivia that the house was secure.

Across the gravel her suitcase rumbled, the stones scattering as she made her way toward the car.

With the suitcase in the trunk, Olivia sat in the driver's seat. She put her key in the ignition and then turned on the headlights. *I'm away to my own place.* Her stomach lurched, but she backed up the car and pretended she didn't notice.

* * *

Once she'd gotten into her house and secured her front door, Olivia rolled her suitcase down the stairway to the guest suite. The police had already left that part of the house.

I won't go into the grand suite, at least until the police have packed up all those photos from the darkroom.

Time for a shower and bed. I'm exhausted.

* * *

Olivia woke with a start, the sun shining in the window. *I don't know what's in the refrigerator.* She swung herself out of bed, pulling on the clothes she'd worn the day before. *I'll unpack my clean clothes after Cayenne leaves.*

We must have coffee. Olivia crossed her fingers. *I'll make a pot and figure out the rest.* Looking out the back window, she inhaled deeply. *My apartment doesn't even hold a candle to this place. Lily Rock and this house already have a hold on me.*

Once in the kitchen, Olivia looked toward the path to the vegetable and herb garden. Her eyes circled the loamy plot, stopping at the far corner.

That's where M&M found the marijuana plants. Where is that mutt anyway?

She turned her attention to the fridge. *Oh good, Wilson must have been a big breakfast eater. There's plenty of food in here. I can fry bacon for Cayenne. I'll defrost this loaf of sourdough from the freezer and make use of this lonely stick of butter on the side door.*

There's even fruit. She inspected two apples in a basket sitting on the counter. No spots, not too soft. *With a touch of sour cream I can make a fruit salad. I wonder if there are any nuts to add . . .*

Olivia heard a scratch from the back door. *I hope it's him.*

She opened the door quickly, hoping to say hello to Mayor Maguire.

Instead of the labradoodle, a ruffled-looking Michael Bellemare stood in the doorway. He rubbed his hand through his hair, his whiskered chin bringing a smile to her face. *Much better than clean shaven*, she thought. *Makes him look so manly*.

Olivia shrugged and looked down. Sure enough, Mayor Maguire sat by Michael's knee, his tongue hanging out the side of his mouth.

"Hi, M&M," Olivia said, stooping to give the dog a hug. "I've been missing you."

After letting the dog sniff her ear, she stood up to open the door wider so that Michael and M&M could make their way indoors. She walked into the kitchen. "Coffee?" Olivia asked Michael as she reached for the pot.

"Sure," he said.

Olivia rummaged through the cupboard. "I have canned milk. Is that okay?"

"It'll work," Michael said.

After checking the date on the can, Olivia opened it and poured some into the coffee mug for Michael. She stirred in the sugar before sliding the mug across the counter toward Michael. "Absolutely ruined," she remarked as he took it by the handle.

"But perfect for me," he said, taking a sip. Michael glanced around the kitchen. "Held up pretty well over the year." He ran his hand over the finely crafted cupboards. "I think these look even better than when I installed them."

Olivia sniffed, then she changed the subject to more pressing matters. "Cay is coming for breakfast, so I have to scoot you out of here quickly. You know. Girl talk."

Michael held the mug to his lips for another sip of coffee.

Pulling the mug away from his mouth, he asked, "How does that work? Does a transgender person learn to speak in one gender then another like a language?"

Olivia stopped slicing open a package of honey-smoked bacon. "You'd have to ask Cay," she commented quietly. "I've found assuming what people think and feel rarely works." As the words left her mouth, Olivia immediately regretted saying them.

When she turned to face Michael, she could tell by his expression that he had misinterpreted her remark and personalized her meaning. "Oh, I never assume anything about you, Olivia. Believe me. I learned my lesson."

Olivia smiled tentatively. "I *am* sorry, you know, about how I left."

And how I thought you wanted to know me better.

"So you say." Michael turned toward the back door. "I'll be going now. Don't want to stay where I'm not wanted. Mayor? You coming too?"

Mayor Maguire looked at Michael for a long while. He dropped his head as if to apologize and then turned around to nibble at the fur on his tail.

Michael laughed. "Did you just give me a furry cold shoulder? What's up with everyone today?"

By the time Michael closed the back door behind him, Mayor Maguire made his way to his customary spot under the kitchen table. Olivia offered him a piece of bacon, which he readily took. *I may not understand the man, but I do get the dog.*

He took my coffee mug with him, Olivia realized. *A good excuse for him to come back, or is he just being forgetful?*

* * *

By the time Cay and Olivia had eaten their breakfast of scrambled eggs, toast with butter, and a side of bacon, they'd reestablished their connection. Munching her last bit of toast, Cay settled back into her chair to look at Olivia, as Mayor Maguire finished the last piece of bacon offered to him under the table.

Cayenne opened the conversation. "It seems like living in Playa suits you. Do you have time for gigs along with work? Sage told me about your band, Sweet Four O'Clock. I like the band's name, by the way."

Olivia smiled. "It took us a few months to reconnect after I left in such a hurry. By the way, Sage didn't say much about you and Arlo. How are things going? I've missed you both."

"Great. Actually, more than great. Arlo kind of likes my newly developed parts," Cay said, pointing to her chest where her breasts lay visible under the denim shirt. "I've taken hormones for so long now that he's getting used to the new me. Of course I'm still taller than he is, but that's true for a lot of couples."

I'm uncomfortable talking about Cayenne's breasts. Let's change the subject. Olivia smiled at her. "You're not still mad at me?"

"I'm over it," Cay said. "You can't tell a person how to live their lives. It was obvious to me, once I thought about it, that you needed to keep moving and that Lily Rock felt too confining."

Finally someone understands. "It's not Lily Rock, it's me."

When Cay didn't have a follow-up question, Olivia had one of her own. "Does your company still clean this place, like you used to for Marla?"

"I do all the cleaning myself, just like when I started with Marla. I don't have a key, if that's what you're wondering . . . if you need it back for the next tenant."

"Oh, no! I have no problem with you keeping a key."

"I didn't use a key with Lana," Cay continued to explain. "Her camera guy usually opened the door when I got here, and then he'd close up after I was done. It worked quite well as long as I stuck to my midweek schedule."

"What do you mean?"

"One time I tried to reschedule and clean on a Friday instead of the usual Wednesday. I thought the cameraman was going to fire me. I really did. He fumed, so I just skipped the week instead of trying to pick another day. I made up for the extra work the following Wednesday at the usual time."

"So it was mostly the guy you saw?" Olivia asked.

"Basically I worked through him. His name was Wilson Jones. Everyone in Lily Rock knew he was Lana's boyfriend and cameraman."

"Did people talk about him much?"

"Of course they did. The circumstances were a bit odd, both of them being new to Lily Rock. They alarmed the Old Rockers right away. But there was also that thing they did."

"You mean the going naked and exposing Lana's chest thing?"

"It kind of annoyed me a lot, if you must know."

Olivia heard Cay's voice shift as if she were overcoming unwanted emotions. "You do sound upset."

"I thought I'd feel better since Lana died and all, but I don't. It's kind of personal. Sure, you want to know?"

"I'm sorry, Cay. I feel so awkward around you when it comes to talking about personal matters. I don't want to pry."

Cayenne's face froze. Then her eyebrows raised in the quirky way they did when she was amused. "I suspect you're avoiding any talk about body parts and sex. Happens to a lot of trans, with family and friends especially. One way to cure that? You tell me more about your sex life. That would certainly fill in my curiosity. Then we can be girl-friends."

"And that won't be happening," Olivia laughed. "The talking about sex part, not the girlfriend part. But do say more about your feelings and Lana—I mean if you want to."

Cay needed no more urging. "So I cleaned once per week." She pointed to the bedroom toward the front of the house. "When I got to that part, the large suite, Wilson would unlock it to let me in. They had already tidied everything up, so my work was easy. The only thing for me to do was change out the bathroom towels and bed sheets, vacuum, dust, and be on my way."

Cayenne continued, "Until one time a couple of months ago. I knocked on the bedroom door and realized it had been left unlocked. I could see right away that the room had not been tidied up like the times before. Stuff was thrown on the floor. For the first time the room looked, you know, lived in. I picked things up. When I bent over to shove a storage box back under the bed, I heard a voice behind me yelling, 'Stop that! You have no business looking at my things!'

"Lana de Carlos herself stood before me dressed in a silk bathrobe. She looked like a movie star with her hair bundled on top of her head. I left the box right where it was. She acted defensive, like a skunk."

Probably smelled like weed too.

"I'd never run into her before. I'd only heard that a woman named Lana de Carlos had cancer and she posted about her chemo and treatments. I was in such a hurry to get out I forgot my vacuum, so I had to turn around from my truck to knock on the door and ask for it back. She gave it to me. But not without chewing me out another time."

"Sounds like Lana wasn't your favorite," remarked Olivia.

"No, she was not. Her yelling made me feel like an

unwanted intruder. Lana treated me like I was put in her world to serve her every need. She probably treated everyone that way. Instead of names, we had titles like cameraman and cleaner. She treated me like an outsider, an enemy she didn't respect."

Before Cay could say more, Olivia's cell phone lit up. Janis Jets's identification showed on her screen. Olivia answered the call. "Janis?"

"What are you doing?" demanded the police officer.

Olivia looked across the kitchen table. Cay had disappeared. *I hope she didn't leave.* "I was just talking to Cay. Why did you call?"

Janis Jets exhaled a long sigh. "I was just checking on you. Michael said you scooted him out of the kitchen real quick this morning for an important meeting with Cayenne. Listen to me carefully, Olivia Greer. I want you to do some searching for Wilson Jones but that's all. Don't go asking a bunch of questions to alarm the Lily Rock residents. And whatever you do, when you find out info about Wilson, you are to report to me. You are not to go finding him on your own. No poking your nose in. Have I made myself clear?"

"You don't have to shout, you know," Olivia shouted back. Then with some deliberation, she ended the call.

"I can talk to anyone I want," she said aloud. Annoyed at Janis's implication, Olivia added, "Sometimes I just hate Lily Rock!"

By the time Olivia cleared the table, Cayenne reappeared from the bathroom, her face composed, looking more relaxed. "I'd better get going."

Olivia stood in front of her friend. "Hug?" she asked gently.

Cay's long arms reached around her, enveloping Olivia's entire body in the embrace. "I missed you, friend."

Olivia took a step back to look at Cayenne, realizing something had gone unsaid. "Is there anything more you want to tell me?" she asked quietly. "We didn't get to finish our conversation before."

Cay nodded. "You may think this is silly, but I notice details in how women dress. It's more research than anything. About Lana's hair . . . Let me start again. After she yelled at me, I started following her on social media out of curiosity. I didn't trust her, which made me want to know more. She posted lots of photos, including when she cut her hair before chemo. She had her boyfriend shear some off and then she shaved the rest. Lana cried—I mean, she really sobbed. Her head was completely bald by the end of the week-long video updates. But a week after that part of her story, when I saw her in the bedroom?" Cay's voice sounded filled with disgust. "Her hair was fully grown, lush and thick, piled on her head, and it was no wig!"

Olivia patted Cay's shoulder, stepping back to look at her hair. Cay wore a beautiful human hair wig, secured expertly into a three-strand braid down her back. *No wonder she looked so closely at Lana's hair*. Cayenne's Native American heritage, her Appalachian Cherokee roots, were echoed in her hairstyle choice.

It was only a year ago in the fire that Olivia realized that Cay's hair was a wig. At the time Cay had rushed headlong into the Paws and Pines Animal Shelter to save the trapped dogs and cats from the unchecked fire that consumed their habitat.

Olivia's spine tingled, recollecting the sight of Cayenne as she ripped off her wig to run toward the all-consuming flames, her bald head shining in the moonlight.

That night Cayenne allowed Olivia to see her true self, the person no longer restricted by gender expectations. Olivia knew it was a sacred moment. She'd not spoken to anyone about it at the time; she'd not even mentioned it again to Cayenne and she wouldn't say anything now.

"When it comes down to it? It's always about the hair," Olivia remarked, looking into her friend's dark eyes.

Cayenne laughed. "That would be the truth."

8

"HE'S PSYCHIC"

It took a few days for Olivia to feel at home in her house. She spent time in each room with one exception. Olivia could not bring herself to enter the grand suite alone.

Two days passed before she finally came to terms with the idea. *I'm ready to look into Lana's lair.*

Michael stopped by Friday morning to rehang the door. Standing nearby, Olivia watched him reach up to tackle the hinge at the top, admiring his tool belt slung low over his jeans.

"This won't take long," he mumbled, holding a screw in the side of his mouth.

"Do you want something to drink?" When he didn't answer right away, Olivia took advantage of her opportunity to observe. *Since he isn't already staring at me, I can have my turn to stare at him.* She watched the bicep of his muscular arm flex as he reached over his head.

"Maybe later on that offer." He ducked his head to smile at her.

She felt his eyes following her as she walked away. *He*

watches me like I watch him, so that neither of us gets caught doing the noticing.

Instead of watching Michael work, Olivia returned to cleaning surfaces in the bathrooms and kitchen. She took the freshly laundered quilts to the back deck, spreading them out over chairs in the sunshine. *Sun and soap smell perfect.*

"All done here," Michael said, sticking his head outside.

She looked up from her task. "Thank you so much." She smiled.

"No problem. Does this mean you want me to be the go-to guy for your next tenant? I'm happy to do it."

I want to say yes. I do.

When she didn't speak right away, he glowered at her. "Okay, I get it. You don't want me involved. Just thought I'd ask." He turned, making his way back into the house.

"Stop," she called, following him inside. "I would appreciate your help with the house. Who knows it better? And it would give us a chance to check in now and then, you know, on the phone."

As if not believing what he heard, Michael shook his head. "You mean it? We can talk like civilized people? That's a change . . ."

Awkward. I've been such a baby about all this. No wonder he's confused.

"Good," he said with small smile. Michael made his way toward the kitchen door. His tool belt slapped against his leg as he hurried away. *I bet he thinks I'll change my mind again,* thought Olivia. *That's why he's leaving in such a hurry.*

In the kitchen she washed a few dishes in the sink. *I'll check the mail and then time to get to work.* Olivia dried her hands and folded the towel over the handle on the refrigerator. She made her way toward the front door.

Stepping outside she caught sight of the array of bouquets lying on the ground next to the front deck. Mayor Maguire stood sniffing the flowers, his nose placed in the center of a fading red rose.

Changing her mind instantly, she asked, "Hey M&M, wanna go for a ride?" *I can go into the room later. Right now I want to get in the car and drive. I'm dying to get away from this house.*

She grabbed her shopping list from inside and met Mayor Maguire out front. After locking the door, the two walked toward the car. With Mayor Maguire in the passenger seat, Olivia slid behind the driver's seat. She put the key in the ignition and the engine turned over. Once in gear, Olivia and Mayor Maguire made their way toward the main road.

Mayor Maguire hung his head out the Ford's passenger-side window, his jowls flapping in the breeze as they drove toward town. Olivia reached over to pat his haunch until a sign along the road caught her attention.

"Paws and Pines Animal Shelter," she mumbled to the dog. Underneath the old sign, one with frilly painted letters had been hung. *Mountain Herbs.* I wonder if Arlo opened a shop . . .

Curiosity piqued, Olivia took a sharp left turn down the dirt road. Dogs from the shelter barked in the distance. Mayor Maguire barked his return greeting.

Driving past the animal shelter entrance, Olivia parked in the paved lot located behind the indoor kennels. Having lost interest in greeting his tribe, Mayor Maguire stopped barking, pawing at the passenger-side door.

"Give me a minute," Olivia said.

She put the car in park and slid out of the driver's seat. The mayor continued to paw inside the passenger-side door. Once Olivia opened his side, the dog eagerly jumped out, making his way toward the entrance of the Mountain Herb dispensary.

Olivia caught up with him and read the sign near the door: "Press buzzer for entry." She pushed the buzzer. In a moment a voice came from the speaker underneath. "Yes?" asked the disembodied voice.

"Is Arlo around?" Olivia inquired.

"Is that you, Olivia?"

Before she could answer, Mayor Maguire barked his greeting.

Arlo laughed, his voice hollow over the loud speaker. "You're with the mayor? He has the code. Just check out his collar; the number for entrance is printed on the back of his tag. You can get in any time you want as long as you're with him."

Punching in the code only took a minute. Olivia followed Mayor Maguire as he sauntered past the small dispensary and cabinets, down a hallway. They found Arlo leaning against a high-top table, which held mounds of leaves from a recent harvest.

Looking up, Arlo took a step to give Olivia a big hug. "So great you found me," he said, squatting to pat Mayor Maguire's head. "I wanted to tell you about my new place at the pub the other night, but it didn't seem to be the right time."

Is this where my mea culpa to Arlo fits in? It feels like my apology tour should be over pretty soon. "I'm sorry for not saying goodbye last year," Olivia said. "I can't say that enough, apparently."

Arlo shrugged. "Don't worry. I get why you left. You felt trapped. But now you're back, so let's celebrate. Want to sample some of my product?"

"No, thanks. But I am happy your business is out in the open. Are you still partners with Meadow?"

"Not officially. She's not that into weed. We do consult now and then. But since you left, I have full Old Rocker and town council approval, and if you must know," Arlo stepped closer to whisper in Olivia's ear, "the Old Rockers like my blend."

"There you go," laughed Olivia. "A marijuana entrepreneur who gets the stamp of approval from the town council. Now that's progress."

"There are no more licenses available, at least for up here. They put a cap on how many weed businesses are allowed, in case you were interested in competing," Arlo clarified.

Olivia grimaced as she bent over to pat Mayor Maguire's head. *He's so competitive.*

As if hearing her judgment, Arlo stammered, "Just wanted to make sure we understood each other. In Lily Rock you never know who will be your friend or who is your competition." He pointed at two stools behind the counter. "Have a seat. Let's catch up a bit." He then turned to open another door, which Mayor Maguire trotted through.

"Where does that lead to?" asked Olivia.

"The other kennels. The mayor visits the dogs down the hall. He likes checking things out to make sure we meet quality review."

"I see. Good to know M&M has another day job." Olivia sat, putting her purse underneath her chair. Arlo sat across from her, his arms folded on top of the table.

"Cay told me you kissed and made up, so to speak." Arlo clenched and unclenched his fingers. Still a nervous habit.

"We really enjoyed catching up. How are you doing, by the way?" *He seems his usual nervous self. I bet he smokes his own blend on a regular basis to reduce that anxiety. Maybe that's how he got involved with weed and CBD in the first place.*

"I'm okay," said Arlo, hesitating for a couple of seconds before adding, "Actually, I am a little worried about Cay."

"She looks great to me. You two seem to be communicating; you have a legitimate business right now. What's going on?"

Fidgeting in his chair, Arlo cleared his throat. "Did Cay tell you about her issues with the hormones?"

Olivia thought back to their conversation, remembering she'd dodged much of the personal talk. Had Cay been trying to share something important? "She did mention hormones. She takes them, I assume, as a part of her transformation?"

"For several years, Cay has gotten shots and taken female hormones. That's why her body has changed, you know, up here." Arlo swept his hand over his chest. "The problem came up a few months ago when she felt a lump. She went to the doctor, and they did tests."

"Cancer?"

"No, not cancer, fortunately for us. Cay did some research while she waited for her biopsy. She learned that lots of trans have cancer from hormone treatments. The doctor told her that many trans people have to remove breast implants due to cancer and go off injections."

I really don't want to ask but . . . "Does Cay have implants?" Olivia felt her cheeks flush. *I've intruded into their personal space. But I but don't want to shut down the conversation like I did before with Cay. If people want to talk about their body parts, far be it from me to stop them.*

"No, Cay didn't need implants. The hormones were enough." Now Arlo blushed. *I hope he's done talking about this.*

"After Cay got a clean bill of health," Arlo continued over

the discomfort, "she started following a trans community online. They shared their experiences with hormone-induced cancers, which upset Cay. She lost sleep and became quite irritable. Then she started paying more attention to Lana de Carlos's posts about her cancer journey. She checked Lana's accounts several times a day. It became an obsession."

I wish I could ease his anxiety. "That's good, you know, that people shared their concerns in a like-minded community. Maybe Cay was trying to help Lana in her own way."

"It may have started that way, because knowing the stories of other trans people online who had cancer made Cay feel she understood Lana. But after a while Cay got more and more agitated. When Lana wasn't online, she was often in the woods behind our house. She told me she was hunting for squirrel and rabbit to clear her mind, but she never came home with anything, not that I'd eat a rabbit.

"Then last week, Cay broke down and raged about unfairness to trans cancer victims and how the trans community has trouble getting decent medical care. I mean, she was as angry as I've ever seen her." Olivia watched Arlo clench his fists, his knuckles turning white.

"How did Lana play into all of this?"

"I'm not sure exactly. I got the feeling that Cay wanted to talk to Lana personally, not just clean her house. She'd go over at odd times to see if she could catch Lana."

"Did Cay have any luck?"

"I don't think so. That camera guy, Wilson something or other, kept his eye on Lana, never let her out of his sight. So Cay didn't get a personal conversation as far as I know."

I wonder if Cay told him about the yelling in the large suite and her wig observation? It doesn't seem like it . . .

Olivia paused to think, then added, "Maybe Cay wanted

Lana to sponsor a trans person on social media. You know people do that to bring attention to other causes. That would have been a kind thing for Lana to do and for Cay to initiate."

Arlo nodded. "You're probably right."

What is he trying to tell me that he's not saying? Olivia sat in silence for a moment, running through Arlo's account of everything in her mind again. "I'm happy that Cay's okay," Olivia said instead, reaching over to pat Arlo's hand. He released his fingers, turning his palm over to grasp her hand.

"Me too," he said. "I missed you, Olivia. You're a good listener." He gave her hand a squeeze and then stood up. "I'd better get back to work. Now that you have the door code, you can come at any time."

"And if I forget the code, I only have to bring the mayor," Olivia added with a smile.

A brief search in the kennel revealed Mayor Maguire sniffing nose to nose with a small terrier. "Hey M&M, we gotta go," she called to him. He turned at the sound of his name, following Olivia out the door to the parking lot.

"See you two later," called Arlo from his office.

Olivia opened the car door for the dog to jump in, noticing the window was open. *I forgot to close the window when I locked the car.* She walked to the driver's side and glanced at the back seat. A manila envelope with her name on it caught her eye.

That's a bit strange . . . Olivia opened the door and retrieved the envelope.

Sliding her finger under the flap, Olivia slid the contents out of the envelope. *The last time I found a surprise envelope with my name on it, it was a letter from Marla.* Olivia shuddered.

Three photographs were in the envelope. Two were of

Lana in bed. Each shot had been staged from a different angle, displaying her pale face, shaven head, and scars where breasts had been removed. Olivia winced, unable to look away.

In one photo there was sagging skin where the breasts had once been. Scars appeared on both sides of Lana's chest, causing Olivia to gasp. The pain, the awful pain.

One other photo showed Lana lounging with a man. He stretched his arm above his head to take the selfie. Lana held a joint in one hand as she stared at her companion. His day-old scruff and sleepy eyes captured the moment with intended sexual overtones.

The last photo depicted Lana standing on a rock, her reconstructed breasts bared, the scars still apparent. She'd not attempted to cover the wounds, which had healed but were still evident. At the bottom of the last photo, someone had written in dark ink: *Whatever happened to Wilson Jones? He took all of these photos, and now he's missing.*

Olivia's gut clenched. *I can't believe how these photos make Lana's pain so personal.* Who was making money on all of this exposure? Had someone taken advantage of Lana's cancer diagnosis and filmed the process for financial gain? Maybe Lana and Wilson parted ways after the reconstruction surgery . . . but maybe not.

After the surgery maybe Lana didn't want to keep filming, so Wilson got angry. They could have fought, and maybe Wilson killed her in the heat of passion. That would explain why Wilson had vanished and was nowhere to be found. But then there was Cayenne.

Maybe that's what Arlo was trying to tell me earlier, why he was so nervous. Had Cayenne gotten involved with Lana? Had Cayenne attempted to talk to the woman to find out if the cancer diagnosis was authentic, and then realized Lana was making money off of it? Cayenne could have gotten really angry if she thought Lana was faking her cancer journey. Could she have strangled Lana in a fit of rage?

The sight of the red scars and the woman with her shirt over her head shocked Olivia. At first Lana was just a tenant, but now she felt like more. *I can't leave Lily Rock now, not until I find out why Lana died. I don't think I can rest easy, let alone rent my place to another tenant until the truth about Lana is known.*

Olivia felt her spine tingle. *Like it or not, Janis, I'm on this case and you can't stop me.* She slid behind the steering wheel. After the engine turned over, she put her car in gear, glancing over at Mayor Maguire with his head out the open window.

Olivia reached over to pat his haunch. "If I didn't know any better, I might think you dragged me into staying in Lily Rock, you silly mutt. At first I thought you were trying to matchmake Michael and me, but now I see you wanted me to get involved and solve another case."

Mayor Maguire made three turns in the seat and settled into a ball, his tail wrapped around his body. He opened one eye and then closed it again.

"You expect me to find justice for Lana," Olivia said aloud. "I guess it's finally time to look in her room, but first I have an errand. We're going to see Janis right now and take her these photos. Maybe they'll help with the case, and maybe she'll realize that you and I can be her deputies. What do you say?"

"Bork," replied Mayor Maguire, barely raising his head.

* * *

By the time Olivia arrived at the constabulary, downtown Lily Rock teemed with tourists. After several trips around the block, she pulled into a parking spot in front of the Lily Rock Library. Through a large plate-glass window she could see Meadow's head bobbing behind the checkout counter.

As soon as she let him out of the passenger door, Mayor Maguire bounded over the boardwalk toward the constabulary. Realizing she'd not come along, he stopped to look over his shoulder.

"Hold on, M&M, I'm on my way," Olivia called after him.

A man guiding a stroller with one hand and holding a small poodle with his other arm stopped in the middle of the boardwalk. "Is that dog on a leash?" he demanded, pointing ahead to Mayor Maguire.

"No, and just so you know he's not my dog specifically—"

"You people are all alike. You think you make the rules. There are leash laws in this county, even if it is Lily Rock."

Olivia stopped. The tourist's angry accusation had attracted attention from passersby. Other people stopped to hear them quarrel. Some stood next to the mayor as if to protect him from unnecessary harsh words.

"Now just a minute," came the sharp voice of Meadow McCloud from the open window. She strode around the library counter to make her way outside. "You will not yell at the citizens of Lily Rock in that tone of voice, and you will never ever speak that way in front of the mayor." Meadow, hands on hips, glared at the man, whose face turned chalk white at her admonition.

"I only meant—"

"I don't care what you meant," insisted Meadow in her most authoritative librarian voice. "You will apologize immediately. We don't like tourists in our town telling us how to go about our business. If you want to be welcomed in Lily Rock, then you need to learn our ways."

Still looking confused, the tourist shifted his poodle to the other arm. "You said the mayor. Who is he?"

"Right there!" she pointed toward Olivia's feet, where Mayor Maguire now sat, his tongue hanging from his mouth.

The tourist shook his head in disbelief while Mayor Maguire took a moment to saunter toward the baby stroller to peek inside.

The father reached into the stroller to gather the baby in his free arm. "Get your dog away," he told Olivia.

Mayor Maguire sat on his haunches, looking back toward Olivia as if to ask, "Am I in trouble?"

"Look here, Mr. Tourist," Meadow sputtered. "Take the example of the mayor. When someone annoys us in Lily Rock —and it does happen occasionally—we sit down and take a pause instead of yelling. Look at our mayor, he isn't causing a fuss."

The tourist grumbled under his breath as Mayor Maguire rose to stand in front of Olivia. By placing himself between her and the angry stranger, he protected her from any more interaction.

Now with the baby in one arm and the poodle in the other, the man looked around the crowd for support. "There's a leash law," he repeated in a pleading voice.

"I thought you understood," Olivia interrupted. "He's a dog and he's our mayor. His name is Maguire. He's well known here in Lily Rock and he's been nationally televised." Olivia patted the dog's head. "He goes where he wants and when he wants. If you lived in Lily Rock, you'd know all about our famous mayor. Plus the other thing we keep kind of quiet. Everyone in Lily Rock knows . . ." she paused to take a breath, ". . . that Mayor Maguire is—

"Psychic!" claimed the crowd in unison.

Totally outnumbered and defeated, the tourist kept the baby under his arm as he tumbled the poodle into the stroller. He rolled his dog down the boardwalk toward the street. The baby's bare feet kicked against his side as cars honked.

"He might as well get in his car and head down the hill," said Meadow to Olivia. "Once he messes with the mayor, he's in trouble with all of us in Lily Rock."

"You said it," laughed Olivia, pulling the dog close to her side.

The crowd dispersed as Olivia waved goodbye to Meadow. She followed Mayor Maguire to the constabulary. When Olivia stuck her head in the entrance, Janis Jets's voice boomed at her, "What's the ruckus outside? You causing trouble again?"

"Something about a guy and a leash law," mumbled Olivia, pointing to the mayor.

"Oh please. We don't let tourists bring their rules up the hill, especially when it comes to our mayor. Did you tell him the dog is psychic?"

"Along with a dozen other people."

"Then I don't need to follow up. The tourist has been informed by the townspeople. That's how I like it."

Olivia smiled. *I don't want to call this place home, but I do love it so. They're my kind of quirky, and besides, even if I didn't choose Lily Rock, the mayor of Lily Rock chose me.* Before she could think more about her change of heart, Janis interrupted.

"Why are you here anyway?" demanded the officer.

"I have information on Lana's death," Olivia said firmly.

"Okay, Miss Nosy Parker. Tell me what you got."

Olivia sweetly smiled. "The mayor and I have actual photographic evidence and a note that you may be interested in."

Janis ushered Olivia and Mayor Maguire to the back room. "Give me those photos. It's time for us to have a serious conversation." Janis Jets closed the door behind her.

9

THREE BUNCH PALMS

After Janis Jets's tirade trying to push Olivia out of the investigation, Olivia stood in the main office hiding a smile. *One minute Janis wants my help, the next minute she doesn't. I can bring Lana de Carlos's murderer to justice, no matter what Janis says.* She felt her jaw tighten.

"Stay in your lane," Janis had shouted at her.

But I don't have a lane, at least not yet. If I don't help with the investigation it may take months, which will keep me from moving forward—an empty house and no renter. I can't in all good conscience offer my place to someone without knowing who killed the previous tenant, now can I?

Good thing I didn't tell Janis any of that. Listen and nod, that's my motto when she's on a rampage.

As her hand reached for the exit door, the sound of the swishing glass doors caught her attention. Janis stepped through, already saying, "Where has Antonia gone? I can't keep that girl in her seat."

Olivia smiled, reaching for the door again.

"Have you seen the mayor?" asked Jets, looking around the room.

At the sound of his name Mayor Maguire scooted from beneath the desk, padding over to the open window, where he stood up on his hind legs, his front paws braced on the windowsill.

Looking through the window facing the alleyway next to the constabulary, he pressed his nose against the glass.

"Here's your water, Mayor," Janis called to him, reaching behind the reception desk for the bowl, which stood ready. She shoved the metal bowl near his back paws. Mayor Maguire dropped away from the window to slurp up the offering.

"He seems pretty thirsty," Janis remarked, looking at Olivia with accusing eyes.

"He ate this morning, and I haven't had water myself in hours," Olivia replied somewhat defensively.

"Is that a hint you want water?" Janis walked through the doors, returning with two unopened plastic bottles. "Okay, so I explained why you can't be a part of my investigation, but you didn't get a chance to tell me why you wanted to see me in the first place. So I need to ask, what do you have that I need to know?"

"I've got photos," Olivia insisted, reaching into her bag. "Left on my car seat while I was talking to Arlo at Mountain Herbs."

"So you didn't lock your car. Haven't I warned you about that? You of all people, with two dead bodies at your house in a year, should know Lily Rock has its share of confused neighbors who will break into anything, especially when not secured."

Olivia sighed. "I did lock the car, but I forgot to close the window. I was hurrying to catch up with M&M," she offered as an excuse.

"Oh sure, blame it on the mayor."

"Can we just stop this?" Olivia's temper leaked through her words, exasperation with Janis's ridicule clear in her voice.

Both women glared at each other while Mayor Maguire, unimpressed, had finished drinking and curled up under the desk. Olivia could hear little puffs of air coming from his lips. *He must be asleep.*

"On the one hand, you are such a big pain in my behind," Janis erupted, "but on the other hand? You look so innocent. Folks think they can unburden themselves to you without consequences. They talk. You listen. You're good at that, and it can be useful when finding out information from suspects."

"That's an interesting theory," mused Olivia aloud. "Or maybe I'm pretty good at figuring things out and have a wicked intuition and a big heart. That could be the case." *Janis just changed her mind about my help. Just like her. She goes hard with the lecture and then does a 180.*

"Okay, that may be true. I will give you that. But what about these?" Janis snatched the photos from Olivia's hand. She looked them over, her eyebrows raising and lowering.

A low growl interrupted the conversation. Mayor Maguire scooted out from under the desk to glare at Antonia. She'd appeared in the open door, her hand clutching her purse.

"Leave it, Mayor," commanded officer Jets.

"He's scary," Antonia whispered, as she took a cautious step toward her desk.

"The mayor doesn't recognize you, and for some reason, he protects *this* one." Jets pointed to Olivia. "We let him pick his projects, and for now, Olivia is his main focus. Don't ask me why. She doesn't even live in Lily Rock. Why are you late, by the way?" Janis focused on her assistant with a glare.

Mayor Maguire walked toward Olivia. He sat near her feet, leaning over for a pat. Olivia obliged.

Antonia gave a sigh of relief. "I was here earlier but

stepped out for coffee. Before I took my break, you got a phone call from down the hill. They have some sensitive information about the Lana de Carlos murder."

"They couldn't just forward it to my email?"

"I guess not," said Antonia, drawing closer to the desk. She glanced over at Mayor Maguire, who no longer appeared interested. "Here's the number." Antonia shoved a slip of paper into Jets's empty palm, glancing at the manila envelope in her other hand.

"Give me a minute, I'll be right back."

Olivia nodded at Antonia, just to keep it friendly. "How long have you worked here?"

"Only a few weeks. I came up for a getaway and—"

"You decided to stay," Olivia finished her sentence. "It happens to the best of us."

"You don't live in Lily Rock," commented Antonia, "or so I'm told."

"I live in Playa in Los Angeles. I inherited a house in Lily Rock—long story—so I rented the house to Lana de Carlos. I only came back up the hill to look over my property and to get it ready for the next tenant."

"How long will you be here in town?"

"Only as long as it takes to solve this murder and find a new tenant. Interested?"

"Oh, no! I can't afford it." Antonia blushed as if money were a sensitive topic.

Janis stepped back into the room. "According to forensics, Lana was strangled. That's not news. The odd part is that she was otherwise in excellent health. In fact, Lana had no trace of cancer in her body nor of any chemo drugs whatsoever."

"Oh, she must have been in remission. That is so sad!" Antonia's eyes filled with tears.

"Not exactly, the coroner said Lana never had cancer nor

chemo treatments as far as her tests could tell. There was no trace in her blood screening."

"Then she wasn't really sick?" Antonia's eyes grew wide in shock.

So Cayenne was right. Lana and Wilson faked her cancer journey.

"But we still don't know who killed Lana," remarked Olivia, "or if the crowd outside the house knew Lana faked her cancer just to gain more followers."

Olivia watched Janis Jets chew her bottom lip. Then Jets clutched the envelope under her armpit, pivoting toward the back office. "You know where to find me," she called out over her shoulder.

* * *

On the drive home Olivia considered her options. *I can tidy up the house, especially the main bedroom. It will keep me busy and look innocent. At least Janis would stop having opinions about my every move.*

Or I can head back to Playa to check on my mail and talk to my temp service. That would give me some space to think and it would put Janis off my real intentions.

Out of sight, out of mind, or so they say.

The next day Olivia packed her suitcase with freshly laundered clothes. She also put in a call to Janis Jets to set her mind at ease.

"I'll let the investigation go and leave the rest up to you. Let me know when I can clean up and rent my house. I left all of that camera equipment for your team."

"Now you sound reasonable. Have a safe drive home." Janis hung up without any more comments.

Olivia felt tears come to her eyes. *I'll tell Michael right away.*

"Time to go back to my job," she explained when she dropped off Mayor Maguire at his house that afternoon. Since her apartment down the hill did not allow pets, Olivia had no illusions about taking M&M with her.

Michael stood in the doorway, looking down at the dog. "But what about your house and a new renter?" He stepped back as if to let her inside. "Why don't you two come in? Let's sit on the deck and figure out how I can help while you're away."

He's trying to be nice, I'll give him that. It's just easier to run away. All these goodbyes make me feel like crying.

Olivia followed Michael into his living room. The smell of wood smoke filled her nostrils. She looked around, taking in the welcoming comfort of his space.

"You sure know how to design a house," she admitted. "I gotta give you that."

Michael pushed the button to open the glass wall, exposing the redwood deck.

"M&M," she called. When he didn't come, she asked, "Do you think he'll be mad at me for going back to work?"

Michael pulled out a chair for her to sit. "He may be mad for a while, but it won't be forever. Neither of us can resist you for too long no matter how hard we try."

She heard the catch in his voice. He smiled at her, holding her gaze with his. Michael Bellemare had not mentioned his feelings in so many words since her return.

"So do you want me to keep an eye on your place while you're gone?" Michael kept his face noncommittal.

"I do. You have the codes and the key. It would work for me, if you don't mind."

"No problem at all. I didn't know after we talked when

you first came back, so I had to ask. Good to hear we still trust each other, at least when it comes to our property."

I'm not gonna say anything more about trust. That's still something I'm unsure about. I do know he'll take great care of his masterpiece though.

After admiring the view and enjoying some chitchat, Olivia stood. "I have to go. Gotta tell Sage and then get on the road before rush hour." Michael stood in front of her, his arms at his sides.

"A hug goodbye," he offered.

"Why not," she said with a smile.

She felt his arms wrap around her, pulling her close.

I could get used to this. It's a comfort to have a man in my life, one who cares about me too. A tingle went down her spine. She burrowed into his shirt to hide her flushed face.

As she tugged away from his embrace, he looked at her fondly, dropping his arms to his sides.

"I'll find my own way out," she told him with a smile. "This won't be like last time. I plan to come back in a week or so to check out the house. There's still stuff to do."

Olivia did not stop to look for Mayor Maguire. She glanced back one more time, noting Michael. He leaned into the railing, looking out to the forest beyond. Then she opened the door and closed it softly behind her.

On her final stop, Olivia discovered Sage sitting behind her desk at the music academy.

"Hi, Olivia. Good to see you," Sage greeted from the desk.

Something in Sage's eyes and her smile remind me of Mom.

"I have to go down the hill for a few days to check in with my agency and to get the mail," Olivia blurted out.

"Okay then," said Sage. "I know where to find you. Are

you sure that's all you want to tell me?" Sage's face softened as she waited for Olivia's reply.

She didn't ask when I'd be back, and why does she have that expectant look in her eyes?

"That's all for now," Olivia assured her.

A fleeting expression crossed Sage's face. *Is she disappointed in me because I'm leaving again?* Turning to go, Olivia added, "Gotta get going to beat the LA rush hour. Be well."

She rushed out of the office to her car. Getting behind the wheel Olivia felt tears in her eyes. She brushed them away as the ignition turned over.

On the drive down the hill Olivia felt a sadness overwhelm her. Since her reappearance only a week ago, she had apologized and reconnected with all her friends. Now she just felt confused. Trapped by her feelings and her need to move forward. By the time she made it to Temecula, she felt better, though a little drained.

Time for some music. It will make the rest of the drive go more quickly.

An hour and a half later, she parked on the street, dragging her suitcase from the trunk. When Olivia unlocked the door to her one-bedroom apartment, she rolled her suitcase across the threshold. Home at last.

A quick look around the small place assured her that everything was the same as when she left. Unpacking the suitcase only took a few minutes. She called for takeout dinner and sat back on her sofa with a deep sigh.

She could hear neighbors arguing from above her; not the distinct words but the tone of voice told the story of their dispute. Olivia felt restless. *I would be hanging out with someone at the pub if I were in Lily Rock. I could be arguing with Janis Jets or playing with Mayor Maguire. Have I lost my taste for this life?*

* * *

When Olivia checked her messages the next morning, she found that her current employer had left a message announcing that her services would be terminated sooner than expected. The woman she'd been hired to temp for would come back to work by Friday. Apparently, the woman's new baby had successfully transitioned over to the nanny.

Olivia nodded when she heard the news. *They'll find me a new position, they always do.*

Not sure what to do next, Olivia sat outside on the narrow balcony facing the street. She stared at a single forlorn eucalyptus tree, planted on the green strip near the sidewalk. *I miss the pines.*

I wonder what Sage is doing . . . Olivia pulled her cell phone out of her pocket and called. Sage picked up.

"Want to talk about the band?" Olivia asked.

"Let me finish with this student, and I'll call you right back. Five minutes."

Olivia poured herself a cup of coffee waiting for her phone to buzz. As she sat back down in her chair on the balcony, her phone buzzed. She picked up.

"I meant to tell you," began Sage, "Arlo wants us to play at the pub on the Friday before Labor Day weekend."

"Does he now?"

"He offered us 500 bucks, plus tips, of course."

"That's pretty good. Better than our usual 300."

"So I was thinking," continued Sage, "you could come up the weekend before, and we can put a set together. I have a drummer and a bass player in mind that I'd like to audition. It would mean less money for us, but wouldn't that pump up the band a bit?"

"Yeah, it would. I like the idea a lot."

"I told Michael we may be playing," Sage said shyly. "He was pleased."

The hair rose on Olivia's neck. "And it's his business because?"

"Oh, we were just talking, you know, over coffee."

"Michael is handling my caretaker responsibilities for the house while I'm in Playa. Has he said anything to you?"

"I just talked to him this morning. He mentioned something about the grand suite. Janis said they have to locate Lana's next of kin. So far, the police haven't come up with anything on the internet about Lana except for her social media."

Sage added, "I've heard you can hire people to clean out all of your background information. Maybe Lana did that so that her followers couldn't discover her previous identity."

"I didn't know you could hire someone to do that."

"You can. I guess some companies keep the internet nice and tidy just in case someone googles your name."

"I'm shocked that Lana could afford to hire that kind of company. From the looks of things, she kept her life tech heavy but otherwise free of expensive stuff. Do you think the missing boyfriend supported her with his own cash?"

"I think Wilson was poor. He could barely afford to take me out for a drink, let alone support Lana de Carlos. I mean, your rent could not have been cheap. That alone would require some kind of income."

"My rent was not that high. I was in a big hurry to divest myself of all things Lily Rock, at least then."

"You might want to reconsider the price. Your house, especially since it's designed and built by Bellemare, brings a lot of attention up here. You could rent by the week and ask a lot."

"Is that so?" Olivia twisted a strand of her hair. "How's Meadow doing?" *I'm thinking she may be the one who dropped those photos in my car. They made Lana look like a fake. With the blood tests, it seems pretty certain she didn't really have cancer.*

"Meadow seems a lot more chipper lately. After Lana died, she quit complaining to the town council."

Surely Meadow was not a suspect in Lana's death.

"Okay, enough Lily Rock gossip. What songs are we picking for our first set?"

* * *

By the end of the week, Olivia had not taken another temp job. *I just don't feel like meeting a bunch of new people right now.* Friday morning she walked downstairs to pick up her mail. To her surprise, catalogs and envelopes addressed to Lana de Carlos had been forwarded from her address in Lily Rock.

Thumbing through the mail at her kitchen table, Olivia stopped at one particularly interesting white envelope addressed to Lana. She held it in her hand. *Should I open this or hold it for Janis? I suppose Lana's mail could be part of the ongoing investigation.*

"I could steam it open like they do in a mystery book," she said aloud. Rejecting that idea Olivia slid her nail under the flap, which released without a tear. Inside, she found a paper on the letterhead of Three Bunch Pines, a resort and spa located in the desert a couple of hours away.

The letter invited Ms. de Carlos to return and spend

another weekend. They offered 30% off for their valued customers.

The following morning it took Olivia an hour to tidy up her kitchen and pack clothes for the weekend. She'd already called Three Bunch Palms the evening before, placing a reservation in the name of Lana de Carlos.

"Oh yes, Ms. de Carlos. We will be delighted to see you this weekend. Would you like your usual bungalow?" the receptionist asked.

"Oh, I would," answered Olivia promptly. "Remind me of the number again."

Ready to leave Playa for the desert, Olivia hoisted her suitcase from the bed. The trip to Desert Hot Springs would take nearly three hours with traffic. *I'd better pack a snack for the road.*

By the time she arrived at the Three Bunch Palms resort, she'd spent nearly four hours in the car and she was ready to stand up and stretch.

"I have a reservation," she told the sleepy-eyed attendant who leaned out of the air-conditioned hut. "My name is Olivia—" She stopped herself mid-sentence, remembering that she was here impersonating Lana. "But I go by Lana." Instead of giving herself away any further, she reached into her purse to pull out the reservation she'd printed from the internet. "Here you go. This is my reservation."

The man looked the paper over quickly and then handed it back. "All the bungalows are numbered. You know where to go." He slammed the window of the hut before Olivia could ask any more questions.

She found a parking space underneath a palm tree whose branches offered minimal shade in the desert heat. With her rolling suitcase at her side, Olivia made her way down the winding path. A map of the property had been posted on a wooden announcement board. *There's my bungalow.* She continued to follow the path.

On her stroll she glimpsed people sipping cold drinks, sitting in white spa robes under blue umbrellas. Pergolas, spaced out over the expanse of grass, harbored more people who rested in lounge chairs. So pompous and yet restful.

Some of the people in the pergolas had closed their curtains, probably getting a massage.

Olivia looked over her shoulder. *There must be a swimming pool around here somewhere.* Checking on another map, which had been conveniently posted near the pathway, she noted the location of the pool before moving on. *I could use a swim—posing as Lana de Carlos, of course.*

Overall the spa grounds were welcoming, wandering past the mission-style bungalows located alongside the banks of the natural hot spring river. People could step out of their bungalow and into the water with little effort.

No one looked up as Olivia passed by.

To the right, she glimpsed a restaurant. On the second-floor balcony overlooking the palm trees, people relaxed in their spa attire, some with an extra towel wrapped around their heads. *I wonder what kind of food they serve.* Her stomach growled.

Following the signs to her room number, she stopped in front of the nondescript bungalow. She looked at the stucco wall next to the door and found numbers stenciled on a flowered tile.

Two lounge chairs had been placed in the shade of an umbrella near the bungalow. *Great place to sit and read.* Olivia propped her suitcase on its wheels to reach for her card key.

She waited for the green light to blink. Only red showed on the monitor. She tried again. Finally after the third try, she reached into her pocket to pull out her cell phone. Before the front desk answered, the door creaked opened.

A handsome man in his late thirties stood in the doorway. When he saw Olivia, he opened the door more fully, revealing his rumpled swimsuit and blond hair, professionally sun bleached, dipping over his sleepy eyes. He stared at her in surprise.

"Who the hell are you?" he asked, his eyes traveling to Olivia's worn suitcase. "You aren't my usual masseuse."

"I'm not here to give you a massage," Olivia told him in her most authoritative voice. "I booked this bungalow for the weekend. What are you doing here? Miss checkout time?"

The blond man scratched his sculpted stomach for a minute as he lifted his finger underneath the elastic of his swim trunks. "Why don't you come in?" he offered. "I can fix you a drink while we sort this out."

Nice try, buster. "What's your name?" she asked, recognizing him from the photos left on her car seat.

Smiling wickedly as if he'd caught her attention and thought he might get lucky, he didn't hesitate to say, "I'm Wilson. Wilson Jones. And you?"

In one smooth movement Olivia grinned back at the man, lifting her cell phone to her ear once again. She kept him off guard, continuing to smile. "Let me just check a moment to see if I have the right room," she lied as he watched.

Apparently still hopeful that she might follow him inside, Wilson held the door wider. "Come on in. You don't have to stand in the heat."

With her eyes locked on Wilson, Olivia spoke into the phone. "Janis? I don't have time to talk. Just want you to know I found Wilson Jones. Yep. Right here. He's standing in a doorway, showing off his tan, thinking I'm here to give him a massage."

Wilson Jones stared at Olivia, mouthing, "Who's Janis?"

She waited and then added in a calm voice, "I'm not inter-fering. Do you want to talk to him or not?" Olivia handed her cell to Wilson. "She wants to talk to you. Something about your rights."

Wilson took the phone, holding it up to his ear. Janis kept him on the phone for a few minutes when Olivia heard police sirens in the distance. *Janis must have Riverside County sher-iffs on speed dial.*

10

THE BIG LENS

The arrest went smoothly. Riverside County police had Wilson Jones in the back of a cruiser within a half hour, allowing Olivia to return to her car, suitcase in hand.

I guess the spa weekend is out, but boy, did I do a good job or what? Found ol' Wilson Jones. Right in the flesh. She swung herself behind the steering wheel, ready for the journey back to Playa.

Olivia's phone rang.

"It's me, Jets," said the matter-of-fact voice. "I don't know how you did it, but after your call, I alerted the Riverside police, who took Wilson Jones into custody. They picked him up and they're holding him for further questioning."

"I could have stayed out of your business, but you gotta admit, I found the guy." Olivia didn't even try to sound humble.

"I will admit nothing. Like I was saying, Riverside County has him in custody. Would you mind coming back to Lily Rock?" Jets's voice lowered.

Is she pleading with me?

"I could manage to drive up the hill . . ." Glancing into her rearview mirror, Olivia steered her car to the off-ramp. "My bag is packed and I don't have a job pending. I'll do it for you, no one else."

"Stop being uppity. My patience has worn thin. But I do need to hear how you found Wilson when none of us had a clue."

"All will be revealed in a few hours," Olivia assured Janis, clicking her phone off. *Sometimes I get the last word.*

It was eight o'clock and dark by the time Olivia drove onto the gravel driveway in front of her house. To her relief there were no Lana de Carlos followers to be found. *Maybe they're off to find another influencer. Plus no fresh flowers on the pile of old ones. I'll have to clean that up soon.*

She locked the door behind her and turned on the lights. With the house illuminated, she made her way down the stairs to her room. Only then did she call Janis. "Still at the constabulary?" she asked in her most innocent voice.

"What took you so long? I'm at home feeding the cats. Why don't you come to my office tomorrow morning? We can talk then."

"Will do, Detective Grumpy," Olivia chided. This time Jets disconnected first.

Sprawled on her bed in the guest suite, Olivia ran through the day and the capture of Wilson Jones in her mind. It wasn't until midnight that she finally fell asleep.

* * *

The heat of the sunshine through the window spread over the foot of her bed. Olivia yawned. She reached over to grab her cell phone. Five missed calls from Janis brought a grin to her face.

She rose from bed and headed for the bathroom.

Olivia brushed her teeth and then got into the shower. *I wonder . . .*

Why was Wilson Jones hiding in a bungalow in the desert? Wouldn't he have put more distance between himself and Lana instead of hanging out in their usual weekend spot? What did he gain from a dead Lana anyway? Influencers must make a lot more money than I realized, judging by all the fancy lighting, cameras, and recording equipment. That had to be a big cha-ching.

Finishing her shower, she got dressed. With one piece of crisp toast in her hand, she opened her laptop to do some research. It didn't take her long to find what she was after. Slapping the computer closed, she grabbed her purse and let herself out of the house.

By the time Olivia walked into the constabulary, she had new ideas. "Where's Officer Jets?" she asked Antonia, who hovered over her computer, intently at work.

"Back there." Antonia gestured with a thumb over her shoulder. Olivia heard a click and realized Antonia had unlocked the door from her cell phone. *Pretty slick.*

Jets called out from the back room. "That you, Olivia? Meet me in room three. I'll bring some coffee."

Olivia found her way, sitting with her back to the door.

Jets put down a steaming mug in front of Olivia as she hurried around the desk and sat down behind her tablet. "You need to call me back," Janis sputtered. "Got to finish up one thing first, and then we can talk."

She didn't mention that I was late. She took a sip of coffee. *Nice and strong.*

While she waited for Janis to finish, she pulled out her cell phone. No messages from Sage or Michael. *Better text them and let them know I'm back in town.*

Janis finished her task and looked up at Olivia. She leaned

on her elbows and said, "So tell me, Ms. Nosy. How did you find Wilson Jones when no one else in our department, the Riverside County Sheriff's Department, or the Hot Springs local police had a clue? It was like you knew where he was."

"I found Wilson without even trying," Olivia explained with a cheeky grin.

Janis's eyes pierced through Olivia's nonchalance. "So tell me everything, beginning with the drive down the hill back to your native habitat. How is Playa, by the way?"

"The job finished up a week early. Odd how that happened."

"You can call it odd, or you can call it karma. Punishment from the universe, that's what I'm sayin'. Tell me everything."

By the time Olivia finished explaining how she'd been forwarded Lana's mail and then took a chance and booked an overnight at the spa, Jets pulled out her laptop again. Typing furiously, she asked, "What's the name of the spa resort again? Something about bunches of palms? Ridiculous!"

Eventually Olivia filled in all of Janis's questions to Janis's satisfaction. An hour passed. Finally the policewoman closed her laptop with a click. "I'm getting hungry for lunch. How about you?"

Olivia stood as Janis opened a desk drawer, putting the laptop into it and then locking the drawer. She shut down her desktop computer and removed her security identity card. "All tucked up," she said before walking around the desk. "Let's go."

Together they walked past Antonia's desk.

"We'll be at Casey's," she told Antonia.

They strolled down the boardwalk toward the popular eatery.

At the entrance the hostess waved them to two seats at the

counter; Janis sat on the end. She picked up the menu. "I love the corned beef."

"I had the vegetable sandwich on whole wheat a while back. It was pretty good. I also had a big fight with Michael that day about Marla's murder."

With her menu tucked back into the holder, Olivia spun her chair toward Janis.

"Did you find out anything about Lana while I was gone? I mean, is that even her real name?"

Jets nodded. "Lana was Lana. She came from Chula Vista and she did a bit of this and that before she became famous on the internet."

"This and that?"

"Mostly topless bars and pole dancing, if you must know. A girl has to make a living."

"Not that there's anything wrong with that," Olivia added, knowing full well she might have been in Lana's position if not for her temp jobs.

Once Olivia ordered, she looked toward the door of the back exit. A photo of Mayor Maguire stared down at her. He wore a necktie and a cowboy hat. Underneath, the plaque read, "Mayor of Lily Rock."

"M&M has his photo in every shop, restaurant, and public facility in town. I'll give you guys some credit. You sure know how to convince people that he really is the mayor."

"Because he is," said Janis. "You have not experienced the mayor's full influence in this town. He's mythical, like a furry unicorn without the horn. Plus Lily Rock loves animals, not people. That may be the only thing we all agree on."

"But why does everyone think Mayor Maguire is psychic?"

"Because he is," said Jets without a moment's hesitation. "It might make more sense to you if you broaden your understanding of psychic. Mayor Maguire knows what people need and he shows up to help them make the next move. I guess some would call that intuitive, but we in Lily Rock? We go all out and just say he's psychic."

Janis leaned closer to Olivia. "Before the food gets here, I have one more important question for you," Janis whispered, her face close to Olivia's. "Who do you think dropped those photos, the ones left in your car? We couldn't find any fingerprints on the envelope."

"I've been wondering about that all morning," Olivia admitted. "I thought one of Lana's followers did it, you know, copied photos from Lana's social accounts and then popped them into an envelope—and I'll get to that part in a minute. But it isn't that hard to find my old Ford in Lily Rock. A person would only have to ask, and they would hear, 'Olivia Greer drives an old Ford. She nearly killed herself the first time she came to Lily Rock for a weekend getaway.'"

Jets laughed. "We do tell your story just that way. But you aren't that unusual. We have stories for everyone in Lily Rock."

"What's your story, pray tell?" inquired Olivia.

"If you haven't heard it, then I'm not the one to ask." Janis shook her head, a sheepish grin coming over her face.

"But you have to admit," Olivia said, "I am the only one who drives a Ford sedan up here. My car sticks out because the rest of the residents drive trucks."

A look of surprise came over Janis's face. "You're right. I hadn't thought of that. Trucks with the occasional SUV sprinkled in. That's a good observation. I'll give you that. You may be the only *resident* with a Ford sedan." Janis smirked at Olivia, whose eyes grew wide. She'd been caught including herself as a resident. Janis reached for the pass and intercepted.

If I'm not more careful I'll be trapped in Lily Rock with Michael Bellemare doing a victory dance in the Lily Rock end zone.

Brushing past her discomfort, Olivia continued. "The thing is, I took a good look at Lana's internet postings this morning. I found the same three photos on her website."

"Now that is interesting. Why would someone drop the photos in your car if they were easily accessible on the website?"

Olivia swallowed, searching for the right words. "I suspect that the person who left those photos in my car knew that I didn't follow Lana. They didn't want to risk me not seeing the photos for some reason."

Jets nodded, clearly taking in what Olivia had said.

"But why you? Why did they drop the photos on your front seat? Why not leave them here at the constabulary where I'd pick them up?"

Before Olivia could respond, their sandwiches arrived, plopped down by the waitress behind the counter. "There you go, ladies. Here's the check." She slid the paper under the napkin dispenser.

Janis picked up the bill immediately.

"I've got this. On my expense account."

Olivia smiled. "Whoever dropped those photos may have figured I would leave them with you before heading back to Playa. In answer to your question, I'm not sure why I was put in the middle."

Olivia paused over her whole wheat sandwich. She put it back on the plate without taking a bite. "What if the photo-dropper didn't want to give you the pictures directly? Instead they dropped them in my car *knowing* I'd hand them over to you instead."

Janis mumbled under her breath as Olivia gave her a moment to process her words.

"Remember Thomas, Meadow's new boyfriend?" Olivia said. "He showed me lots of Lana photos when I first met him. He has a big camera with a huge lens. Long-distance." Olivia stretched out both hands indicating the size of the camera lens.

Jets winked at Olivia. "Are we really talking about his camera?"

The women laughed. "I'm talking about his camera; I'm not sure if Meadow was when she described it to me."

"Okay, get on with your suspicions," said Jets, taking a deep breath to stop laughing.

"Thomas seemed interested in Lana de Carlos. I mean overly interested in a woman with a breast cancer survival story. Oh sure, Meadow wanted to hire him to get pictures to show the town council so that the Old Rockers could ask Lana to leave. I think that part is true. But that doesn't mean Thomas didn't really enjoy his photography work, aka he's the perfect peeping Tom."

"Okay, let me get this straight. Meadow hired Thomas. On the one hand, he may not have been following Lana at the time. But on the other hand, he may have figured making some extra cash for doing what he already loved would be a no-brainer."

"I am going with the other hand. I think Thomas or even Meadow left those photos in my car so that we'd ignore him and go after Wilson Jones. I mean, the two with the couple in bed could not have been taken by Thomas. They were obviously well-staged selfies."

"So you're saying the photos point back to Wilson, leaving that Seeker guy off the hook. It does sound like Meadow may have been in the mix with the drop-off. All right, stop picking at your vegetable sandwich, and let's get going. Maybe we can interview the peeping Thomas guy with the big lens before he covers his tracks."

Olivia gulped the last bite and washed it down with some water. "Yes, ma'am," she said in a serious voice.

When they exited the coffee shop, a small crowd had gathered by a pickup truck parked in front of the library. Sure enough, Mayor Maguire peered down from the flatbed, extending a paw to Lily Rock visitors, who lined up one by one to pet the dog. Next to the truck, Meadow dispersed magnets with the mayor's face printed on the front. "All those with ice cream cones for the mayor can move to the front of the line," she announced to the mayor's admirers. "Welcome to Lily Rock."

"Since Meadow is busy in town with the mayor," commented Jets, "let's take your illustrious Ford and visit her boyfriend."

"Did you background check Seeker while I was away?"

"Yep, I did some internet snooping when you mentioned him the first time. He's a retired schoolteacher from LA who takes his photography pretty seriously."

"Come on, he's for real too?"

"He doesn't sell his stuff, but he considers himself an amateur photographer, an artist, if you will. When I dug further I found a couple of arrests. Not everyone appreciates a guy taking photos of their kids without asking."

"So he retired from teaching and is in his late fifties, you'd say?"

"About that. Thomas must have decided to live in Lily Rock to get away from it all. A lot of people make that decision, you know, reinventing themselves on the drive up the hill."

Olivia thought for a moment. "I didn't reinvent myself

when I came here," she said aloud. "But I do feel like a different person than a year ago—does that count?"

"Actually no," said Jets firmly. "You aren't lying about yourself, conveniently forgetting the difficult things. You're peeling away unnecessary defenses. Totally different. At least from my point of view."

By the time they reached her car, Olivia had a moment to consider what Janis had said. She unlocked the vehicle, sliding onto the driver's seat. Janis sat in the passenger seat, pulling on her seat belt.

"Aren't you the philosophical one today," Olivia said, starting up the car.

"Just drive, Ms. Snoop. I'll give you the directions."

"No need, he lives right across the street and up the hill from me."

Ten minutes later, Olivia was winding her way farther up the hill.

Thomas Seeker's house looked modest and well kept. A freshly painted wraparound porch provided ample seating and a good surrounding view of Olivia's house below.

Olivia pulled into the driveway, the crunch of gravel announcing their arrival. Before they could both get out of the car, Thomas himself stood on the front porch, shading his eyes from the sunshine overhead.

Janis Jets quickly exited the car. She strode toward the front porch, holding her badge and credentials for Thomas to see. "I'm Janis Jets, officer of the Lily Rock Constabulary. I have a few questions to ask you about the death of Lana de Carlos."

Nodding his head, Thomas looked calm and collected. He pointed to three freshly painted wicker chairs set on his front porch. New cushions were plumped and ready, almost as if he'd expected company.

By the time they were seated, Thomas had brought out three glasses of iced tea with lemon. "Never know when someone will drop in," he commented, putting a napkin under each glass.

Janis raised her eyebrows at Olivia.

Thomas seated himself, placing his iced tea on the table in front of him. "How can I help in your inquiry?" he asked in a very polite voice.

"First, you can tell us about the photography business and how you came by the photos of Lana de Carlos and her naked breasts. You know, the ones you showed Olivia?"

When Janis said "naked breasts," Olivia saw Thomas flinch. The direct question delved right under his polite veneer. *Are those tears in his eyes? Talk about peeling away the illusion to get to the truth. You go, Janis!* Olivia leaned back to watch the master at work.

"Tell us where you took those photos from and if you had Lana's permission. Were you her part-time photographer, you know, when Wilson Jones was unavailable?"

That question surprised Olivia, and apparently, it also surprised Thomas Seeker. Before Jets could keep talking, he interrupted, "Oh, no! I did not work with Lana de Carlos." He bit his lower lip and added, "I would find that work extremely distasteful."

"Distasteful or not, we know the photos are yours. So explain why you took them and how they ended up in Olivia Greer's back seat a week ago."

"If you'll excuse me . . ."

Instead of answering Jets's question, Thomas left the table to walk into his house.

Olivia took the opportunity to lean closer to Janis. "You sure know how to make a grown man cry. Did you see him tear up when you accused him of taking naughty photos of Lana?"

"I don't care about his artsy photos. I just want to know what he was up to that made him kill Lana." Janis turned in her chair to look across the bluff toward Olivia's house. "Lana lived right there. Her upstairs window is directly below Seeker's upstairs window. I bet I would find his camera all locked and loaded for the next photo shoot if we only had a search warrant."

Olivia swallowed. *Note to self: close the bedroom curtains when I get home.* "The next time he leaves we could break in to his house to look for evidence."

"We are not going to break in. I want to prosecute this Thomas guy legally without having it thrown out of court for breaking and entering without a warrant. This is Lily Rock," Janis said dryly. "We may not lock our doors, but we do play by the book when it comes to bad guys."

Before Olivia could disagree, Thomas returned from inside the house. Only red-rimmed eyes gave away his earlier distress. After seating himself, he spoke in the most winsome voice. "I did have a little trouble down the hill a couple of years ago. I suppose you know, Officer, that I was arrested. The life of an artist requires stepping outside boundaries for the sake of personal expression."

Janis Jets put on her interested face. "Better that you tell me right up front about your priors."

Thomas pulled his shoulders back, assuming a dignified tilt to his chin. "I didn't mean to invade that woman's privacy."

When Janis didn't say more, Thomas continued. "I thought she looked so beautiful on the beach, sunbathing with her children, and I took a few photos. She became distraught when she happened upon them on the internet. I don't know how she actually found them. Of course, they were taken in Malibu. You just can't trust people to do the right thing there."

Janis side-eyed Olivia, who pretended not to notice. Instead of asking more questions about Thomas's previous arrest, Janis kept up her questioning.

"Did Lana feel the same way about her privacy? Did you post her photos on the internet as art?"

"She was not happy with me, let's just put it that way. Her boyfriend actually threatened me; he had such large hands." Thomas skirted away from the topic of the internet, directing his interest toward Wilson Jones.

Holding up his hands, he added, "Do you actually think I could, even if I were so inclined, strangle a woman to death with these? You need to look at her boyfriend. He's the one—so powerful." Thomas shuddered as if fearing for his own safety.

"Well, that does help. I'm relieved to hear you tell the story of the other time. Only the one time you were arrested?" Janis asked, her face impassive.

"It may have been two times . . . or perhaps three," Seeker admitted, ducking his head.

"You know I can access your priors with a couple of clicks on my computer?"

Seeker's chest raised and then dropped. "I do know."

Jets pushed her chair back in one sudden movement. "We're going now, but I warn you, stay in town and don't go down the hill. I may have some more questions."

After the women bid their goodbyes, they drove back to the constabulary office.

Janis spoke first. "I think he may be right. I'm going for Wilson as our main suspect. Seeker is nervous and a bit icky, that's for sure, but I don't think he's the killer type. I am a bit curious about his habit of posting his photography without consent from the subjects. I'll look into that."

Olivia nodded. "I agree. I don't see him for the murder either. But there is one thing that bothers me more. He looked so ready for our arrival this afternoon. It was like someone warned him we were coming."

"He did look prepared. He kept us safely outside his cute little cabin."

"So did Meadow warn him? She could have seen us leave Casey's Kitchen together. Maybe she was the one."

"It could have been Meadow. She's a brilliant woman hiding behind a denim jumper and an old-school hippie turn of phrase. She may have suspected he'd be interviewed and told him to be ready for visitors to drop in any time." Janis shrugged. "Okay. I'm exhausted. Let's call it a day. Drop me off over there."

She left Janis standing in front of the constabulary.

Alone in the car, Olivia drove back to her house, thinking about the photographs. Then she punched in a cell phone number she'd been trying to ignore since she'd returned to Lily Rock. It rang several times before going to voicemail. Olivia left a message. "I'm here at the house. Is there any chance you'd come over tonight for dinner? I want to run something by you."

Olivia ended the call. It would be good to see Michael. She could run her suspicions about Wilson and Thomas past him to see if he had any insights. *Sure, Olivia. Like that's the only reason you want to see him.*

11

ONE FRENCH FRY TOO MANY

By the middle of the week Olivia had not heard from Michael, neither in a text nor an appearance. *Maybe I should ask around. I don't want to seem too interested in his whereabouts, but I am concerned. I mean, he could text me, right?*

Olivia reached for her cell only to have it light up in her hand. Janis Jets.

"Good morning, Officer," Olivia said cheerily. "How can I help you?"

"Just calm down with the pleasant talk. I have news."

"Tell me everything," she said brightly into the phone.

"We've got him!"

"Got who?"

"Wilson Jones, you idiot, who else? He's on his way to Lily Rock to take up residence in our most exclusive cell, which includes a view of the parking lot behind the library."

Olivia felt her focus shift from Michael's whereabouts to Wilson Jones. She'd spent two days in her home, not seeing or talking to anyone except Mayor Maguire. *When unattended, my thoughts always shift back to Michael. I'm glad Janis called.*

"How is Wilson getting to the constabulary?"

"Official transportation, including three cops and a big siren. How else did you think he'd show up? Riding on the back of a squirrel or something?"

Olivia grinned. *I like this Janis Jets, the hardwired for sarcasm one who makes me laugh.* "I guess the better question would be why did the county police release him to you?"

"You think we're amateurs here, do you?"

"Honestly, I think you put the *pro* in *pro*fessional. Not like I've had any experience with the county cops in LA or even Playa. I pretty much keep to myself, which makes you my first police official."

"Interesting, since you have caused so much trouble here in Lily Rock, I assumed you did the same wherever you went. You tell me that's not the case? I'm rarely wrong about troublemakers."

"You've already done a background check on me, haven't you? You know."

"Okay. I have done a check. You are squeaky clean. It was kind of disappointing, if you must know. I wanted a reason to keep you at a distance, and there wasn't one. You don't even have a parking ticket unless . . . Do you have an alias?"

"I do not!"

"Okay, then get yourself down here within the hour. I want to talk to you about the guy who lived in your house who mistook you for his massage therapist. Maybe you can give us lowly cops some insight on how to proceed with his interview. Wilson Jones committed this crime. I am certain he killed Lana de Carlos. He's got motive and means. We just have to pin down the timing."

"I thought Seeker was also a suspect?"

"That weasel doesn't have the gumption to swat a fly, let alone strangle a woman three inches taller."

"If you say so."

"I do. Come on down and see my arrest. Let's see how Wilson reacts when he sees you in the flesh."

Olivia hung up the phone. At least she had something to do while she waited for Michael Bellemare to answer her text. So many of her thoughts had gone in his direction the past two days. *What a confusing man!*

* * *

When Olivia arrived, Antonia sat behind the constabulary desk, looking at her computer. Mayor Maguire sat under the desk next to Antonia's feet. "Hey, Mayor," Olivia greeted the dog, reaching down to pat his head. "I thought you and I were a thing. Hanging with Antonia now?"

Though it wasn't uncommon for the mayor to make his way around Lily Rock, sleeping in a bed or on a porch wherever he felt the need, Olivia still expected him to stay with her. *That's what happens when you take someone for granted.*

As she straightened her back she saw Antonia clear the page she'd been staring at on her computer. *I feel like the mom who catches her teen looking at porn.*

"Hey, how are you today?" she asked politely.

Flipping her ponytail with a quick head movement, Antonia put up a forced smile. "I'm okay. Lost track of my boyfriend. I think he's ghosting me." Tears formed in her enormous violet-blue eyes.

"He hasn't texted you back?" Before Antonia could answer, Olivia felt a knot in her stomach. *That's what Michael is doing to me. He's ghosting me, turning his back, pushing me to the curb.*

"How long have you been seeing this guy?"

"Nearly a year now. We had plans, you know, for the

future. He got into a bit of trouble, but that's no reason to just stop texting. You can text from anywhere, right?"

Are you hearing this, Michael Bellemare?

Antonia looked away from her computer and rubbed her chin with the back of her hand. "You don't have to wait, the door's been unlocked. Janis said to send you in as soon as you arrived." Antonia reached into her desk, pulling out a pair of scissors. They slipped from her fingers barely missing Mayor Maguire's head. "Oops. Sorry, doggie."

Olivia sighed. Mayor Maguire may like Antonia. "Hey, M&M," Olivia called to the dog. He raised his head for Olivia to give him a pat.

"Hey, Toni," came a holler from the speaker on the desk. "Is Olivia there yet?"

Startled at the sound of Jets's voice, Olivia flinched. "Wow, I haven't seen one of those office speakers in years. I thought cell phones put those things out of business."

The young girl ignored Olivia, pointing to the open door. "You've been requested," she said sweetly. The girl sounded chipper and very businesslike; her tears were gone. Apparently, being ghosted by her boyfriend no longer occupied her thoughts. *I guess pretty girls like that ghost and get ghosted all the time.*

She found Janis Jets standing in interview room one holding two mugs of coffee, one in each hand. Olivia glanced around the room, taking in the paneling and glass. "Any two-way mirrors here?" she asked Janis.

"The whole place is one big mirror," explained Janis. "But before you sit down, I want to show you my guest. They dropped him off in the back—a big clandestine operation. Not even Antonia knows he's here. I feel like I have a prize species from the zoo, an exotic breed deposited by the county right in one of our cells."

Leading Olivia down the hallway, Janis stopped at the first cell. The glass door revealed Wilson Jones with his feet up on his single bed. He stretched his muscular arms behind his head, eyes closed, mouth hanging slightly open, fast asleep.

"Can he see us?" asked Olivia.

"Of course he can see us. Not every mirror blocks the view from one side. Some of our glass doors and windows provide a view from both sides. Aren't we clever?" Janis pointed to the cameras located at the corner of the hallway. "We also have cameras everywhere in this building. Michael set us up with state-of-the-art security. Toni can see all the rooms on her computer . . . when she bothers to look, that is."

"So she knows Wilson is here?"

"If she's turned on her equipment," muttered Jets, "which she doesn't always do." Jets pointed toward the front office. "I'll check on my assistant and inform her that one of our cells is occupied. She can start baking cookies and knitting him socks."

Olivia waited patiently while Janis was gone and observed Wilson as he slept. Talking to him after turning him in to the cops would be very interesting.

When Janis returned she had a grin on her face. "Toni was surprised. By the time she switched on the computer with the camera, she burst into laughter. I was right. She often forgets to turn on the surveillance in the morning. That girl!"

Jets turned back to the glass window. She clicked a button on the panel and spoke into it. "Wake up, Wilson Jones. We want to talk to you."

Arms still stretched over his head, the sleeping man shook his shoulders and then swung his legs over the edge of the bed. He stared groggily at the two women, who stared back.

"Hey, I know you," Wilson mumbled, locking his eyes on Olivia.

Jets interrupted, "Sure you do, buddy. Now stand up, use the facilities, and we will be back to get you for our little chat. Don't take too long now, ya hear?"

Minutes later, Janis ushered Wilson into the private interview room. Two chairs had been placed on one side, with the third chair facing across the table. Jets invited Wilson to sit in the single chair, motioning for Olivia to sit next to her.

Clicking her recording machine, Janis spoke the date and time, pausing to add, "This is Janis Jets along with Olivia Greer. We are interviewing Wilson Jones as a suspect in the murder of Lana de Carlos." Janis pushed the device toward Wilson.

Olivia watched the man nervously shift in his seat as Janis calmly adjusted herself in the chair. "I didn't do anything. I got nothing to hide," Wilson insisted. "I did not kill Lana. She was my girlfriend. I loved her!" As he spoke the word love, his voice screamed out the declaration, as if he wanted the entire world to know.

Immediately Janis's cell phone buzzed on the table. The name "Antonia" appeared on the screen.

"What's up?" asked Janis. "Sure . . . Talk to you later," she mumbled lightly before disconnecting. "I have a few opening questions for you, Mr. Jones." Janis began the interview with specific details, confirming Wilson Jones's name, age, and where he lived.

"You listed my house as your permanent address with the post office," Olivia interjected. "I didn't even rent to you."

"Yeah, I moved in with Lana a month or so after we met. There was nothing in the lease that said she couldn't have a roommate, I checked." Wilson smiled at Olivia, pleased with himself.

"You mean you were her boyfriend?" interjected Jets.

"Whatever! Lana could have had a dozen people living with her. There was nothing in the lease, like I'm telling you. Maybe you should write that next time if you want to be so picky about it." Jones glared at Olivia. "I didn't kill her," he snarled. "I wasn't even on the hill the day she died. I was waiting for her at Three Bunch like always. Every weekend we unwound at the spa from our hard work during the week."

"Hard work?" Jets asked.

"Yeah, the filming and stuff. Plus, I took care of Lana, you know. She was sick most of the time with cancer." Wilson paused to look toward the mirror, shifting his feet under the table. He blinked and then turned his head to look at Janis Jets. His voice shifted its tone. "Taking care of a sick person takes up a lot of time and energy." Wilson hung his head and they were unable to see his expression.

He's playing along with the story that Lana was really ill. Does he think we believe the story on the internet?

Jones continued to explain, "Sometimes we'd film twelve-hour days, into the night even, to get the right shot. Then Lana would need to rest, so we'd drive down to the hot springs. That water heals people, or so they say."

A puzzled look came over Jets's face. "So you took all those naked photos in public while Lana was recovering from chemo? That was her idea?"

Janis is playing right along.

Wilson sat back with slight smile. "Lana didn't mind taking her clothes off. It was part of her story, you know, the breast cancer. She kind of liked flashing herself all over town."

"I see." Jets's expression did not change.

Seeming uncomfortable with the silence, Wilson kept talking. "We had a great plan too. We even wanted to get a shot with that crazy dog you call your mayor, but unfortunately, Lana died, and we didn't get around to it. We could have hauled in some money on dog sponsors. Dog products are," he gestured by rubbing his middle finger against his thumb, "quite lucrative."

"What do you mean lucrative?" Janis inquired.

Olivia gulped back her indignation. Using Mayor Maguire to attract an internet sponsor seemed unethical at best. *The Lily Rock hero may require his own attorney if people are going to take advantage of him.*

"Lana and I got sponsors for her story. We'd advertise comfy sleepwear, special linens, pillows, medical equipment. We even talked up the local weed company up here in Lily Rock. They delivered, and we told all of her followers about the product. Your local economy should have been thanking us instead of complaining."

Before Janis could ask another question, Antonia arrived at the door with three glasses and a tall pitcher. Lemon slices floated on top of the water, making Olivia wonder if they were just gossiping around the table like old friends or actually conducting a police interview.

"Thanks, sweetie," Wilson said, smiling up at Antonia.

She blinked, a tentative smile going to the corner of her wide lips.

Just a ladies' man, thought Olivia. *It doesn't matter where Wilson is, he turns on the ol' charm.* There was something about Antonia that encouraged patting her on the head and calling her words of endearment like honey and sweetie. *Such a pretty young thing.* Even Mayor Maguire was entranced by her. Hadn't he taken Antonia under his protective paw?

When the interview was over, Jets ushered Jones back to his cell. On her return, she closed her laptop with a thump. "Let's get some lunch," she suggested to Olivia.

"Do we ask sweetie to come with us?" Olivia inquired smoothly.

"Don't be ridiculous. Wilson Jones is a pig and much too old for her. Toni feels like a lost kitten that needs protection. A real man magnet."

Olivia followed Janis out the back door of the constabulary.

"Not telling Antonia where you're going?" she asked innocently.

"Tired of that girl," muttered Jets.

The two women waited in line outside the front door of Casey's Kitchen. A familiar man exited the diner holding three takeout containers. "Hey, Brad," called Janis. "Over here, I want to talk to you."

Balancing all three containers, Brad smiled his hundred-watt grin, bumping into people in his rush to reach Janis and Olivia. "Hey, ladies. I'm just getting some lunch for Arlo and me. No matter how we try, the pub can't beat the fries here." Brad opened the container to reveal hot french fries, the perfect golden color, glistening with oil fresh from the fryer. He offered one to Olivia and then Janis. Both women refused.

"I want to talk to you," Jets repeated, still eyeing his burger and fries. "We'd better have some privacy, so come over to the constabulary after your lunch. I want to know about your business with Lana."

Brad shoved a fry into his mouth, wincing at the heat but swallowing anyway. Before he snatched another from the container, he asked, "What business?" He popped the hot fry into his mouth and waved his hand in front of his open lips to cool down.

"The little delivery business you had with Lana on Wednesdays—before she was killed?"

Brad's face drew a blank. Then his lips curved downward.

"It's so sad she just up and died like that. I wanted to get to know her better. I mean, she was a free spirit, you know, like a lot of Lily Rock folks."

Detaching from Janis and Brad's discussion about Lana's weed habits, Olivia followed her own thoughts. Even with Lana's naked antics and her recovery group-worthy story about breast cancer, Olivia had to admit that her old tenant fit in with the Lily Rock community.

"Janis Jets," announced the diner hostess. "Counter for two," she added, smiling at the police officer.

"They've cleared my place," said Janis, nodding at Brad. "Come by and see me this afternoon. I have some more questions."

"Will do," Brad responded, waving at both women as he strode toward his parked truck.

"Do you think Brad had anything to do with Lana's murder?" asked Olivia, hiding behind her menu.

"I don't think so, but I also know that Brad stumbles into problems without thinking. He may have information to share that he doesn't know is relevant."

Olivia closed the menu. "I guess."

After saying goodbye to Janis, Olivia drove back to her house. She knew that Brad made weekly deliveries of weed to Lana and Wilson. Had Mountain Herbs made a lot of money as one of Lana's sponsors? Maybe Brad got angry when Lana announced she had been cured of cancer. Or maybe Brad found out Lana didn't even have cancer! Brad might have feared that his income would dry up and that he'd been treated like a fool all along.

He could have gotten into an argument with Lana. His

easygoing nature may have been pushed too far. Maybe both Lana and Brad were stoned, and things got rough. Brad could have grabbed her, one thing leading to another, with Lana left dead by her front door.

Olivia sighed. *How many times does it take burning the inside of your mouth before you stop gobbling french fries one after the other?* Had a character flaw of Brad's been revealed right outside the diner? Did he ever learn from his mistakes?

For a moment Olivia imagined Brad's face as his hands slipped around Lana's neck. He could have been trying to scare her, and then he started shaking her back and forth until her face turned blue and she stopped breathing. Anger could do that, make a person unaware of their own strength.

For Brad, Lana may have been the one french fry too many.

12

ANGER ISSUES

Exhausted from her day, Olivia ate a light dinner, followed by a cup of peppermint tea. She sat on her deck, looking out into the forest beyond. *I wish the mayor would come hang out with me again. It's lonely without him.*

As soon as she acknowledged her aloneness, she thought of Michael.

Why hasn't he answered my text or phone message?

She welcomed her conversations with him, and she relied upon him to help out with her house. *I suppose I could call on another Lily Rock handy-person. I can treat this like an inconvenience, not a personal rejection.*

With the last sip of tea, Olivia savored the peppermint on her tongue. *Might as well get this over with. I've put it off long enough.* She walked inside, depositing the mug in the sink. Then she made her way to the grand suite, where she paused before reaching for the doorknob. *I'll just take a look and then call Janis to make sure it's okay for me to clean up the room.*

I don't know why I'm so apprehensive about going through Lana's room. Usually I like getting rid of stuff and cleaning out a space. But Lana was murdered. It makes a huge difference.

Clearing a dead woman's space feels like when my mom passed.

"Why are you spending so much time cleaning out your mom's stuff?" Don had asked.

"She was my mom. Who else can do the work? I loved her best."

Don shrugged. "I still think you're overreacting."

Maybe that was how I learned to hesitate instead of act. Now I pull back instead of moving forward. Of course, "overreacting" for Don really meant "not doing things my way."

Whenever I disagreed with him, he'd accuse me of overreacting.

She turned the knob, walking into the room. Olivia inhaled deeply. *I'm like a dog the way I sniff everything.* The smell of marijuana still hung in the air, lingering behind the closed door. *I need to air out the room.*

She pushed the window on the far side of the room to the side, feeling the cool breeze against her cheeks. *I don't want to work in here until I air it out. In the meantime I can work on the details of a new lease agreement.*

* * *

When she awoke on Thursday, she already had a voice message from Antonia. "Hi, Olivia, Janis suggested that I rent a storage pod for Lana's stuff. She says we can start packing everything right into the pod. I can come over and help you as soon as they deliver the unit. Give me a call."

She sure sounds chipper and efficient. Not a terrible idea either, at least I can get Lana's belongings onto the driveway and out of my home.

Olivia put down the phone, moving toward the bathroom. She brushed her teeth and stepped into the shower. As she pulled on clean clothes, she heard the *beep, beep, beep* of a vehicle backing up from the street. *That must be the pod delivery*. She hurried upstairs, shoes in hand.

From the great room window she could see a large semi-truck unloading a storage container near the side of the house. *I guess Antonia wasn't asking my permission. She was just giving me a heads-up.*

Her doorbell rang. "This is for you, lady." A man in brown shorts and white T-shirt held a clipboard.

"That was quick." Olivia scribbled her name at the bottom of the sheet. "Any keys?"

"Here you go." The man handed her two keys for the storage unit, then sprinted to his truck before Olivia could ask any more questions.

Back in the house, she considered her day. *One way or another, I want to be so busy I don't need to think about Michael Bellemare and wonder if he ghosted me.* Staring at her cell phone, Olivia smiled in satisfaction. She had only sent one text and left one voicemail over the past several days. *At least I don't look needy.*

As she dressed, Michael kept popping into her head. *Maybe I could knock on his door, just to make sure he's okay— or maybe I can mind my own business. Put him out of my head. I'll go check out the pod instead.*

Staring at the storage unit on her driveway, Olivia felt her gut clench. *I can't face the room yet.*

She returned to the house to get her keys and lock the door behind her. Then she got in her car and drove away. *I want to talk to Sage. She should be at work by now. We need to make arrangements to rehearse before the Labor Day concert. That's my excuse for avoiding that room and I'm sticking to it.*

Keep busy, Olivia told herself. *I'm constantly either avoiding the room or worrying about Michael. I feel like one of those Push Me Pull You toys in a book my mother read me. I don't know if Michael is pushing me away or if I'm pulling him back. What I do know is that I don't want to sort that room out by myself.*

In the music academy parking lot, Olivia parked in a spot designated for visitors. She slid out of the car to walk to the trunk where she grabbed her autoharp. *Check the windows and lock the door.*

From the empty reception room of the academy office, Olivia could see straight through to Sage's desk.

"Hello there." Sage smiled her welcome.

Olivia held up her case with the autoharp tucked inside. "I brought the autoharp. Do you have any time to rehearse today?"

Sage nodded. "In fact, let me call the bass player. I think he's around all day, and he can connect with the percussionist, who also lives on the hill. How about two o'clock? We can rehearse here in our community room."

"Can I leave this behind the door?" asked Olivia, still holding the autoharp midair. "It's hot in the car, and I want to stop to get groceries."

"Please do." Sage's head bent over the computer on her desk. Then she looked up again. "Is everything okay? You haven't called me in over a week. I just wondered."

Olivia gulped. *Another opening for me to tell her about our mom. But she'll be angry that I've withheld the information for so long, and then she won't be my friend. Nope. Not right now. Not a good time.*

"Everything is fine," Olivia said, waving her hand over her head. As she walked back through the reception room, she noticed two high school students waiting. Both heads hung down, necks curved forward, as their thumbs clicked over smartphones.

* * *

It took several trips from her car to the kitchen to put the groceries away. Perspiration formed on her neck, slipping down her back. Olivia opened all of the windows to air out the house, feeling the cool breeze brush past her hot cheeks.

Looking toward the grand suite, she remembered another task. *I have to check in with my temp office.* She sat at the dining table with her laptop open to read her email. The agency director had posted three positions that looked good to her. *I can find my next tenant in two weeks. Then I can go back to Playa to start the next job.*

What else can I do . . . She clicked on local websites to get an idea of how to price her rental. *I can talk to Cayenne, but I'll post on Craigslist to see if I have any takers before firming up a price. New photos would help. One step at a time.*

Olivia closed her laptop and picked up her cell phone to make a call to the constabulary. Antonia answered.

"The pod was dropped off. Can I start hauling Lana's stuff out of my house?"

"Hi, Olivia. Sure. I'm getting off of work early and can come by to help you out. Janis expects me to help."

"I'd love your help, but I have a rehearsal at two. Could we do it on Friday?"

"Even better. I'll see you Friday morning. What time?"

"How about nine?"

"See you then," Antonia signed off.

Oh good, I have help with the room and a definite time to begin.

Olivia checked her phone. Half an hour until band rehearsal. She looked toward the door to the grand suite, which stood ajar. From the kitchen she grabbed a wrapped bundle of sage resting in a ceramic dish.

"This is for those times when you need to cleanse a space," her mother told her. "When a person leaves or when you need to clear your head from unwanted thoughts, use sage." *Sage like my sister. Mom didn't name her. Mom didn't think her baby lived. A coincidence? Sage is perfectly named. She helps clear my thoughts whenever I'm near her.*

With the flick of her wrist, Olivia lit a match and then held the fire to the dry ends of the herb bundle. Watching it burn, she extended her fingers to grip the end while avoiding the heat.

She held the burning bundle aloft and headed toward the grand suite. Grasping the cording around the bundle, Olivia moved to the far corner of the room. With a wave of her arm, she stepped from north to south, then east and west observing the smoke settle into all the corners. Extending her arm into the air as far as she could reach, she waved the bundle over her head, watching the waft of smoke fall in circular patterns before settling to the floor, only to disappear from view.

Yet the scent of sage still lingers.

My new tenant will be welcomed in a clean space. Olivia placed the sage in a clay bowl to burn on the windowsill. Then she picked up the bowl again. *I forgot the secret closet.*

She pushed on the panel, which opened the door to the space. The sage still burned, a small puff of smoke lingering in its wake. Stepping through the door, she stopped. Her hand flew to her neck. *Why do I feel afraid?*

Eyes darting over the wall opposite the window, she realized there had been a change. *Where are the photos?* All of the hanging pictures had vanished, leaving the cord with clips strung across the empty wall.

With the sage still smoking in her hand, she inspected the rest of the room. *Where are the cardboard files, the ones that used to be under the tables?*

Fear crept up her spine. *Someone has been in this room and taken what was here. Not the police, Antonia would have told me.*

Olivia placed the pottery bowl on the edge of the table, her hand shaking. *I'd better take a closer look at the main room.*

At first glance she felt relief. The cameras and bed furnishings looked the same.

Making her way toward the open window, she put her hands on the sill to look past the threshold. Someone had removed the screen. *Maybe I can find some footprints.*

She leaned out the window, her hands placed firmly on the sill. Hot weather made everything dry outside, including the dirt. *It looks like someone brushed over footprints with a pine branch.* Olivia squinted. Sure enough, the imprint of pine needles covered the dirt in a pattern as if done intentionally.

With her head under the window, Olivia felt her phone buzz. She pulled her head back and reached into her pocket, barely missing a bump on her head.

"Are you coming?" asked Sage's impatient voice.

I forgot about the rehearsal!

"On my way." Sliding the window closed, she set the locks. *I'll deal with the screen later. So my next task is to reactivate the security system. I can pick new passwords and not worry if Michael is here or not.*

On the drive to the music academy a wave of nausea came up to her throat. She swallowed to push it back. *Someone broke into my house. The photographic evidence has been tampered with. I really have to stop leaving my windows open.*

She arrived at the academy just as classes were letting out. Young people crowded the walkways as Olivia sprinted toward the performance hall. Two men stood at the far end of the room. Catching sight of her, the percussion player, who shouldered a large conga, dipped into his gig bag. He placed a set of maracas and a tambourine on a table nearby.

Next to the upright piano, Sage tuned her violin, moving her finger up and down each string, holding the instrument under her chin.

"I brought your autoharp. It's sitting over there," Sage told her.

Olivia strode to her autoharp, sitting on the piano bench to tune.

The bass player greeted her first. "Hey, I heard you at World Music. Awesome set. Your voice is mesmerizing. Made me want to confess everything I'd ever done."

Olivia laughed. "I've been told that before. Something about my singing makes people want to spill their guts. Probably to shut me up," she added with a grin.

"Maybe," he admitted. "I think your voice reminds people of emotions they choose to forget."

"Or maybe her voice reminds people of buried truths," commented Sage from across the room.

He snapped his fingers. "I know. You're like Jesus and that woman in the Bible, the one he meets at the well. As soon as he talks to her, she starts telling him about all of her old husbands. Your voice is like that. Like Jesus."

He is some kind of rubber Christian . . .

"Oh please, Paul," Sage interrupted. "Don't tell Olivia that! She'll get all self-conscious and stop singing, and we'll no longer be a band with a vocalist. No more Jesus comparisons."

Paul grinned. "You mean she'll go viral, and we'll get left in the dust?"

"Something like that," Sage agreed.

Dave Franco, the percussionist, nodded to Olivia. He shoved an extra wood stool her way. She traded the bench for the stool to be closer to the group. Sitting down again she ran her thumb over the strings, still tuning. "This will just take a minute," she assured everyone.

Tapping an app on her phone, Olivia plucked the metal autoharp key from her bag. She twisted the pegs to adjust several strings. Then she clicked the app off, finishing the fine tuning by ear. Strumming a G, C, and a D7 chord, Olivia smiled. "Got it," she told everyone who had gathered to watch.

* * *

An hour and a half later, the band finally rested. They'd covered any number of old-time tunes, some with Olivia singing. The bass player added vocal harmony to a couple of the songs, which gave Olivia the chance to let her voice soar.

"Sing it again," hollered a teen from the back of the room. "You sound fantastic!"

Now that's nice. A person under the age of twenty likes our music.

"I can teach you the tune later if you have time," Olivia called to the young man.

To her surprise, he gave her a thumbs-up.

After the set she watched Paul load his instruments in gig bags. The boy from the back of the room stood shyly by the piano, waiting for her to notice him.

"How about we knock off for a while and go get a drink at the pub?" Paul wiped sweat from his brow with the back of his hand. He made the invitation to everyone, but his eyes were on Olivia.

Olivia turned to the boy and smiled. Then she spoke to Paul. "I want to show this guy the chords for that one song, and then maybe I'll stop by."

Paul nodded. "Sure is hot in here."

Sage, with violin case slung across her back, stepped closer. She wiped her forehead with the back of her hand. "We don't like to use the air conditioning unless absolutely necessary."

"An environmental stand?" Olivia asked.

"More like a financial necessity."

A puzzled look came across Paul's face. "I've been wanting to ask you . . . did your mama name you Sage after the herb?"

"Yes, she did." Sage grinned. "My mama, as you say, is Meadow McCloud. You know her? Meadow named me after the dried herb that cleanses; it's a Native American tradition to smudge with sage. My mom would say, 'Your name reflects your spirit. You have brought me clarity since the first day we met.'"

A look of surprise came over Paul's face. "I've certainly heard of her. She's a legend in Lily Rock, handler of Mayor Maguire, the whole deal. And an Old Rocker, right?"

"Yep, that's her, my mom."

"Are you ready?" the young student asked, reaching out to touch Olivia's autoharp. She gestured for him to sit on the wooden stool while she stood near him.

"Here, hold this in your arms," she suggested, handing him the autoharp.

He lay the instrument flat on his lap.

"That's one way," she nodded, "but try this way, against your chest with your arm reaching around to press the buttons."

In a few minutes she had the young man playing a simple tune with two chords. His face lit up with joy.

"That's pretty awesome. I play trombone and it took me a lot longer to make even the slightest sound."

"That's why the autoharp is so user friendly," she told him. "Do you sing?"

He nodded, his face flushing. "Not a lot, but I can carry a tune."

She looked at the young man. *I like showing people how to make music.* "Bring me a folk song that you like sometime and we'll figure out the chords and sing together. You'll get the hang of it in no time."

Saying goodbye, Olivia walked to her car, where each of the band members were getting into their cars to drive their own vehicle to the pub. By the time they arrived and parked, it was Sage who moved ahead to grab seats at a large table by the open fireplace. She gestured at Olivia from across the room.

"Put your coat here," Sage told Olivia. "Before you sit down, Cayenne is waving. I think she wants to talk to you."

Olivia acknowledged Cay with a wave back, and Cayenne pointed to an empty seat at the bar where she was serving. Olivia elbowed her way through the crowd to sit down.

"Soda water with lime?" Cay asked.

"That would be perfect. And how about a burger with truffle fries too? I am starving."

"Been working hard?"

Olivia told Cay about the teenager who wanted to learn about the autoharp as Cay placed her order. "We've been rehearsing for our Labor Day gig."

"Arlo wanted to book you guys. He's been hearing about Sweet Four O'clock from some friends. I guess you and Sage are pretty good."

She flushed with pleasure. "I guess," she admitted, ducking her chin.

"But you must be good," insisted Cayenne. "Arlo doesn't invite everyone to play at the pub." She slid a basket with

Olivia's order into her hands, pointing to the salt shaker. "Want some?"

Olivia shook her head. "I have to take this back to the table. Will you have a chance to talk later?"

"Sure," said Cay, wiping her hands on her bar apron. "I want to talk to you more about that Lana chick. I've been thinking, you know, about her wig."

Olivia took a large bite from her burger, nodding for Cay to continue.

"I think those pictures were photoshopped, you know, for effect. I mean, why would Lana be telling the story of her surgery and shaving her head when she still had hair? The dates don't match up."

Olivia took a bite of a fry. "You're right. It doesn't add up. You could call it poetic license. They manipulated the timing of the events to tell her story."

"I see where you're going." Cay nodded. "For example, people probably loved naked photos in the forest. But let's say Lana had to start chemo before she got her followers ready for that journey. She and the hotshot photographer might have pushed back the dates a bit, just to set the scene for her followers."

"I guess so. It seems awfully complicated to me. Why not tell the story as it happened in real time, photos and all? That makes more sense."

"But it's not postmodern." Cay grinned.

Olivia took her plate. "Oh right, postmodern. Just another excuse for disorganized." She looked over her shoulder to add, "Here I am, still talking to you. The band must be wondering where I've gone."

"Before you go, I want to share my . . . feelings." Cayenne scowled at Olivia. "Arlo tells me to share my feelings more, which isn't always comfortable for me. So anyway, I am furious at that Lana woman."

Alarm trickled up Olivia's spine. "You only met her that one time, right?"

"It only took one time to make me doubt her story. I think she lied about her cancer. I'm not sure she was even sick. She just put on a show to get attention and followers. Did you know she kept her cancer wigs in that box under the bed? I didn't even get to everything in the box before Lana interrupted me that day. I felt disgusted."

Olivia looked Cayenne in the eye, sensing the fierceness of her anger. The tall woman had buffed arms and a muscular chest underneath her clothing. She'd transitioned into a woman, who hid a powerful darkness that could erupt at any time.

"Is it the lying or cancer that bothers you most?"

"Both," snapped Cayenne. "I told you I have friends who have gotten cancer because of the hormones they take to transition. Just imagine for a moment how that would be. You take a pill to help you become who you were meant to be, only the hormones turn on you and give you cancer. Plus, there are implants. Plenty of trans people use them. Now the implants need to be removed because of the health risks, taking away, yet again, a prime part of your new identity."

"So you think Lana was faking her suffering?"

"I think her faking cancer degrades the genuine suffering of all sick people, especially the trans community."

She's focusing so hard on that glass, polishing as if her life depended on getting it clean.

"Many of us give up and commit suicide, you know," added Cayenne. She turned the glass around again, using the end of her cloth to polish the same areas yet again. Then she held the glass to the light.

Olivia watched with growing concern. *Why is she polishing that already clean glass faster and faster?*

Cayenne now gripped the glass in both hands, pressing the cloth harder and harder. With strong fingers she continued squeezing, and then to Olivia's horror, the glass shattered.

A gush of blood covered Cayenne's arm, dripping down her apron to the counter below.

Cayenne stood motionless, staring with fascination at her own blood running down her arm.

"Drop the glass," Olivia demanded. "You crushed it with your bare hand."

Cayenne shook her head, still staring at the dripping blood. When her eyes finally latched on to Olivia's, she let go of the remaining shards.

Cayenne spoke. "Did you see? My blood. Such a deep red."

Olivia screamed for help.

13

CLEANING UP

Leaping to her feet, Olivia ripped the bar apron off of Cayenne's waist, wrapping it around Cay's bleeding fist. "You're okay," she repeated to the stunned woman. "Pull the towel tightly around your hand to stop the bleeding!" Olivia turned to the bar patrons, who watched in silence. "Has anyone seen Arlo?"

"I'm right here." Arlo ran from the other side of the restaurant. "Hold your hand over your head, honey," he said in a firm voice, his face tight with fear. "Looks like a little blood. Let's take care of that first." *Is he downplaying Cay's angry obsession act with the glass?*

Arlo reached for Cayenne's free hand, which he took gingerly in his own. "Let's step in the back," he told her cautiously.

By the time Cayenne followed Arlo to the back room's kitchen, the pub voices rose, returning to normal. Removed from view, Cayenne no longer caused alarm. Olivia looked around the restaurant. The rest of her bandmates chatted animatedly over empty plates, seemingly unaware of the incident. Her eyes dropped to her burger, which stood cold on the bar counter.

Leaving the plate behind, she inched her way into the crowd toward the band. When she stood next to the table, Paul pulled out her chair.

"What was that all about?" he asked with a smile.

"So you saw Cayenne?" Olivia's stomach felt queasy. "So much blood—"

"I didn't see the blood," Paul said quickly, "just the owner escorting the tall woman into the back room."

Olivia shrugged, unsure how much of the story to tell. "One minute Cay was talking, and the next she cracked a glass with one squeeze of her hand. Blood everywhere."

"Got some anger issues?" Paul commented dryly.

"You could say that," she said offhandedly, hoping to satisfy his curiosity without saying more.

Olivia took a deep breath to settle her nerves. Leaning forward, she made a point of looking interested in the conversation around her, pretending to pay attention while she sorted out what just happened. *I no longer have any doubt. Cayenne could have strangled Lana de Carlos. Those strong hands . . .*

The waiter arrived at the table to drop off the check and clear the dishes. After settling the bill, they walked single file through the pub crowd, Olivia the last in line. She took that moment to glance toward the bar. *Hopefully Arlo took Cay to have that hand stitched up.*

As the band bid each other goodnight in the parking lot, Olivia lingered behind with Sage. "I like the new guys. You did a great job of auditioning them when I wasn't around."

"Speaking of ducking out," Sage smiled, "what went on at the bar while you were standing there? Everything got quiet, but I couldn't see."

"It was Cayenne. She broke a glass. Arlo came right away to take her to the back."

"Will she need stitches?"

"I think so. If I hear anything tomorrow, I'll let you know."

"Same here."

"So I was wondering . . ." Olivia's voice dropped off as she looked intently at Sage. "Do you mind my not living in Lily Rock, you know, to help with the band hiring and organizing—"

"Not so long as you don't mind. We can make this work, you in Playa, me up here. I trust you; you trust me. We've got this." Sage smiled, giving Olivia a reassuring pat on the arm.

With a goodbye hug, both women moved toward their vehicles. Olivia waved one more time as Sage took a right turn toward her truck while Olivia kept going straight.

In the dark Olivia kept her eyes focused on her car. *The new guys gelled our band into something even better than with just the two of us. I'm the only one who doesn't live in Lily Rock. If I were to stay here, we could rehearse more.*

But then I'd have to tell Sage the truth.

* * *

By the next morning Olivia felt determined to clean out the grand suite and divest herself of Lana's belongings. She rinsed her coffee cup in the sink. *Okay, no more excuses. Get going.*

With cleaning products in her plastic tub, she stood in the middle of the grand suite. *I can think about the suspects while I work.*

Brad could have killed Lana, maybe something to do with his weed business. Maybe Lana didn't take him seriously enough or wasn't giving him any business back for free product.

Cayenne might have killed Lana because she thought her social media platform was a scam. Lana faking cancer undermined the experience of her trans community, minimizing their suffering.

Thomas Seeker. He lived right across the road from Lana and he took so many photos of her. That day he invited them for lemonade on his porch felt awkward, as if Thomas kept them outdoors for a reason, maybe to hide something sinister he didn't want Janis to know about.

And then there was Wilson Jones. Janis had him in jail, convinced he was the murderer. He had motive and opportunity. Wilson, the business partner, aka boyfriend, aka photographer, would be a very likely suspect. *I'm not certain about Wilson. He did take advantage of Lana, living in her house and all, but would he actually murder the woman who included him in a lucrative business adventure?*

Armed with a box of plastic trash bags, Olivia opened dresser drawers. Working her way from the bottom to the top, she shoved items into the first bag. When that one was filled, she tied a knot at the top and tossed the bag into the corner. Opening a fresh plastic bag with a flourish, she continued to work.

A bark outside interrupted her focus. *Mayor Maguire?* She hurried to the front door, where she found not just the dog but also a smiling Antonia.

"You look beautiful this morning," Olivia told the girl, who wore skinny jeans and a pink scoop-neck top. Wrapped around her long neck, a pink flowered scarf flowed to both sides, toward Antonia's chest.

"Oh, I thought I'd dress up a bit," smiled Antonia, fingering the scarf at her neck.

"I like the colors." *She's so used to compliments.*

"It's a gift from my auntie. She loved scarves. I have a drawer full at home."

Olivia bent over to pat Mayor Maguire. "Hey, buddy. Good to see you." She felt a pang in her heart. Whispering into the dog's ear she said, "I used to be your favorite."

The dog licked the side of her face. *Apology accepted.*

Olivia gave Mayor Maguire one more pat and then gestured for Antonia to follow her to the grand bedroom. "This is our chore," she said, pointing to the room. "You've never been here before, am I right?"

"That's right," Antonia said, a flush coming to her cheeks. "I have seen the room in photographs, you know, from Lana's posts."

"You followed her, right?"

"Pretty regularly. I think Lana was courageous, fighting the cancer."

"I remember now that we talked that night at one of the vigils. You were standing in the back of the crowd. I think you were wearing that scarf."

Antonia looked over Olivia's shoulder, absentmindedly fingering the fringe around her neck. "So sad about Lana," she whispered. "Her courage during the cancer journey inspired me."

"You and a million others," commented Olivia dryly. She handed Antonia a trash bag. "Let's get to work. You can start over there by the cameras. Just start packing all odds and ends. So many electronic gadgets. I'll get the cases so that we can pack the equipment for safe transportation."

Antonia ducked her head as she shook the bag open.

By the time Olivia emerged from the bathroom, Antonia had piled up three plastic trash bags. The two beds, cleared of linens, aired in the sunlight streaming from the window. Antonia tied the plastic bags and dragged them toward the hallway. "Tell me where the laundry is," she called back over her shoulder, "and I'll put the sheets in the washer for you."

"You don't have to launder them," Olivia answered hastily. "The cops can decide what to do with them when they're done. That's the usual procedure, right? The linens may have DNA."

Antonia dropped her bundle and then picked up the bags again. "I figured they already got their DNA samples. I suppose you're right. I guess I'm overly tidy."

Olivia shrugged. *She has a thing for clean linens.* "You can put the sheets and everything in a couple of bags. Then haul them out. I need to finish in the bathroom."

By lunchtime, the room had been transformed. Both mattresses had been turned and the nearby windows opened. The women worked together dragging the therapeutic chair to the storage pod. The hospital bed would be next. All of the camera equipment had been returned to cases. Olivia took the last two bags in hand as she made another trip to the pod unit in her driveway.

"Olivia," someone called.

She spun around to find Thomas Seeker standing by her front door. He wore his usual jeans and faded green T-shirt, along with a mild-mannered expression of curiosity.

"Hey, Thomas," Olivia said, brushing her hands against her jeans. She smiled, doing her best to look polite.

"Are you leaving town?" he asked, pointing to the trailer.

"I am leaving town, but not today. The police told me I could pack up Lana's belongings."

She looked at the man, making a quick decision, surprising even herself with the next sentence. "I want to post photos of a clean house for a new tenant. Would you be interested in doing a shoot for me, you know, for some cash?"

I bet he's going to turn me down because he's too much of

an artist to take such a menial job. To her surprise, his face lit up at her offer.

"I would love to do the shoot for you at no cost; we're neighbors."

For free? Really? Maybe he isn't such a big creep. I might have misjudged him. To be cautious she said, "Let's keep this as a financial arrangement. I can pay you and write off the expense on my taxes. That way, we're on the up-and-up. Okay with you?"

"Perfectly fine. I charge 200 per hour."

Olivia gulped. From free to overpriced in one short conversation. "I can manage the cost. It shouldn't take more than a couple of hours, right?"

"I'll have a look inside and give you an estimate," he said, moving toward her open front door.

Before she could object, Thomas walked past her right in the front door.

A low growl met him within.

Sprinting inside she saw Thomas standing with his back against the wall, his hands in front of his crotch. "Now now, doggie," he cajoled in a nervous voice.

"Stand down, M&M," Olivia said in a firm voice. Why did M&M growl at him? Usually the mayor was the epitome of hospitality.

Thomas lowered his hands. He reached one palm under Mayor Maguire's black nose for him to sniff. The dog leaned forward as if to sniff and then took a step back as if he was offended by the smell.

"Probably caught a chemical from my darkroom," suggested Thomas. "I'm not really a dog person. Don't tell Meadow."

"Not really a dog person . . . does that mean you like cats?"

"Oh, I like kitties just fine."

"You may be forgiven then." Olivia did not want to pick on the man who obviously didn't fit in anywhere and never had.

Antonia entered the room in a rush, a plastic bag dragging alongside her left boot. "This is the last one," she said breathlessly to Olivia. Stopping suddenly, she looked at Thomas Seeker.

"Antonia, this is Thomas. Thomas, this is Antonia. I assume you haven't met?"

Thomas reached out his pale hand as Antonia reluctantly let him touch hers. "Hello," she added hastily.

"You look familiar to me," said Thomas. His eyes lingered on her face and then dropped to take in her slim body and long legs encased in expensive leather boots.

Olivia leaned back to watch with interest. "Thomas is a photographer. He's going to shoot pictures of the house so that I can put them up on the website to attract the next tenant."

"And I would love to include Antonia in my shoot." Thomas leered at her, forgetting his manners as he moved in for a closer look at the young woman.

Antonia looked away, disinterested in his approach. "Sorry, I can't stay. I have to get back to the constabulary. Officer Jets is expecting me. See you later, Olivia."

At the name of Officer Jets, Thomas Seeker stopped in his tracks. Mayor Maguire let out a low growl. Before Olivia could admonish the dog, Thomas shoved past Antonia toward the great room.

"Thanks so much for your help," Olivia told Antonia. "You can put the last bag into the storage unit. I'll call when I'm finished. Will you arrange for all of this to be picked up soon?"

"Yes, I will. Just text or call, and I'll have everything taken care of. You are so organized. I'm sure the police lab will be relieved when everything arrives in such good order."

If only Michael could have helped. Olivia checked her cell phone again. *No messages.*

Olivia watched Antonia pull out of the driveway. Then she turned quickly, walking back into the house. *Is he checking the house for lighting?*

Olivia looked in the great room without finding Thomas Seeker. She stepped into the grand suite next. "Thomas," she called. But no one appeared.

Since the stairs were just outside the suite, she walked downstairs toward her room, opening the doors to the spare rooms and the laundry. Still no photographer.

When Olivia returned up the stairs to the grand suite, she finally found Thomas standing in the middle of the room. He looked nonchalantly toward the timbered ceiling as he hummed to himself under his breath.

"Where were you?" asked Olivia.

"I've been here waiting for you," he said.

Big fat liar.

"Such lovely architecture. This house is quite a gem. You inherited, I hear, from a high school friend who married rich?"

The familiar sense of guilt flooded over Olivia. Thomas knew her entire Lily Rock story, from finding Marla's dead body to inheriting her wealth. *Thank you, Meadow.*

"Lucky me," she answered, trying to remove the irritation from her voice. "So, where do you want to begin with your photos?"

"Now that I have the lay of the land, so to speak, I'll go to my house and get my camera and meet you back here in an hour?"

"That would be great. I'm ready to rent the place as soon as possible now that Lana's belongings have been removed."

She waited for Thomas to follow her out of the room. By the time they stood at the front door, questions filled her head. *Where had Thomas been hiding while I looked for him and called? Maybe the grand suite bathroom?*

Once back in the house Olivia made her way toward the bathroom. Nothing appeared out of place. *Hey, wait a minute. What's that hanging off the shower nozzle?*

Stepping into the wet room enclosure, she reached up to touch the nozzle. Loosened from the wall extension, it fell into her outstretched hand. She screwed the nozzle back on and directed it toward the wall where she would not get wet. She tried the water. *Still works.*

She stepped out of the wet room and headed for the bedroom. Inhaling deeply, she realized there was no more marijuana scent, just the fresh breeze. *Maybe I'll call the painter to freshen up in this room. That would be only fair to my next tenant.*

Hearing a noise come from the kitchen, Olivia froze for a moment, then hurried out of the room, down the hallway. She cautiously moved toward the kitchen door to look inside.

"Hey, M&M. Are you hungry?" A smile came to her lips. *He stayed with me after Antonia left. Good doggie.*

Mayor Maguire ambled toward the kitchen, where he pointed his nose toward the drawer where she kept his dry food. Olivia opened the drawer, reaching in to grab the bag of food. She found his bowl on the floor near the back door. Heaping kibble into his bowl, she placed it near his water. "There you go."

The dog immediately sniffed his food and then consumed his entire bowl of dinner in a matter of minutes. "Well, you were hungry." She picked up his empty bowl and placed it in the sink. "I'm so happy you stayed."

14

"YOO-HOO!"

On Sunday morning, Olivia slid out of bed with a groan. She rubbed her eyes, pushing away a sleepless night. Even the comforting presence of Mayor Maguire had not brought her the usual slumber.

With a yawn, she walked to the bathroom to look at her tired face in the mirror. After showering she made her way to the kitchen to fill the coffeepot with water. Mayor Maguire followed, waiting by the back door to be let outside.

She watched the dog explore the trees outside her kitchen window. Looking past him, her eyes rested on Michael's cabin. *Normally I'd invite him over for a cup of coffee this time of the morning.*

The curtains to the left of his porch had remained closed for several days. Olivia closed her eyes. *Something about Michael's disappearance is not right. Maybe I will call him again. Who cares if I seem needy?* Curiosity had been replaced by apprehension.

The first sip of coffee always tasted the best. Olivia savored the strong roast in her mouth before turning to look out the window again. Then she opened her door as Mayor Maguire sauntered in. "Time for breakfast?"

Preparing the dog's food gave Olivia time to think about her lack of sleep and Michael's disappearance. She'd gone over and over Lana's death in her mind, never able to settle on who could have strangled her tenant. Leaning over to put the bowl on the floor, Olivia straightened up.

With a deep sigh, she considered what was going on with Michael. *Maybe Michael isn't ghosting me. Something might be really wrong. He could be lying in his house, unconscious or worse, without anyone knowing.*

I've been pushing Michael away thinking he wanted to rescue me. He always shows up even when I don't need help. But what if Michael needs me to rescue him?

Michael wouldn't ghost me for no reason. He'd confront me and nag me but not just walk away. It's been days now. And why haven't I asked anyone else where he went? Because I didn't want to be teased. Like Janis, for instance—she might know his whereabouts. She could have a perfectly reasonable explanation. Or I could have asked Meadow. She knows everything about everyone in Lily Rock. But instead, I kept it to myself as if I didn't care.

Mayor Maguire stood by the back door again. Olivia reached into her kitchen drawer, where she kept extra keys. Michael had given her his house key as a peace offering a year ago. *I'm going over to his place right now.*

"Let's go, Mayor," Olivia told the dog as she opened the door. His tail raised at the sound of Olivia's voice. He wagged it back and forth in the air, rushing out ahead.

Before Olivia could follow the dog, someone called from around the front of the house. "Yoo-hoo. Anyone home?"

"Oh no." Olivia stepped back in the kitchen. She closed the door, leaving Mayor Maguire to fend for himself outdoors.

I'd know that "yoo-hoo" anywhere. What does Meadow want? I'll cut her visit short.

Meadow stood on the front doorstep, a basket in her outstretched hand. "I thought you may like some of my home-made muffins with raspberry jam," she said, pushing past Olivia.

With nothing else to do but close the door behind her visitor, Olivia took the basket from Meadow, forcing a smile to her lips. "Thank you, Meadow. What brings you here on such a lovely Sunday morning?"

"I was on my way home from the church, and I thought I'd drop by." Meadow looked around, heading toward the great room sofa. "I just love the design of this house; Lily Rock is so fortunate to have a Bellemare from Chicago living in our town."

In a singsong voice Meadow kept talking, one sentence tumbling into the next, like a row of dominoes falling in line. "You were lucky to inherit such a new home in Lily Rock. So many of the cabins are just a work in progress. People dread being the ones to pick up after dead relatives, what with all of the used furniture and knickknacks. I like your place so much. You don't indulge in collecting, do you? You know, like those ceramic squirrels and mice and dishes. I have my grandma's set of spoons, which take up an entire wall the living room . . ."

Meadow chatted on and on as she seated herself in the middle of the sofa. Olivia noted how her opinion of Michael had done a 180. Only a year ago Meadow and the Old Rockers couldn't stand the name of Bellemare. They'd done their best to drive him out of town, resenting his lush designs and the attention he brought by living in their insulated small town.

Olivia sighed, returning to Meadow's voice, which droned

on. *Without being entirely rude, my only choice is to wait for a pause in the conversation and then jump in.*

"You're right," Olivia said as soon as Meadow paused for a breath, which took a while. "I don't collect knickknacks, and I do have to get out of here very soon. I have a rehearsal with the band! We're getting ready for a Labor Day gig at the pub."

"Oh, really?" Meadow's glasses had slipped down the bridge of her nose. She looked intently at Olivia, sussing out a lie. "I see. Well, I just wanted to check up on you. Two dead women on your property must be upsetting."

"I didn't find the second dead body," Olivia argued.

"Oh no, dear, I know that. I just wanted to make sure you were well. I do have herbs in case you have any issues, you know, with sleeping or appetite."

I must look as tired as I feel after two restless nights in a row.

"I'm fine. I've been drinking coffee all morning."

"Well then I'll be going. I see you are in a hurry . . . but Olivia?"

Here it comes. She's finally going to get to the real question she's dropped by for.

"You spoke to Thomas the other day? I don't want you to get the wrong idea about us, you know, as a couple. We only went out a few times. He's rather stodgy for me, if you must know the truth. I prefer a man who is more of a free spirit."

"And one who's not a peeping Tom?" added Olivia innocently.

"Just as I thought. You got the wrong idea! Thomas is an artist. He takes wonderful photos of people, he really does. I don't understand why some get so uppity about his process."

"Maybe because he takes the photos without asking permission?"

"Doesn't everyone do that nowadays on their cell phones?

Take photos whenever they feel like it, regardless of who might be in the picture?"

Meadow's not far wrong. Social media has made it possible to post photos with little to no consequence.

"Thomas came into my house yesterday and looked around without asking." *Not so innocent, is he, Meadow?*

"Surely that doesn't surprise you. Everyone in Lily Rock wants a tour of this magnificent house. Marla didn't live long enough to have a welcoming party for the town. Then you rented to Lana and the window of opportunity closed. We're just curious, Olivia."

Olivia sat back to consider Meadow's words. She'd under-estimated Lily Rock's proclivity to get into everyone else's business. They naturally wanted to know about Michael's architectural triumph and her newly inherited home.

Meadow was right. Marla had been in a hurry to build, passing her permits and inspections before anyone on the town council could object. By the time Michael finished his design and took over as general contractor, the rest of the town could barely catch up.

"You're not mad at Michael anymore?" Olivia asked.

Meadow's cheeks puffed up and then deflated. "I was mad at him at first. He did everything by his own rules, in such a hurry. But after Marla passed, Michael became such an upstanding member of Lily Rock. He donates to the music academy scholarship fund, for instance. Plus he's very generous at Christmastime. We—the town council and I—have a new respect for Michael. But enough about him. What I want to say is about Marla. You never had a memorial service for her. The town had no chance to celebrate Marla's life with a gathering, even a party. A year has gone by and no recognition."

Olivia sighed. *I am a terrible friend. But maybe I can*

correct the problem right here and now. I can afford to be generous, especially if I include Meadow.

"I think you're on to something. I've been . . . how would you put it . . . remiss. Why don't I throw a party? A kind of housewarming and a memorial celebration for Marla, too. We could invite the entire town before I find the next tenant. That would achieve two goals: satisfy people's curiosity about the house and honor Marla's memory. Maybe people could say a few kind words about Marla at the event. You didn't know her very well," Olivia gave Meadow a nod, "but you seem to appreciate how she brought Michael Bellemare's talent to the town. That's something."

Meadow's jaw dropped in excitement. "That's a wonderful idea! You could hire Arlo and Cayenne to cater the food, and Sweet Four O'Clock could play. I would be happy to organize the open house for you."

Olivia shuddered. *Meadow having free reign of my house . . . She'll know everything about me in a couple of hours, and then the entire town will be in my business.*

Before Meadow could start talking again, Olivia stood, turning to face the front door. "Thanks for the muffins and jam," she said, giving the woman a quick kiss on the cheek.

"Let me know when you're ready to have that open house," Meadow reminded her. "You can tell Sage. She is an excellent go-between."

Spoken like a true mother. If only Meadow knew the truth.

Watching Meadow walk to her truck, Olivia quickly closed the front door. She headed toward the kitchen to resume her interrupted quest. "M&M," she called from the back door. The dog bounded to her side immediately, his tail held high as he awaited Olivia's next instruction.

They walked the path to Michael's house together. Trees

rustled above. One crow stood on a lower branch, his beak holding a berry. When he saw Olivia, he cawed, causing the berry to bounce on the dirt below. With a swoop, the crow picked up the lost berry, climbing higher, wings taking the bird from view.

Olivia knocked on Michael's door. No answer. She tried again. Still no answer. Then she pulled his spare key out of her pocket. A sense of foreboding froze her hand in midair. *Is he inside, unable to answer the door?* Her knees trembled. The memory of Marla's dead body felt so close.

She looked down at Mayor Maguire, who stood alertly at her right knee. *That's when I first met you, M&M,* she thought. *You were there when I found Marla right past the herb garden.*

Olivia could not bring herself to push the key into the lock. Fear of what she would discover held her back. Then she heard a twig snap behind her. Had the crow returned for another stray berry?

Frozen in place, she brought her arm back to her side, hiding the key in her palm. Mayor Maguire turned around, his ears perked to listen. Olivia turned to face the trees, looking around for the cause of the broken branch. A voice came from the woodpile at the side of the house.

"Hey, Olivia. Want to come inside for a cup of coffee?"

Mayor Maguire leaped into the air. He spun in a circle at the sound of Michael's voice. He barked, running toward the man in the flannel shirt. Before Michael could divest himself of the firewood he held in both arms, the dog jumped, expecting to be caught.

Michael dropped the wood to catch the dog, a smile covering his face. "Okay, buddy. Good to see you too."

Olivia watched the reunion. *I wish I could have greeted him that way.*

"Haven't heard from you for a while," she said, stepping toward the dynamic duo.

"I've been away," he said, gently placing Mayor Maguire down on the path. "Took a hike for a few days, did some backpacking. Got home late last night. I saw your text."

"You didn't take your phone on the hike?"

"I took it. Just didn't have any reception. Up for the coffee?"

If I say yes, then we'll go back to our usual banter. If I say I'm too busy for coffee, he'll take the hint and move on.

"I'd love a cup of coffee. Had a difficult night—so much has happened, I can't keep the details straight in my mind. I missed having you to chat with." She'd admitted that she missed him before she could take the words back. Did she regret it?

Michael patted Olivia's shoulder in a friendly gesture. His hand lingered for a moment before he removed it, walking past her to his front porch. With Mayor Maguire at his side, he turned the door handle. "Did you drop by because you were worried about me?" His face held a hopeful grin.

"When you didn't answer my text and voicemail, I got concerned," she explained.

"Concerned?" Michael scratched the back of his head. "You weren't concerned, you were worried! About me!" His pleased expression was exactly what Olivia hoped to avoid.

She laughed. "You may be the most conceited man I've ever met. I've been busy and forgot all about you, if you must know the truth. It just occurred to me I hadn't seen you for a few days, so I thought I'd drop by."

"Sure, you tell yourself that, but Mayor Maguire and I know differently, don't we, buddy?" The dog's tongue hung out under his whiskers.

"The dog knows nothing," Olivia insisted.

"If you say so. Come on in. The coffee should be ready by now."

Olivia took a step into the house. She smelled the fresh brew and her stomach growled. Her coat came off first, then her boots.

Michael returned with a full mug to find Olivia seated in front of the fireplace. "Here is your disgusting brew. Black, no cream or sugar. You're a tough cookie, Olivia Greer."

I like the way he uses my first and last name. Kind of like his own personal endearment. I don't think he does that with anyone else.

"I do like strong coffee," she admitted.

He turned to head back to the kitchen but hesitated before saying, "I'll get my mug, plus I have someone I want you to meet."

Someone else is in the house . . .

When he returned, he held a mug of steaming coffee in one hand and the elbow of a tall blond woman with the other. She smiled at Olivia.

"I've heard so much about you. Olivia, right?" She extended her hand.

Olivia's brain put all the details of the last week into place.

He's got a girlfriend. He's been camping with her. She must have spent the night. She's the blond Sage saw him with at the pub when I first arrived.

Olivia looked at the woman, watching Michael's bland expression at the same time.

She shook the woman's hand with a quick grip before looking toward the door. *How soon can I leave?*

"My name is Wanda. Wanda Bellemare," the woman responded.

Michael's sister, maybe? Olivia looked at her closely.

Though she and Michael were of the same height, they did not have a familial appearance. *Maybe they're adopted siblings.*

Michael explained. "Wanda is my wife."

"Your ex-wife, dear," Wanda corrected him with a punch in the arm. "I've been happily unmarried to this man for the last five years. Best years of my life!" She grinned at Olivia, daring her to disagree.

Unsure what to think, Olivia's gaze dropped to the wood planks underneath her feet. She curled her toes in her socks, taking time to gather herself. *Is she the ex-wife with benefits?* Sighing deeply, she nodded toward the door.

"I won't stay. You two probably have a lot of catching up to do."

Michael cleared his throat. "Don't go, I can explain."

Before yanking on her boots, Olivia pulled out Michael's house key from her front pocket. *Should I return the key?* She held it in her palm and then slipped it back into her jeans pocket.

I am a good neighbor, and good neighbors can keep a set of keys as a backup. Olivia waved at Michael and Wanda as she let herself out the door.

15

THE LADIES' MAN

That evening Olivia did her best not to think about Wanda and Michael. Whenever her thoughts wandered in their direction, she'd say, "Stop it. Just go to sleep."

The following morning, bleary-eyed from lack of sleep, she stood staring out the kitchen window toward Michael's house. *Let it go! Dwelling on my feelings for Michael doesn't help. There is no sense in overthinking a relationship that never really happened. I must have imagined his feelings for me. Get back to work.*

After eating his breakfast, Mayor Maguire stood by the back door. "Time to move on," Olivia said to him. She watched the dog mosey along the path toward Michael's cabin. *Oh well. M&M makes his own choices.*

With her to-do list in her hand, Olivia decided to call Thomas Seeker. The photos of her house had become a top priority. She needed pictures to post on her website for that potential new tenant. *I can use the photos as an excuse. While he's here I can ask him questions that may lead to him telling me the truth about his relationship to Lana de Carlos. I'm not sure if Thomas ever spoke to Lana face to face. Maybe he just took her photo from behind bushes.*

Rather than calling, Olivia changed her mind and texted Thomas. While she waited for his response, she tidied up the kitchen. Satisfied with her work, Olivia locked up her house and headed downtown.

At the constabulary, no one greeted her, so she sat down and called Janis Jets on her cell phone.

"What do you want?" asked Janis impatiently.

"I'm out here in reception," Olivia explained and then hung up. She waited another few minutes and called again. "Are you coming out or what?"

"Don't get your panties in a bunch. I'll be right there. I'm dealing with a crying administrative assistant here, kind of messy."

She must be with Antonia. Wiping up tears is not Janis Jets's superpower.

Olivia waited a few more minutes. Finally Janis appeared through the sliding glass doors.

"Your shirt is untucked," observed Olivia. "What's going on?"

"Who made you the fashion police? Come back here and I'll explain." Jets turned toward the conference room.

They found Antonia slumped over the table, her head held in her hands. Surrounded by balls of crumpled tissues, she dabbed at her eyes. "Hello, Olivia." Tears welled, spilling over her cheeks.

"What's going on with you?" Olivia sat down next to the distraught girl while Janis left the room.

"I've been attacked!"

Olivia looked at Antonia's bare arms and face. She could see no signs of scratches or blood.

"That crazy trans woman, what's her name?" Antonia said. "That tall woman with the obviously fake black wig? Well, she organized a bunch of her trans friends, and they've been picketing the constabulary for the past few days, demanding that justice be done over Lana's death."

Antonia continued, "One of those women got in my face and accused me of protecting him by keeping him in our jail. Just because Wilson is in jail, it doesn't mean he killed Lana. Police make mistakes. I know him; he wouldn't hurt a fly."

"You know Wilson Jones?"

"Well, kind of. He used to be my boyfriend."

Well isn't he the man about town. Wilson dated Sage and Antonia and Lana? "When was Wilson your boyfriend exactly?" she asked.

"Before I came to Lily Rock. We dated for months."

Olivia noted that Antonia's face looked more composed when she spoke of her old boyfriend.

"Wilson only came to Lily Rock on an assignment. He set up an interview with that woman who's the head of the music academy. You know, what's her name? Lavender or Chamomile or something?"

"Her name is Sage."

"Whatever. Wilson was supposed to do an interview about the school and come back, but he ended up staying in Lily Rock. I followed him up here." Antonia looked around the room. *She was so absorbed in her story she must not have realized Janis isn't here.*

A commotion in the hallway drew Olivia's attention to the door. Though Janis could not be seen, her voice could be heard from the hallway.

"Here he is," Janis announced, shoving Wilson Jones into the room with one hand. "I brought him with me so we can figure out this mess." She closed the door behind her. "Learning anything interesting?" Janis asked in a phony tone, implying that she cared.

"I'm not sure," Olivia answered, running her hand through the hair on her neck.

Wilson slipped past Antonia into the chair on the opposite side of the table. He glared at Jets, who stood in the doorway.

Both of Wilson's wrists had been forced together in handcuffs, making him look like a polite child waiting for his next meal to be served. "Can you take off the cuffs?"

"Sure I can," said Janis. "I can also get you a three-course breakfast and freshly brewed coffee. Pardon me while I call the maid, and she can grind the beans. You are a prisoner, or have your forgotten?"

Wilson's head slumped, looking pathetic. Janis moved around the interview table. "By the looks of you, I don't think you have the energy to fight your way out of jail, so I'll give you a break. But don't get used to it." She unlocked the cuffs, and Wilson massaged his wrists.

Janis came around the table to sit next to Olivia. She pointed to Antonia and back to Wilson. "It seems these two are a couple, and they didn't bother to tell me."

"So I've been hearing," muttered Olivia.

"This one," Janis gestured toward Antonia, "knew Wilson before she got the assistant job. She just pretended not to know him when he arrived. Here I thought she didn't see it when they dropped him off, but apparently she watched the entire exchange and managed to turn off the computer screen before I noticed.

"But this morning, I caught them canoodling in his cell, with blankets and takeout. Apparently, they'd spent the night together under the surveillance of the Lily Rock constabulary. If you want proof, I'm sure we have the video recordings."

Olivia shook her head vigorously.

"But I love Wilson," sobbed Antonia.

Olivia looked intently at the young woman. *How can someone cry that much and still look so perfect? She doesn't even turn blotchy or get puffy—just those enormous violet-blue eyes with the tears. Does Antonia know more about Wilson's culpability in Lana's death than she's saying? Is she covering up for him?*

"Is he the one?" she asked. "The guy who ghosted you?"

Antonia checked her tears immediately. *Faucet on, faucet off.* "I told you about that?" Antonia's expression turned blank, the corners of her mouth turning downward in a perfect pout.

She widened her eyes as if remembering something. "That day when they brought him to the Lily Rock jail. I told you then. You seemed to understand about ghosting. But since he's been here a week, we've made up." Antonia's eyelashes fluttered.

Janis Jets drummed her fingers on the table. "I have to get my tablet and make some notes. Come with me, Olivia. I want to talk to you. Leave the lovebirds here, we can watch them from across the hall."

Olivia followed Jets toward her private office.

"Leave the door open. I can't take my eyes off those two for a second. I feel like I'm a chaperone on a high school field trip." Janis slumped into the chair, pointing across the desk for Olivia to sit down. She stared over Olivia's head at Wilson and Antonia, who leaned toward each other as they whispered.

"So, you had no idea about those two?" Olivia asked, gesturing with her thumb over her left shoulder.

"Not a clue. Antonia may look oh so innocent, but she has a sneaky streak that I can't quite put my finger on."

"I know what you mean. At first I took her for a princess, you know, with the big wide eyes and innocent smile. But then today, she let her guard down. If she moved to Lily Rock to be with Wilson . . . how surprised she must have been to find he'd already moved in with Lana."

"Not just living with Lana but making a profit with his naked photographs."

"Speaking of photos," Olivia said, "I haven't had a chance to tell you that Seeker came to my house yesterday. According to him it was just to say hello. When my back was turned he wandered off, ostensibly to check out lighting for a photoshoot I'd spoken to him about. It wasn't until after he left that I discovered the grand suite showerhead had been dislodged."

"You mean broken clean off or disassembled and hanging there like a ripe piece of fruit?" asked Jets.

"Just hanging there as if he didn't have time to put it back together."

"Oh really? Do say more!"

Jets reached for her laptop and then shook her head. "I left it in the other room." She reached into a drawer, pulling out a paper and pencil instead.

Olivia watched Janis scribble. Her mind drew a blank and then she realized, *I might have missed a clue.* "Do you think Seeker put a camera in the shower to spy on Lana and that he made an excuse to get into my house to remove the evidence?"

Janis wrote even more furiously. When finished, she looked across the table at Olivia. "On the one hand, I think you're an idiot to hire Thomas Seeker to do your photos. On the other hand, I think he did have a camera in Lana's shower, and maybe you can get him to admit to spying on her. We'll definitely come over and dust for prints one more time."

"Does this mean that I'm on the investigation team?" asked Olivia, holding her breath.

Jets carefully folded the paper with her notes and put it in her pocket. "I will transfer this information to my laptop later. You're on the team . . . as an amateur only, not in any official capacity."

Jets sat back in her chair, still looking over Olivia's shoulder at Wilson and Antonia across the hall. She sighed deeply. "You should have seen Cayenne's crowd out here all weekend. They kept demonstrating by taking their wigs on and off. For an hour, they were all bald, and then the wigs, and then bald again."

"What was their primary complaint?"

"That Lana de Carlos was a fake cancer victim."

"Is that true?"

"I think it may be. Of course, I believe Cay about the wig and the dates and her observations. It would be nice to have some more specific evidence, like a photo with a reliable date. I kept waiting for Jones to admit he knew Lana didn't have cancer, but he was so convincing during his initial interview. You heard him; he believed Lana was really sick."

Now that I'm on the investigation team, I might as well be all in. "I do have one more thing to tell you," admitted Olivia. "Someone came through an open window at my house and removed all of the photos from the inner dressing room. When I looked outside I saw footprints brushed away in the dirt."

Jets's eyes glowed, her jaw set in concentration. "I bet you have an idea who broke in."

At that moment Olivia's cell phone buzzed. She reached into her pocket to check who was calling.

"Hi, Thomas." She mouthed to Janis, "Speak of the devil."

"Actually, I'm at the constabulary, and Officer Janis Jets has a problem that you might be able to solve. She wants to get your professional opinion on how people alter the dates of photographs."

Olivia listened and then held her hand over the phone's speaker. "He's more than willing to help the ongoing investigation—at least that's what he says."

Jets shrugged, reaching her hand over the desk to take the phone.

"What Olivia means is that I need the photos you took of Lana de Carlos in the shower and the ones you stole from Olivia's house. I already know you have them." Janis handed the phone back to Olivia.

"I've got you on speaker now," Olivia told Thomas.

"I have no intention of sharing my photos with the police," Seeker said in a firm voice.

Olivia's eyebrows raised. He did not deny taking photos from her house or dropping in through the open window. *I need to confront the little weasel.*

"Well, then I may have to file a report about you hooking up a camera in Lana's shower without her knowing. Don't forget, I can do that because I own the house, and you did not have my permission."

Both women stared at the silent cell phone on the table between them. Janis took a sip of coffee while Olivia brushed back her hair with one hand. Finally, Thomas spoke.

"I'll be down to the constabulary in fifteen minutes."

"Bring the photos . . . and the shower camera," demanded Jets, snatching the phone to end the call. "I like being the first one out of the conversation."

Looking across the table at Olivia, she leaned back in her chair.

"On the one hand, I don't think Thomas Seeker has the necessary focus nor strength for strangling a woman on her doorstep. But on the other hand? If he were nervous enough, concerned that we'd find out about his past, he might have killed Lana just to keep her quiet. Maybe she caught him taking photos of her without permission and threatened to call the police."

"Thomas has found a pretty nice home here in Lily Rock. Plus he has Meadow on his side." Olivia shuddered. "You don't think that Thomas would strangle Lana with his bare hands, do you?"

Janis Jets shook her head. "What makes you think Lana was strangled with bare hands? I never said that."

"Well, I just assumed. Actually, I have no idea how Lana was strangled. I didn't think to ask. Much too gruesome an image for me to dwell on. I still have nightmares about finding Marla."

"The coroner had evidence that Lana was most likely strangled by a piece of fabric. They found small fragments of silk in the wound around Lana's neck." Janis held up her fists in front of her. With a quick pull, she pretended to grip someone around the neck, and her face contorted into a grimace.

Olivia shuddered. *I didn't picture Lana with a scarf around her neck.*

"I'm really good at jumping to a conclusion," Olivia admitted as much to herself as to Janis Jets. "I don't know why I never thought about the exact method of how Lana was strangled."

"That is one thing I can agree with this morning. You don't think. Anything else I can clear up for you?"

"How long can you hold Wilson Jones?"

"I've got a team down at the spa resort asking around. If

they remember him, then his alibi will hold. I'll let him go then, but no sooner than that."

"That will make Antonia happy," Olivia smirked.

No sooner had she finished speaking than an alarm sounded, stopping all conversation.

"That's the fire alarm," Jets shouted over the noise, springing to her feet. "I have to check out front to see what's going on. Keep your eye on the lovebirds." Jets pointed to the interview room. "We may need to evacuate to the street."

Olivia held her hands over her ears, shouting, "I'll stay with them."

Dropping her hands, Olivia sprinted across the hall. Within minutes Janis appeared at her elbow. "Nothing out front. Maybe one of the demonstrators set off the alarm while we were discussing the suspects. I'm going to check behind the constabulary through the back exit. I don't see or smell any smoke."

"Wilson and Antonia, you stay put."

The couple nodded, making no effort to speak over the alarm.

Olivia stood in the doorway so that she could watch Wilson and Antonia but also keep her eye on Janis's comings and goings. Her head ached with the loud ringing. *Good thing Mayor Maguire isn't around. Dog ears are so much more sensitive.*

Janis turned up again, gesturing to Olivia. "Bring Wilson and his lady with you. We'll go out the front together."

When Olivia turned toward the interview room, the couple had vanished. She hurried toward the back exit, and sure enough the door stood ajar.

"Janis, they're gone," Olivia shouted toward the front. *Oh no, she can't hear me, she's already gone.* Olivia ran to the glass doors, where she saw Thomas standing by Antonia's desk. He held a thick portfolio under his arm while looking toward the front entrance.

"Hey, Thomas!" Olivia shouted over the alarm, but the man didn't hear her. Before Olivia could step from the hallway through the glass doors to the front, he had dropped the papers on the desk, making a quick exit out the front.

"Stop!" yelled Olivia.

The glass doors finally swung open when Janis Jets came from behind. Apparently she hadn't left the building, she'd just gone elsewhere. "I think we lost Wilson and Antonia. I saw them go through the park."

"We also lost Thomas Seeker. He went thataway." Olivia pointed toward the front door.

"I forgot all about Seeker in the fuss over the fire alarm." Janis pulled her jacket closer to her body, running toward the door where he had disappeared.

She can catch Thomas while I look for Wilson. I'm on the team now.

"You come with me!" Jets directed, yelling from afar. As Olivia followed Jets back to her office, the alarm stopped as suddenly as it had begun.

Janis explained, "I called off the fire department when I realized someone pulled the alarm as a prank." Olivia could still hear the ringing in her ears as she watched Jets shove a small gun in the back of her belt, concealing it inside her constabulary black blazer.

She must be really hot in that outfit, but I guess she has to have somewhere to hide the gun.

"Let's go," shouted Janis loudly.

Once out the front door, Janis and Olivia looked left and then right for any sign of Thomas Seeker or Wilson Jones. Along the boardwalk in front of the constabulary, a group of men and women stood with picket signs, waving them in the air. Two women leaned into each other, arms wrapped in an embrace. A man in his early twenties, sporting expensive cowboy boots, waved with his free hand.

Younger people, a part of the group, wore Lily Rock T-shirts. They looked like the typical outdoor enthusiasts who wandered through town on weekends. All three stared at their cell phones, picket signs resting against their legs.

It wasn't until she did a double take that Olivia noticed everyone wore an identical oversized bandanna around their necks, identifying them as protesters.

"Hot out here," one man said, wiping his forehead with the corner of his bandanna.

"Did you see a guy about this tall, with a beard, running really fast?" asked Janis, gesturing.

The sweaty man spoke. "We did. He was in a big hurry, so we didn't give him a pamphlet." He held out a piece of paper for Olivia.

She read aloud, "Equal rights for all. Trans people are your neighbors and your friends. Implants kill. Cancer is real."

Olivia handed the paper back to the man. "My friend Cayenne is in your group."

"Not just in our group," the man said, "Cayenne formed our chapter and leads all of our protests. She's our trans leader." He stopped to look at the rest of the people. "Just to be completely transparent . . ." he stopped to appreciate his own pun before continuing, "some of us support the trans community, though we are not trans ourselves."

Rather than comment one way or another, Olivia asked, "Is Cay around now?"

"No, she went to get some more handouts. She'll be right back."

"For the last time, which direction did they go?" Janis Jets had had enough of the chitchat.

"Behind the pub, over there." A redheaded woman pointed.

Instead of running in the direction the woman pointed, Janis took a shorter route, sprinting through the Lily Rock park. Olivia followed her, trying to keep up. *That guy is right. It is hot. I wish I could shed my jacket. I look more professional with the coat on, kind of like Janis; only I never want a weapon. If only I weren't a musician, I might be a detective.* She smiled as she kept running after Jets.

Both women ran straight through the park, stopping in front of the Egg and Yolk Breakfast Garden. "Listen," Janis said, holding her finger to her lips.

"I can double the delivery for only half the price, if you'd like. I can give you Lana's usual order too if you can pay in cash. I don't like credit," hissed a familiar voice.

Janis, who stood with her hand resting on the back of her jacket, peeked around the corner of the building. Olivia stood behind her, so close she could hear the other woman's breath.

Sure enough, Brad was the source of the voice. To Olivia's disappointment, he wasn't talking to Thomas Seeker but to the reunited couple.

As soon as Brad saw Janis Jets he fumbled with the wad of cash he held in his hand, stuffing it into the front pocket of his jeans. Antonia, realizing they'd been caught with their dealer, yanked on Wilson's arm. Instead of trying to explain, Wilson pivoted and brushed past Olivia. She balanced herself to keep from falling as she watched his back and then Antonia's disappear down the alley.

Wait a minute! She rushed around the other side of the building, arriving just ahead of Wilson and Antonia to the main street. In too much of a hurry to realize she'd arrived first, the couple rushed past. Without hesitation, Olivia stuck out her leg, wincing as Wilson Jones tripped over her foot and plunged headfirst into the boardwalk. He rolled into a ball, screaming, "My leg. You broke my leg!"

Antonia held her hands to her mouth as if to scream.

Olivia placed her foot squarely on his back. Wilson squirmed and shouted, "I'm not the killer. I keep telling you!" *Where is Janis? She needs to bring the cuffs and make an arrest.* Olivia looked to her right. Janis Jets stood listening to her cell phone. She waved at Olivia while Wilson squirmed in the dirt. Olivia removed her foot as Wilson rolled to his side and then sat up.

Janis shoved her cell in her jacket pocket as she crossed the street to stand next to Olivia. She bent over to look into Wilson's face. "You may not be the killer, but you are by far the dumbest man I've ever met. You stopped to score weed while escaping from jail? Who does that?"

Olivia looked around. A crowd had gathered. Before Janis could get the injured man to his feet, the crowd began to laugh and cheer.

Janis turned to Olivia. "Thanks, by the way. You were a big help."

"You're welcome," said Olivia with a smile. "I hate to state the obvious, but we seem to have forgotten about Thomas Seeker yet again."

"If only Wilson was our guy," Janis muttered, pointing at the man being comforted by his crying girlfriend, "it would be so much easier for everyone. We could arrest him right here. But I just heard from my team at the Two Bunch. He had at least five people notice or talk to him at the same time Lana was murdered. I don't have enough evidence to keep him in jail, unless I charge him for escaping jail, which doesn't make sense in the long run."

Olivia paused to think. "What about Thomas Seeker . . . I have a feeling I know where he went."

Janis Jets grinned. "So you want to help find Thomas Seeker and you think you know where to look? Aren't you a smart cookie. Okay then, we can stop by the constabulary, and this time, I'll follow you."

16

ANOTHER ARREST

The sun made its slow descent behind the trees as Olivia slowed her car in front of Meadow and Sage's house.

"Park on the road," Jets advised from the passenger seat. "I don't want anyone to know we're coming."

Olivia pulled as close to the side of the road as she could, yanking on her brake. "Is that Thomas's truck over there, under the trees?" she asked.

Jets looked closely. "If he's trying to hide, he's doing a terrible job." She released her seat belt and then opened the car door and waited for Olivia. Her left hand crept to her waist to loosen the button on her blazer. Then Jets patted her back.

She's checking on the gun.

"Have you ever used that thing?" Olivia pointed to Janis's back.

"So you saw me put my weapon in my belt?"

"I saw you, and you also keep patting your back, so technically anyone who looks can see you're carrying a weapon."

"That was my point. I have a gun. Everyone sees my gun.

Then I don't have to use it. I use the gun's potential as my greatest threat."

"I see. And here I thought your ability to equivocate was your most dangerous weapon. 'On the one hand . . .'" Olivia mocked Janis's voice to her face.

"That's enough from you. We have a real bad guy here, Miss Amateur Sleuth. Thomas Seeker killed Lana. I just know it in my gut."

"We can sit here and wonder, or we can go knock on Meadow's door and ask him face to face," suggested Olivia.

From their position behind the large oak tree, Meadow's front door was clearly visible. "Let's go," Jets called to Olivia as they began the slight descent from the road toward the porch.

After several attempts at knocking, Janis tried the handle.

"It's locked," she said, surprise in her voice. "Meadow never locks her door. I've had words with her about this for years. There's something odd going on here."

Olivia shuddered. "Be careful. We may catch them, you know, in bed together. Now that would be a sight I'd prefer not to see."

"You are weak, Olivia Greer."

Janis lifted her knee to give the door a hearty kick. The old hinges creaked as both women walked into the living room. A quick inspection did not reveal Meadow or Thomas Seeker. Olivia and Janis stood side by side listening for voices. Janis nodded toward the swinging cafe doors that led to the kitchen, motioning with her hand for Olivia to step behind.

Tiptoeing across the wood floor, Jets reached into her jacket. This time she pulled out her gun. Olivia grabbed an iron poker from the fireplace. *This is my weapon.*

Janis looked over her shoulder and hissed, "Get behind me."

Olivia did as she was told.

With her gun out in front of her, both hands grasping the grip, Janis Jets pushed through the swinging doors shouting, "Police!"

Olivia followed, her heart pounding. Meadow McCloud sat in a kitchen chair; her hands were tied behind her back along with her ankles. The most disturbing encumbrance was the kitchen towel stuffed in her mouth.

Meadow's voice, deep in her throat and muffled by the towel, sounded like a ghost at a Halloween bazaar.

"Don't untie her just yet," hissed Janis to Olivia. "I want to look around a little more first."

While Janis inspected every corner of the kitchen, Olivia took in the mess.

To the left she saw that the kitchen table had been over-turned. Surrounding Meadow were broken bottles and dishes. Her carefully curated herbs had been strewn over the counters intermixed with the broken glass.

Meadow moaned from her chair. Olivia walked over and touched her shoulder, holding her finger to her lips. *Meadow must be furious about this mess*. Every cabinet had been emptied, the contents removed.

Another moan from Meadow brought Olivia's attention back to the chair. Before she could reach out again, Janis grabbed Olivia's elbow. She pointed toward the closed door of the walk-in pantry.

Meadow stopped moaning, her eyes wide with antic-ipation.

Olivia took a deep breath.

Raising her gun in the air again, Janis took a step toward the closed pantry door. Olivia moved next to her, reaching out for the knob. Janis nodded to Olivia who, with a swift pull, opened the door.

"Bingo, we found our guy," announced Janis.

Sure enough, Thomas Seeker cowered in the corner between the canned green beans and the strawberry jam, his face frozen with fear.

Croaking sounds came from Meadow as Olivia and Janis stepped closer to Seeker. Janis shouted out to Meadow, "Calm down, Olivia will get you loose. I've got the perp right here."

Olivia backed away from the pantry. She pulled the dishtowel from the frightened woman's mouth, reaching behind her body to untie her wrists.

Meadow's voice filled the kitchen. "He tied me up and then he ruined my kitchen." Tears rolled down her cheeks as she rubbed her mouth with the back of her hand.

With the pantry door wide open, Olivia watched Janis shove her gun back into her belt. She spun Thomas Seeker around and secured his hands behind his back with the cuffs she pulled from her coat pocket. Catching him by the ear, Janis dragged him from the pantry back into the kitchen.

"Don't shoot. Don't shoot. I'm innocent."

I guess he didn't notice that she put the gun away.

Janis shoved the man down in the one remaining upright kitchen chair. Then she looked back at Olivia. "See what I mean? He's terrified I'll use my weapon—that's all it takes."

Seeker began to cry, perspiration forming on his forehead. Janis turned her back on him to look at Meadow. "Are you okay?"

"Of course I'm okay. That awful man," she pointed to the sniveling Seeker. "He tricked me. I want to press charges . . . and make him clean this mess up!"

Shifting into her most soothing voice, Janis said, "Why don't you go with Olivia and get cleaned up. I'll meet you in the living room with Seeker where we all can talk."

Meadow stood unsteadily. Olivia put her hand under her

elbow. Meadow immediately shook her off. "I can stand just fine," insisted Meadow.

She does look okay. The only thing I can see is that her hair escaped the usual bun.

At that moment Meadow swayed and then grasped Olivia's hand to steady herself. "Maybe a little help," she said, her bottom lip trembling.

As they headed past the cafe doors into the living room, Jets called to Meadow. "No one gets to push around an Old Rocker on my watch. As soon as you're ready we'll file a report."

Straightening her shoulders, Meadow shrugged off Olivia's hand for the second time. Tears formed in her brown eyes. "Well, I can't believe what just happened. I thought Thomas was such a nice man. When he first arrived in Lily Rock, he wanted to be treated like family. The Old Rockers accepted him right away, on my recommendation, of course. I hoped Thomas would stay." Meadow's voice dropped, wiping away more tears.

"And then today, when I was fixing him a cup of tea, he snuck up on me. I thought he was giving me a hug, you know, from behind. But he shoved me into the sink and then forced me into a chair. Before I knew it my hands and feet were tied and he had gagged me with my own kitchen towel. He betrayed me." Fresh tears streamed down Meadow's plump cheeks. "He ransacked my kitchen from top to bottom."

Olivia nodded, moving Meadow down the hall toward the bathroom as she spoke.

Once in the bathroom Olivia stood close as Meadow splashed her face with cool water. The tears had stopped, replaced by a pink flush to her cheeks. Meadow dabbed her face with a dry towel.

Olivia could hear Thomas and Janis talking in the living

room. Olivia comforted Meadow as she helped her comb and braid her hair, all while trying to listen in.

"Let's go back to the living room," Olivia urged. "We don't want to miss Janis tearing that guy a new one."

Meadow inspected the broken skin on her wrists. "You don't have to be vulgar. I'm getting ready. Just let me put some ointment on my wounds."

Olivia inched closer down the hallway, hoping to hear the conversation more clearly. She could still see Meadow straightening her jumper, smoothing the front with her trembling hands.

"Thank you, dear, for saving me from that horrible man. I will be forever grateful."

Putting her arm around Meadow, Olivia gave her a squeeze. "I'll help you clean up in the kitchen as soon as you're ready. Do you want to stay with me tonight? It's my turn to offer you hospitality."

Meadow's eyes widened, surprised by Olivia's offer. "Oh, that won't be necessary. Sage will keep me company tonight. I may even enlist Mayor Maguire's help. He can stand guard on the porch . . . just in case."

Both women walked toward the living room side by side. Janis Jets looked up, smiling at the two of them standing together.

"I didn't do anything," whined Thomas Seeker. "Tell her, Meadow, honey. We were just playacting, right, sweetie? That's what we do, you know, as foreplay."

Olivia felt her stomach lurch. *Ick. Please stop talking about foreplay.*

"Not so fast with your excuses, Mr. Seeker," demanded Jets. "What were you looking for in Meadow's kitchen, and for that matter, what about those photographs, the ones you left at the constabulary? Why did you just dump and run?"

Meadow sat on the sofa opposite Thomas Seeker. She leaned forward but did not speak.

Jets will get him to confess. She'll keep going round and round asking obvious questions until he finally admits what he's done. She is so persistent.

Thomas Seeker cleared his throat as his face hardened. "I dropped the photos at the constabulary to show you that Lana de Carlos was a fake. I had the proof for everyone to see."

Jets followed up on Thomas's statement, asking another question. "Let me see if I understand you. You set off the fire alarm and then dropped the photos, hoping for a quick getaway?"

Adding the part about the fire alarm surprised Olivia. *Once again Janis makes her perpetrators confess. She adds another detail that they admit to because it seems so trivial. Then Janis adds it all up, and whammy, she bears down on them like a wolf, eyes glaring, in for the kill.*

Seeker did not disagree with Jets. He nodded, admitting without words that he'd been the one to pull the fire alarm earlier.

"So tell us how you came by the photographs then, if you're as innocent as you say." Janis modulated her voice to a more conversational tone. Instead of interrogating her suspect, she accompanied him, as if they were both storytellers, each having their own part. "Go on, Mr. Seeker. You know you want to tell the truth," coaxed Jets.

Now the words rushed from Thomas's mouth. "From the beginning, Lana interested me," he admitted, adding, "then Meadow commissioned me to follow Lana and to take photos of her. A good excuse to satisfy my curiosity and get paid."

"I wanted proof for the town council," explained Meadow. "Lana was not a decent woman. She'd take off her clothes in broad daylight no matter who was watching."

"Yeah, that's right," agreed Thomas. "Lana was practically asking to be photographed, so I obliged. No harm in that. She was doing it publicly."

"When did you realize she didn't have cancer?" asked Jets, nodding to both Thomas and Meadow, encouraging them like a mom who knows best.

Seeker continued, "I had the dates of the photos online. Sometimes Lana would have her implants. Some photos showed her flat as a pancake with red scars. And some had the new breasts with big scars where nipples were supposed to go. Pretty revealing. But she'd go back and forth one day to the next. I soon suspected she was using fake breasts, like they do in the movies."

"You mean like prostheses?"

"Yep. Like those."

Janis leaned forward in her chair. "So the only proof you have of Lana's faking is the photos with the times and dates?"

"I only had suspicions until I borrowed the photos from the dark room in Olivia's house. I didn't take anything else. Just the photos, which proved I was right. I detected that the dates were photoshopped and concluded that Lana faked her surgery. But I didn't hurt Lana, you know. I never put a hand on her."

Olivia interjected her question. "So you took Wilson Jones's photos from my house."

Seeker shifted uncomfortably in his seat while Olivia waited for Janis to take over the questioning again, but when she didn't, Olivia continued. "Did you confront Lana with your findings and then put a camera in her shower to get more shots of her at home?"

Thomas's eyes narrowed. His bottom lip trembled. "I did ask her for some money, you know, just a bit to tide me over. I promised not to out her as a fake if she'd pay me."

"So you blackmailed Lana de Carlos?" Janis Jets asked in a firm voice. "And then you kept taking photos just to make sure you had enough evidence. I mean, you could leak the shower videos online, and no one would know it was you. Lana must have been terrified."

Now Olivia spoke. "Lana must also have been furious. If you posted those pictures and videos online she would be outed as a fraud. Poof, no more internet sensation, no more sponsors for the products on her website. She'd be done financially."

"So how much did she pay you?" asked Jets nonchalantly.

"A few hundred," Seeker said softly.

"How many hundred?"

"Seven hundred."

"Per month?"

"Per week." Suddenly Thomas frowned. "I want a lawyer!" he said, the words rushing from his mouth.

"You can call your lawyer, but let me get this straight. You had your own suspicions about the photos Lana posted, and you had your own photos plus the videos from an installed camera in her shower to prove she didn't really have cancer. Plus you got seven hundred bucks from Lana every week to keep your mouth shut."

Thomas nodded, his lips clamped firmly shut.

"And you expect me to believe that you didn't strangle Lana when she threatened to go to the police? She got tired of you, didn't she? Lana decided she wasn't going to pay any more. Hey, maybe she had something on you, like the prior arrests as a public nuisance, you and that camera of yours."

Seeker rose to his feet in one movement, shouting at the top of his lungs, "I did not kill Lana de Carlos! How many times do I have to repeat my innocence? I want my lawyer!"

"Sit down, Seeker. I warned you earlier. You can have

your lawyer as soon as we get back to the constabulary. That can be your first call." She turned to Meadow and asked another question. "Doing better now? Want to give me your account of the break-in?"

Instead of answering Jets's question, Meadow made a bid for time. "Would you like a cup of tea before you take him away? I have a lovely peppermint eucalyptus, which will help soothe your nerves and clear your sinuses. It will just take a moment."

Jets turned to Olivia and mouthed behind her hand, "Is she for real?"

"No time for tea now," grumbled Janis as she grabbed Seeker by the handcuffs, yanking him to his feet. "I have to get this guy back to the station so that he can call his lawyer."

Meadow nodded. She stood up, taking a few steps closer to stare at Seeker.

Olivia listened intently. *I think she wants to ask Seeker her own question.*

"Why did you tie me up like that in my own kitchen?" Tears formed in her eyes. "I thought we were friends."

"Ah come on, Meadow. Won't you back me up here? No harm was done."

"Stop whining and tell me the truth," she insisted, stamping her foot and pointing her finger in his face.

He dropped his head, his knees slumping against the back of the sofa.

"You go girl," Olivia mumbled under her breath.

Seeming to forget about his lawyer, Seeker pleaded with Meadow. "I started my search in your kitchen to see if you had any of those photos I gave you for the Old Rockers. I wanted to have all the pictures of Lana at my disposal so that I could be certain she was faking. You printed some, right? Those were the ones I was looking for."

"Do you mean to say you thought I hid photos with my herbs?" Meadow could not have looked more shocked.

"I just started in the kitchen for convenience. I planned to ransack the whole house, if we hadn't been interrupted."

"That's the most ridiculous story I've ever heard," Meadow stated indignantly. "And if you must know, I'd have given you the three prints if you'd asked. Why would I want to keep them anyway?"

No longer contrite, Meadow stood, her shoulders pushed back, looking ready for a fight.

A grin appeared on Jets's face. "Thank you so much for that little explanation. So now I can hold you," she pointed to Seeker, "for breaking and entering and inflicting bodily harm. And you," Jets pointed to Meadow, "will stop playing coy and give me a statement." Patting Meadow on the shoulder, Janis added, "See you at the constabulary tomorrow bright and early. Now get some rest."

"Of course," Meadow said, no longer resisting. "I'll stop by before my shift at the library."

* * *

As Olivia parked in front of the constabulary, Jets leaped out of the passenger seat to drag Thomas Seeker from the back of the car. She walked him past the remaining three protestors, who held their signs above their heads chanting, "She's a fake, she's on the take," over and over.

Olivia parked the car, locking it behind her in a hurry so that she could catch up with Jets and Seeker. She found them in the constabulary waiting room, where Jets walked Seeker through the glass doors, into the hallway.

Removing the cuffs from his wrists, she shoved him into

an empty cell. The door automatically shut. "I'll get you a phone for that call," Jets told Seeker.

Olivia faced Janis, a question on her mind.

"So how do the protestors play into all of this? What do they mean 'she's on the take?'"

"On the one hand, I know they didn't like Lana and thought she was a fake," Janis admitted.

"But on the other hand," Olivia picked up the conversation as she realized where it was going, "Lana was making a lot of money as an influencer. Money is a strong motivation for murder."

Janis took Olivia by the elbow. "Go to my office and wait there for me."

Once Janis came in, having given Seeker his phone call, she sat across the desk from Olivia.

"Why did you get him to talk without an attorney present? Won't that make it hard for the case to stick in court?"

Jets smiled. "Don't you worry, Miss Amateur Sleuth. I've got this. Watch and learn, the case isn't over yet. Like I said, Meadow's sworn statement will keep him in jail. I wanted that first. For a minute, when she was more worried about making us tea, I thought I'd lost her. But then she got so mad at him, I knew she'd make the statement. I can hold Seeker until tomorrow on suspicion. By that time Meadow will have signed her statement and we can hold him longer. A guy like that, with a couple of nights in jail . . . he'll confess. No attorney will be able to stop him once I'm done."

"So you think you have enough evidence either way?"

"He's the guy. He murdered Lana de Carlos. I'm sure of it."

* * *

By the time Olivia left the constabulary the protestors were gone. *Chasing people through Lily Rock was not on my to-do list this morning. I'll go by and check on Meadow before I head home.*

When Olivia drove up to the small house, she saw that Sage's truck was parked under the trees. Through the open curtains Olivia saw the mother and daughter sitting on the sofa, each holding a glass of wine. Meadow was talking as Sage nodded her head.

Even Mayor Maguire knew his place. The dog snoozed on the porch, his body blocking the door. His head rested on his front paws.

"Good boy, M&M," she told him out her open car window.

After driving home Olivia put on the hot water for tea. She rested her elbows on the counter and looked down the path toward Michael's house. In just a day Michael had cleaned up and organized the front of his cabin.

Firewood had been neatly stacked near the front door. He'd swept away the rocks and debris left by the latest wind storm. Smoke rose from his chimney.

Olivia turned from the kitchen window. *I'd like a fire tonight.* She gathered small pieces of kindling from the indoor woodpile and with careful attention, she began to lay a fire.

After the first flame took hold, Olivia looked around the room, her eyes resting on a novel she'd left open on the sofa. She sat down, pulling her feet up under her body. *I'll read and then get some rest. What a day . . .*

17

NOTHING BUT THE TRUTH

Olivia's phone rang from the nightstand. Her hand reached out from under the pillow.

"You up yet?" asked Sage. "Just wanted to thank you for saving my mom."

Olivia rolled over in bed, the phone held next to her cheek. "What time is it and you're welcome."

"It's nearly ten o'clock, sleepyhead. My mother wanted to invite you for lunch. She's so happy about you coming to her rescue. I told her you'd probably be moving slowly this morning. Looks like I'm right."

Olivia chuckled. "Not sure I can stand the pressure now that I seem to be Meadow's favorite. Do you need help fixing the kitchen mess? I think her body injuries weren't nearly as unsettling as her ransacked cupboards."

"You don't need to help. Just come by. We've already resettled the kitchen, and Meadow wants to cook for you—and make a cup of tea, of course."

"Can I pass on the tea?"

"Not forever, my mom is pretty insistent that her tea is the elixir of longevity and good health."

Olivia laughed. "How about around one o'clock? I need to practice. Are you ready for our pub gig?"

"I am. The band wants to get together on Friday morning to check the sound and play through a few tunes. Are you excited? We make our big debut in Lily Rock in a few days. You realize the place will be packed, with you being the draw, of course. Other than Miss Jensen, who teaches first grade at the elementary school, no one has seen an autoharp player on stage."

"I seriously doubt that I'm a draw. I can't think of one instance when an autoharp brought a large crowd, not even for the Grand Ole Opry when Mother Maybelle Carter performed."

"Judy Collins played the autoharp, and I think I saw Joan Baez with an autoharp one time. Who's your favorite?"

"Dolly Parton plays the autoharp. That woman rocks."

Sage laughed. "I don't think you are the spitting image of Dolly, but you do bring down the house. You know it's your voice, right? That's why people start crying and holding hands. The autoharp is just a crazy side piece."

Feeling embarrassed, Olivia wound down the call. "Gotta go now. Time to shower." *When people start talking about my voice I feel so self-conscious. Thank you, Don.*

Lying on her back in bed Olivia stretched her body, extending her heels, feeling the pull all the way to her lower back. Before she could get her feet on the floor, the phone lit up again. Michael Bellemare.

"Hello," Olivia said brightly, "how are you today?"

"Hey there. Heard you got into a bit of a mess yesterday, chasing culprits through the middle of town, and then you and Jets brought down Lana's killer."

"You just can't take me anywhere," remarked Olivia, a

smile coming to her lips. She laid her head back down on the pillow.

"Don't I know it," Michael said. "I wondered if you had time to catch up this morning, you know, with coffee. We haven't talked since—"

"I met your wife," she interrupted, willing her voice to be calm. "Wanda seems like a nice woman, by the way. You have excellent taste."

"That would be my ex-wife," he corrected her.

"How about we call Wanda your camping buddy? Would that be more accurate?"

"That would be accurate. How about coffee, and we'll talk."

"About what?"

"Anything you want. I'll answer anything you want this morning."

"But will you tell me the truth?"

"That depends. If you make the coffee, then I will speak nothing but the truth. Promise."

"Give me half an hour. See you at the back door." Olivia hung up, her heart skipping a beat. *We have a connection no matter what. Maybe I'll feel less like running now that he's hanging out with Wanda.*

Standing in the kitchen with her wet hair dripping down her back, Olivia poured water into the back of the coffee maker. By the time it finished brewing Michael stood at her back door, holding a basket with a napkin on top. "I made blueberry muffins," he told her, stepping into the kitchen.

"You are a man for all seasons." Olivia smiled, handing him the empty carpe diem mug. "Help yourself."

He reached past her to pour the coffee as he listened attentively to Olivia. She filled him in on the search for Lana's killer. He didn't take his eyes off of her face as he sipped.

Aware of his attention, she hurried her words, feeling her cheeks redden the longer she spoke.

Michael placed the mug on the table. "So let me summarize. We've got Thomas Seeker in jail, arrested for killing Lana. We released Wilson Jones because he was at the spa at the time of her death. Do you think Seeker is the one?"

"Janis does, and she's the expert."

"But Janis doesn't always get it right," reminded Michael. "Remember last year, Janis was convinced that you killed Marla."

"True," admitted Olivia. "But Thomas is so creepy, and he tied up Meadow. No one ties up Meadow. She's not a threat to anyone."

"Except she's a threat to you. Remember when Meadow drugged you, and you slept for two days while she and Skye Jones ransacked your house?"

"According to Janis, Thomas Seeker is our guy. When I left her yesterday she had that look—you know the one, when she's sure she's wrapped up the case."

"I do know the look." Michael nodded. "But I think we have to keep looking at all the suspects, including Cayenne and maybe Brad."

"I can start advertising the house for rent and get back to my life in Playa and . . . Just a minute! I get it now. You're trying to get me to stay in Lily Rock by undermining Janis's case."

Michael's chin dipped as he tried to hide his sheepish grin. "Well, kind of. I mean, you could be right. I do want you to stay."

"Enough to let a killer go free?"

"I'd never go that far. I was just playing with you a little. I like to see you get all flustered. Kind of made my day."

"Fun for you, maybe," she muttered.

Michael took the last sip of coffee. Then he suggested, "Let's drive to the constabulary together. I'd like to get a look at old Thomas Seeker in a jail cell."

"Sure, you can come," Olivia agreed. "Maybe you can give added perspective to the case."

Michael's eyes opened wide. "You actually think my opinions might be helpful? Ah shucks."

Olivia laughed openly.

Michael's eyes brightened. "So I thought you had some questions for me this morning."

He assumes I have questions about Wanda.

"I don't have any questions. I thought I did, but when it came right down to it, I don't. Let's go to the constabulary. I have to hurry because I'm supposed to have lunch with Meadow and Sage by one o'clock."

Michael reached across the table to take her empty mug. "I'll leave and get myself cleaned up. Meet you out back in ten minutes. We can drive together in my truck."

"See you soon." Olivia smiled, watching as he let himself out.

* * *

Half an hour later, Michael and Olivia arrived at the constabulary and exited his truck in the parking lot. As soon as they stepped inside the door, Janis Jets appeared from the back room.

"What a happy coincidence. I need you both."

"How do you always know when I'm here?" asked Olivia.

"We have cameras in the back. I can see everything. Thanks to him." Janis shrugged her shoulder toward Michael.

Olivia and Michael exchanged glances as they followed Janis to the interview room.

"Mike," Janis hissed, "keep out of sight. Get behind the two-way mirror. Observe what he does and says. We'll talk later." Janis shoved Michael in one direction as she took Olivia by the elbow and dragged her in the other.

"You can come with me. Since you were in on the arrest, I'd appreciate your presence at the interview."

"Oh, it's you two again," said Thomas Seeker as Olivia and Janis came through the door. "How many people you got over there?" Seeker gestured to the two-way mirror.

"That's none of your business," commented Janis crisply. Before she could sit down the door opened behind her. Antonia held a laptop and several file folders. "Here's the evidence," she muttered, dropping the armful on the table in front of Janis.

She's not her usual cheery self. Antonia wore baggy jeans and a sweater that came down to her knees. Her uncombed hair protruded from an off-center ponytail behind her head.

Olivia leaned over to Janis. "Looks like your administrator had a bad night."

Janis whispered back, "Not now. Let's focus on that guy." She glared across the table, beginning her interrogation.

Seeker spread out the file folder of pictures on the desk, taking a careful look at each one. "Yes, these are the ones I took over a period of five months. See here, Lana de Carlos's natural hair."

Janis leaned in. "Lana has the same, as you say, natural hair, in all five photos. What's that mean to you?"

Exasperated, Seeker shoved himself away from the table. "It's obvious. Or it would be had you done your homework and looked at her website. She posted lots of hair photos to depict her journey with cancer. From bald to wigs, Lana always had something going on to make certain her followers watched her carefully. But when I took photos of her from across the street when she wasn't aware, her hair was the same no matter what her website or social media showed. Always piled on her head in a messy array, blond and long."

Olivia leaned over to take one of the photos. *It's weird seeing another woman in her robe on my doorstep. Thomas is correct. The photos, dated every two weeks, depict Lana in a kimono stepping out to get her mail, and her hair is always the same. The dates range from late March to late May, three months before her death, which means she should have been bald-headed or wearing a wig.*

Jets spoke again. "So you're telling me that these photos are proof that Lana lied about her cancer. And you want what exactly for giving me that information?"

"I want you to dismiss any charges Meadow brings up, which were a complete misunderstanding on her part and—"

"And you want me to turn a blind eye to your previous arrests regarding taking unauthorized photos," Jets snapped.

Seeker nodded his agreement.

"You must think I'd be willing to cut a deal since you changed your mind about the attorney." Jets thumbed through the papers Antonia gave her. "Here it is in writing. So now I have a few more questions."

She'll come at him like a viper, offering new information and then recoiling to watch his response.

"Can you tell us why you killed Lana?" *The viper strikes!* Janis continued, "Maybe she was tired of being blackmailed, or maybe she did her own research on you. Not like your arrests are a secret. Did she threaten to tell the police in order to get you off her back?"

"I didn't blackmail or kill her. That's why I decided not to hire an attorney. I'm innocent and I don't have the cash to hire a good one." His voice dropped. "I thought we could come to an understanding, just the two of us." He folded his arms over his chest.

"Well, that's the thing. I appreciate that you changed your mind about getting a lawyer, but I suspect the fee wasn't the only reason."

The man sighed deeply. His chin drooped. "If I hire a lawyer, I'll most likely end up back in court."

"Once they see your previous arrests, there will be little to no chance of you staying out of jail," added Jets.

"They warned me the last time," admitted Seeker.

Janis turned to Olivia. "You most likely know that the state of California has a list of laws for people they call peeping Toms." Janis faced Thomas Seeker again, waving another folder in the air. "You're right. If you tell us the truth, you will have a better chance of a shorter sentence. Another thing that would help? We discovered Lana dead on Sunday, August 16. Can anyone corroborate your whereabouts on that day?"

Thomas held his head in his hands. "I'm alone most of the time in my darkroom. There's no one to give me an alibi—the story of my life."

He's kind of pathetic, most likely been a misfit since childhood. I bet he started taking photos to feel more powerful, to make himself feel less of an outcast. The only person in Lily Rock who invited him to dinner was Meadow. She has a heart for the one left out.

Unfazed by Thomas's refusal to say more, Jets continued to prod. "What are you not telling me?"

He sighed, tugging at his T-shirt neckline. "You know most of it. But what you don't know is that Lana made a lot of money being an influencer. She netted thousands of dollars a month. But it wasn't just from her sponsors."

"Say more."

"Lana had a Please Fund Me account. Do you know about those?"

Jets leaned forward. Olivia sat back to watch.

Thomas continued, "Lana set up a Please Fund Me on the internet, asking her followers to donate money. That expensive chair in her bedroom is an example. She told her sad story on Please Fund Me, asking for donations to meet the expenses of her cancer diagnosis.

"Money poured in, which she used to buy equipment. People gave her a couple grand so that she could buy the electronic chair to sleep in during her recovery. Then she advertised the manufacturer of the chair and offered a discount to other buyers. The discount would be kicked back to her account. Along with paying Lana to advertise, she made quite a profit. Pretty good setup and very lucrative." Thomas reached for a glass of water. After taking a sip, he added, "With her pathetic fake photos of her mutilated breasts, she raked in the cash."

"How much do you think she 'raked in'?" asked Janis, making air quotes with her fingers.

"Over a hundred grand for the chair alone would be my estimation."

Janis tapped the file folder on her desk. She slid the photos into a pile. "Were you part of the Please Fund Me operation?"

"I knew about it. So long as everyone believed that Lana had cancer, no one would be the wiser. But by the time I outed her, she knew she was in real trouble. If I went public suddenly, her little money-making scheme would go belly up."

"Punishable by a fine and in some cases imprisonment," added Janis, leaning over the table. "The funny part is, I'm surprised you're even alive to tell me this story. I mean, if I were Lana, I'd want you dead. Did she? Threaten your life? Is that why you strangled her in the heat of the moment?"

Olivia's heart raced. Janis had a point. Maybe she'd uncovered Thomas Seeker's true motivation. What if Lana did threaten Thomas, or maybe she had Wilson threaten him instead. Olivia waited for Thomas to reply.

His chin jutting up in defiance, Thomas shook his head. He set his lips in a straight line.

Tired of Seeker's antics, Janis Jets abruptly pushed her chair out and stood. "Okay, so you aren't going to say any more, but you did give me some information that I can use. Now back to your cell you go. Hope you have a good book. I'm gonna keep you for quite a while."

Janis waited for Seeker to stand before she took him by the elbow and ushered him out the door. Olivia waited in the hallway for Michael to exit the other room.

"Love what we did with the place," he said when he reached her. Michael smiled over Olivia's shoulder as Janis approached. "The sound system and two-way mirror really work."

"Not the right time to pat you on the back, builder man. Why don't you two get going? I have work to do."

Michael frowned. "I thought you wanted my opinion about the interview."

"I have other things to do. For one I have to look up that Please Fund Me business." Jets abruptly walked to her office, leaving Olivia and Michael in the hallway.

He shrugged, checking his watch. "Okay then, I'll take you back to your house so you can get ready for lunch with Meadow and Sage."

They took the back door of the constabulary to the street. Michael held the door for Olivia as she hopped into the truck.

He walked around the truck bed to sit behind the steering wheel.

As Michael drove through the center of town he said, "Or I can drop you at Meadow's."

Olivia checked the truck's dash for the time. "That would work. I'll get a ride home from Sage, no problem. Thanks for coming along. I'm curious, after listening to the interview, what do you think of Thomas Seeker?"

Michael's hands spread out over the steering wheel. He gripped the leather covering tightly. "I don't like that guy, but honestly, I don't think he strangled Lana. Men who hide in bushes and peep into windows aren't necessarily violent. At least that's what I've heard."

Just what I thought.

Olivia pointed toward Meadow's house. "M&M is still standing guard."

Michael pulled the truck up in front of the house. Olivia opened the doors and jumped to the gravel driveway.

"See you later," she called over her shoulder.

"I guess I'm not invited to lunch," Michael hollered through the open window.

Olivia waved over her head without an answer.

She heard him reverse the truck over the gravel and then drive toward the main road.

"Hi, M&M." Olivia bent over to pat the dog's head.

Meadow opened the door to greet her with a big hug. "I am so grateful to you for saving me from that dreadful man."

Olivia hugged Meadow back, placing a kiss on her cheek.

"Lunch is served," called Sage from the kitchen door.

The table had been set for three, with mismatched old crockery and bright, flowered cloth napkins. A board covered the middle of the table, filled with an array of cheeses, olives, and rolled meats. On the side were two loaves of Meadow's freshly baked bread, along with another board filled with seasonal fruits.

"The last of the strawberries," Meadow observed, watching Olivia's face light up with surprise. "I hope this suits your appetite."

Olivia glanced at Meadow. *She's growing on me. A true eccentric, Meadow McCloud.*

A shudder fell down Olivia's spine. *But what about Sage? When she knows about my secret, I'll lose her and Meadow.*

"Have a seat," Sage said, pointing to the chair.

The three women lightly chatted and laughed as they assembled their plates with all of the delicious offerings for lunch. "May I have more iced tea?" Olivia asked.

"Of course." Meadow poured the tea over fresh mint leaves. "This is mint tea, without any special ingredients." She winked.

Olivia held up her glass as she looked around at her companions.

The women reached to the center of the table to clink their iced tea tumblers.

After taking a long drink, Olivia asked Meadow, "So why did Thomas tie you up and ransack your kitchen? I still don't understand."

"He was just toying with my affections, trying to see how much abuse I would take. Awful man. Said something about his fastidious mother. I told him I wasn't his mother, but he kept pulling things off my shelves, yelling at me like I'd know what he was talking about. A lunatic, if you ask me."

"Mothers are significant," Sage commented.

I need to change the subject.

Olivia asked, "Has anyone spoken to Cayenne since she cut her hand at the pub?"

Meadow's smile faded as she turned to look at Sage. Reaching over the table, she patted her daughter's hand.

She's reassuring Sage about something.

Sage shook off Meadow's touch. "I haven't seen Cay in the past few days."

Olivia drank the last of her tea. *I'm such a coward.*

18

TWO-SPIRIT

Driving away from the lunch with Sage and Meadow, Olivia felt discouraged. *With the investigation nearly wrapped up, it's time for me to leave Lily Rock. But I can't leave here and return to Playa until I tell Sage we're sisters. And after I tell her, why would Sage ever trust me again?*

Once she opened the door to her house, exhaustion set in. *It's been a long day. It's time to settle in for an early supper and then bed.*

She showered and dressed in comfy clothes: her loose-fitting shorts and a T-shirt. *I'll make a green salad with some cheese and strawberry vinaigrette dressing.* After making her salad, Olivia took her plate filled with greens to the deck and sat down for dinner, the pine trees her company.

As the sun set, Olivia yawned. *I'm going to read a bit and then get some sleep.* She washed her dishes in the sink, leaving them in the drainer to dry. Checking the back door and the front, Olivia finally made her way to her bedroom, exhaustion following her like a shadow right to her bed.

That night Olivia woke with a start. She'd dreamed about Cayenne, her strong hands wrapping around the throat of a blond woman whose wig fell, covering her face. *Was that a clue or just my mind working through possibilities?* Rolling over to her side, she fell back to sleep.

By early morning Olivia woke to the sunshine from her window. She quickly dressed and then made her way upstairs to the kitchen. Filling the coffee maker with water, she looked out the window and waited for it to finish the cycle.

Then she sipped her morning coffee, still standing by the sink. Again her thoughts wandered to who killed Lana de Carlos.

Michael may be right. I don't think Thomas Seeker would strangle Lana. Too up close and personal for his taste. And then there's the very odd incident in Meadow's kitchen.

Ol' Thomas had some mommy issues, according to Meadow. Once he got cornered, he went off the rails. Sure, Thomas tied up and gagged Meadow, but he'd not come close to doing any permanent injury. The broken vials and wasted herbs were the act of a child having a tantrum.

But Cayenne, she was a different story. Cay held back her anger, feeling more like the aggressive dog at the end of the leash. When she found out that Lana undermined the trans community with her fake story, Cayenne could have been the one to coil a cloth around Lana's neck before she could bring her anger back to heel.

Plus Cayenne wore scarves. In fact the entire community of protestors who stood outside the constabulary that day all wore scarves. Any one of them might have killed Lana de Carlos.

Or what if, like *Murder on the Orient Express*, the trans group all conspired to kill Lana? Of course they seemed more like pamphlet pushers than killers, but you never know.

Olivia shuddered. *Please don't let Cay be a part of this crime.*

After she finished her coffee, Olivia grabbed her keys and headed to her car. She drove toward the brew pub. *If Cay is there with Arlo, I can talk to her and see if she'll tell me what provoked the glass-breaking incident. Even if Cayenne isn't there, Arlo would know where to find her.*

Standing in front of the pub, Olivia looked through the glass door. No one in sight. Then she pushed against the bar across the glass and opened the door.

"Anyone here?" she called into the empty room.

"I'm in the back," came Arlo's voice.

Olivia walked behind the bar to the kitchen area. She found Arlo sitting at the counter, staring into his empty coffee mug. "Hey," she said gently, "how are you?"

"Hey yourself. What brings you here on this beautiful summer morning? We're not open for another hour."

"I'm looking for Cayenne, haven't seen her for a while. Thought the two of us could catch up this morning."

"She's out supervising her crew." Arlo sighed. "Cay inspects each house and business before noon."

"She's a busy person."

"Cay is a very hands-on business owner. Her crew loves her, probably because she's not afraid to pitch in right alongside them."

Hands on . . . Olivia felt a shudder down her spine.

"What with the pub and the cleaning business, you both must be busy. How is the weed dispensary doing?"

"Oh, we make some cash there, enough to afford to live in Lily Rock."

Olivia rested her elbows on the counter. "I've been fortunate, having a house handed to me on a silver platter. I couldn't have afforded to live here otherwise. It makes me feel grateful but also sad. I feel like I don't deserve any of it."

Olivia smiled. *I have the house and this community thanks to you, Marla.*

"You are pretty lucky, but what we do and don't deserve isn't up to us."

"Don't you sound all deep and wise this morning," chuckled Olivia.

"Cay is rubbing off on me."

"So, where does she go when her inspections are completed?"

Arlo rubbed his chin before answering. "I don't suppose it would hurt to tell you. Cay either heads to the corral to work out one of the abandoned horses at Paws and Pines, or you might find her at the labyrinth. She walks that nearly every day."

"The labyrinth?"

"Up by the old Lily Rock chapel near the base of the hiking trail. The congregation created a labyrinth walk like in medieval times, made of stones and under the pine trees. Cay uses it to meditate nearly every day."

"Are labyrinths like mazes?" Olivia asked.

"Not really. You go in, and you go out on the same path. Plus you walk very slowly. Does nothing for me, but Cay says it clears her mind and keeps her in touch with her inner wisdom. Something like that anyway. When she talks like that, I mostly tune out and nod. Just go up and see for yourself."

"Maybe I'll check the animal shelter first. At least I know a horse and a corral when I see it. I'm not sure I'd know a labyrinth if I ran right over it."

Arlo grinned. "I think that's the point. It's right in front of us, but you have to focus with intention to unlock the mystery."

"Did I mention you sound all wise this morning?"

"It feels good to laugh, especially at myself. Thanks, Olivia. I'm glad you came by. But I have to get back to work. There are french fries to be cut and oil to be heated and vegetables to clean and cook. I'm looking forward to hearing your band on Friday, by the way."

Olivia walked around the counter to give Arlo a hug. "Be well. I'll go find Cay. Thanks for the chat."

* * *

By noon only one woman rode a horse in the Paws and Pines corral, and it wasn't Cayenne Perez. Olivia leaned against the wood rail to watch Sage McCloud canter the quarter horse around the circle. Sage urged the older horse on with a click of her tongue, centering her body to mold into the saddle, adjusting to the rhythm of the big animal's gait.

She looks like Mom. Same body, compact and thin. Thick golden-brown hair, braided down the middle of her back. As the horse strode past Olivia, Sage waved. She kept riding, doing another three laps around the corral before bringing her mount to a fast-paced trot, and then finally a relaxed slow walk.

"You ride so well," Olivia commented as Sage swung her leg over the horse, landing with both boots on the ground.

"I've ridden for as long as I can remember. Doc taught me."

Both women avoided looking at each other. Speaking about Doc seemed to bring them both sadness. "Do you miss him?" asked Olivia.

Sage shaded her eyes with the palm of her hand. "I miss who I thought Doc was. Once I got the entire picture, it was hard to reconcile my feelings. When he passed just after the trial, I grieved for a long while. So did Meadow. I suppose he couldn't stand the strain of being discovered. Once he realized he'd most likely go to jail, his heart attack gave him a way out. I guess that's what happened."

"Not surprising," said Olivia. "I don't think about him much, but then, he wasn't my biological father."

Sage slid the bridle over the horse's neck, giving him a gentle pat on the nose. "I try to forget about all the other stuff. But think about it, Olivia, I wouldn't know you if it weren't for the doc."

"True," admitted Olivia. "And that is a good way to look at it. This must be wisdom day in Lily Rock. I just left Arlo, and he was full of deep thoughts."

Sage gestured to Olivia. "I have to cool down Bronco a bit before taking him back to the stable. Come along with us."

The two women exchanged small talk as the horse walked alongside them, ducking his head occasionally to snatch a mouthful of grass.

"Are you ready for the rehearsal on Friday morning?" asked Sage. "Arlo said he'd open up early just for us."

"I'm ready. Ran through our songs several times."

"I know your mother taught you the songs, but how did she learn them?"

"My mom was a part of the ACN."

"The what?"

"The ACN is the Appalachian Cherokee Nation."

"But didn't you say she was part Cahuilla?"

"She was both. Her mother was part Cahuilla and her father part Cherokee. Both my grandparents were dead before I was born, so my mom made it a point to teach me to sing the old songs. She didn't read music herself . . . all in her head of course, nothing written down."

"So your mom wasn't full-blooded?"

"Her other half was a mixture of Scottish-Irish heritage. I

suppose that's why I come by the music and the singing from Appalachia naturally."

Sage, lost in thought, stared at her boots as she walked. She opened her mouth and then closed it quickly. After a pause she said, "Music has always been a part of my life. I didn't learn to fiddle from anyone in particular. I just listened to recordings. It's pretty amazing that we both play the same tunes and that we play them so well together." Sage stopped and turned toward Olivia as if waiting for her to agree.

Olivia's stomach twisted into a knot. She smiled at Sage and said, "It happens that way. The traditionalists claim folk music has to be handed down from one person to the next. But I think listening to recordings may prove to be just as useful. Maybe we heard the same music growing up. That would explain it."

Sage nodded, a look of disappointment crossing her face. Then she led the horse back toward the barn. Bronco immediately picked up his pace. "He's ready for a nap, and I have to get back to work."

Olivia asked, "Before you go, have you seen Cayenne?"

"I haven't seen her for days."

"I wanted to touch base before I leave town. I've learned that lesson, at least!"

"But we forgave you for the last time, right?"

"Everyone did forgive me, or so they say," admitted Olivia. As Sage and Bronco moved ahead of her toward the barn, she stopped to wait.

When Sage returned she carried a bridle in her hand. "Come with me to the tack room. I'll leave this and walk you to your car."

"Did you drive over?" Olivia asked.

"I got a ride. Do you have time to take me back to the academy?"

"Let's go."

Olivia unlocked her Ford as both women hopped into the front seat, Olivia behind the steering wheel. On the way up the curving road, Sage broke the silence.

"Olivia," her voice cracked. She took a deep breath and continued, "I get the feeling you want to tell me something."

Not until after the band gig, then I can tell you about Mom and leave right away.

"No. I'm good. I think Janis has her guy in jail, the one who killed Lana. So I'll tie up a few more loose ends and head back to Playa."

"I heard that Thomas Seeker is in jail. I hope he's the guy. It's nerve-racking thinking there's a killer in our midst who's gone undetected. But I have to admit, I thought you might have changed your mind about leaving Lily Rock."

"I'm not running away this time. I know I'll be back a lot more often. I have you and Meadow to thank for that. I feel like I belong somewhere for the first time since Mom passed."

"Just so you know, you can always stay with us when you come to Lily Rock. By the way, how are things going with Michael?"

"We're doing okay. He has other matters on his mind right now." *I'm not gonna tell her about meeting Wanda right now.*

Olivia pulled the car to a stop as Sage hopped out, slamming the door shut. "See you early on Friday," she said through the open window. "Hope you find Cay."

Olivia drove back onto the main road and followed it upward to where Arlo told her the labyrinth was located. In the full sun, Lily Rock, shining in the noon sunlight, looked alabaster white where the rays bounced off her smooth surface. *A benevolent force of nature, watching over her namesake.*

Olivia hung her arm out the open window, feeling the air

grow cooler. Her ears popped as the altitude gradually increased. A sense of calm came over her, relaxing the muscles in her neck and shoulders. *So beautiful.* She slowed her car to gently follow the curves of the road.

On the left, Olivia saw the sign *Lily Rock Chapel and Labyrinth.* Turning her car onto the dirt path, she followed the arrow to the parking lot. Shoving the gearshift into park, Olivia slipped out of the driver's seat to stand in front of the chapel entrance. She glanced up toward the rustic steeple, which rose from the roof of the old timber building.

Holding her hand over her eyes to block out the sun, Olivia looked for the labyrinth. Just past the chapel, she saw the back of a tall figure. *That must be Cayenne.*

Walking closer, she didn't call out to the woman walking slowly, hands clasped behind her, deep in thought. *I can wait until she's done. There's a bench, I'll sit there.*

Mesmerized by Cayenne's slow progress, she watched her take each deliberate step, one after the other, with a pause in between. Finally, Cayenne reached the labyrinth's center, where she turned her body around, stepping directly into the shadow of Lily Rock.

Cayenne raised her open-palmed hands above her head as if to honor the town's namesake with a full-body pose. After holding her head back for several minutes, Cayenne let her arms fall gracefully to her side. Then she made her slow walk back on the same path she'd come.

Olivia kept staring at Cayenne. *A person can take a journey without actually going anywhere.*

Instead of greeting her friend aloud, she waited in silence. *I feel like I'm in church, sitting in a pew that happens to be an outdoor bench.*

When Cay returned to the labyrinth entrance, she stopped and turned to face Lily Rock one more time.

Lowering her head Cayenne paused to bow, then her head came up. Then she turned to Olivia.

"To what do I owe this pleasure?" Cayenne asked with a smile. "Arlo must have told you where to find me."

To Olivia's surprise, her chest grew warm with emotion at Cay's greeting. "You knew I was here . . ."

"I sensed your presence. Thank you for waiting, by the way." Cayenne walked over to her. "Instead of sitting here, let's walk to the grove so that other people in the labyrinth can have more privacy."

They rose from the bench together, walking side by side on the trail. After several minutes, Cay pointed to a spot in the woods.

"We can sit under that tree," said Cayenne.

"I never knew about the labyrinth," Olivia said, leaning against the rough tree trunk. Cayenne sat facing her, her hand touching the earth by her side.

"I'm responsible for the labyrinth construction. About five years ago, I gathered people together to place the stones for the path. Some people came from the church, a few tribal elders from down the hill, and a Jewish rabbi also helped. It's designed with a mathematical equation, you know, not just a bunch of rocks thrown around helter-skelter."

"Maybe sometime I could learn how to, you know, walk it."

"You just do it, no learning necessary." Cayenne patted Olivia's hand. "But let's talk about what you came for. I know you have something on your mind."

That's the second time in one day someone has assumed I have something on my mind. Am I that transparent?

Instead Olivia asked, "How's your hand, by the way? I see you have a sizable bandage."

Cay's gaze shifted upward, toward the trees. "Much

better. I'll have full mobility after a few weeks. Thanks for asking."

"I do have a question, you know, about your take on Lana's murder. Did you hear they arrested Thomas Seeker for the murder?"

"This is Lily Rock," Cay said, smiling. "As soon as Janis snapped the cuffs on him, the word was out. Why do you think I've been up here at the labyrinth for so long?"

"I don't know," admitted Olivia.

Cayenne's eyes looked ahead as she contemplated her next words. "Because I feel guilty."

Olivia held her breath. *Is she going to confess to killing Lana?*

Cay quickly added, "Not what you think! I didn't kill Lana, though I wanted to. Lying about her illness to make money?" Cay shook her head. "Everything's a reality show nowadays. I am just coming to that understanding."

Olivia believed Cay. *What a relief . . . but If Cay didn't feel guilty about killing Lana, then what did she feel guilty about?* In a hesitant voice, Olivia asked, "So why do you feel guilty?"

Cayenne cleared her voice. "You know I'm a Two-Spirit, right?"

Olivia nodded. "My mother used to talk to me about Two-Spirit people, those in the tribe who refused to be identified as male or female."

"I thought you knew me when we first met. You weren't afraid or embarrassed, you just accepted me. I knew from that moment I could trust you. So then I can tell you, I don't feel guilty because I killed Lana, I feel guilty because I couldn't stop the person who did."

"Did you observe the murder?"

"Not with my eyes, just in here." Cay pointed to her

chest. "I knew it was only a matter of time until it happened, and because I felt angry for my trans community, I didn't step in to stop the violence."

Olivia ducked her head. "So you know who killed Lana?"

"I do."

"Will you tell Janis Jets?"

"I won't."

Sometimes Cayenne can be so frustrating. Why doesn't she just tell me or Janis already?

Ignoring Olivia's indignation, Cayenne looked upward, into the forest.

"The murderer needs to confess. Words from their heart spoken aloud will bring peace to the community. Janis Jets making an arrest will only create more animosity. If the confession can be made from the heart by the one who committed the crime, then all of those hurt from Lana's lies can be healed."

I can't argue with that. It feels true, though Cayenne's way doesn't feel exactly logical. Yet Janis Jets's way doesn't feel exactly true either. Being Two-Spirit must give Cayenne a particular perspective not available to others. I can learn from her.

"Is this when I ask you if you have an alibi for the time of Lana's death?" said Olivia, hoping that Cayenne would laugh.

"Of course. I was here at the labyrinth. All alone. No one else can corroborate my truth. But Olivia, that doesn't mean it isn't true; we both know that."

As the sun rose behind the pines, Olivia and Cayenne sat in silence. Lily Rock loomed in front of them. She leaned over to Cay. "My mother used to say 'the truth will set you free.' Is that what you mean about the person confessing on their own?"

Cayenne smiled at her. "Your mother was Indigenous?"

"A part of her was, not all."

"Then you know. That's all I can tell you. Knowing is more than being able to prove something."

Olivia frowned. *I only wish I did know. What is she talking about?*

Cayenne rose to her feet. She held her bandaged hand with the other, leaning forward to say, "Your part in discovering Lana's killer will become clear soon enough. But for now, we move forward one step at a time."

19

SAME TIME NEXT YEAR

That afternoon Olivia felt distracted. *I'm nervous about the gig on Friday. Stage fright, that's what I've got. No matter how many times I've sung the songs, every audience is different. I wish I could get that first walk on stage over with. After that I'll be okay.*

Time to pick out my gig outfit.

She walked to her bedroom closet where she kept an array of dresses and hats. *My gig clothes. One of these dresses should work.*

The creamy-white cotton sundress with the spaghetti straps. That would be perfect. She let her fingers run through the embroidered lace of the hem, holding the dress up to herself. *That will do.*

For the next couple of hours Olivia's mind did not settle down. *I wonder what Janis is doing. Is it time for me to tell her I don't think Seeker is the killer? I'm not looking forward to her*

dissent. Better make a cup of tea instead. Her cell phone buzzed.

"Just thinking about you," Olivia said to Janis.

"I want to talk to you if you can fit it into your busy schedule this afternoon." Jets's voice sounded dry. "I'm still putting together the timing of the Thomas Seeker incident," Janis added. "Come in later. We can talk and see if the facts line up."

"Okay. Anything new?"

"We still have Seeker in custody. He sticks to his claim that he didn't intend to hurt Meadow and that they were just 'playing around.'" Olivia could imagine Janis air quoting the playing around part even over the phone.

"When I confiscated all of his cameras you should have seen him rant and rave. Boy was he mad! He felt guilty to me. The temper makes me think he's a likely suspect. On the one hand, Meadow claims he was with her when Lana was murdered. Why would she lie after what he did to her and her kitchen? I could hold him in the cell, but I just don't have the evidence. I especially don't want to babysit him Friday night. I want to be there for the big event at the pub."

Olivia felt her gut clench. "Big event?"

"Come on, don't play dumb. Everybody is coming out to hear your band. Arlo is pumped up for a big crowd. Even I'm coming, and I hate folk music."

Olivia sighed deeply. *The band sounded great at the previous rehearsal. With a few more local gigs, we could consider touring. Goodbye Lily Rock, hello world!*

"What about the other hand?"

"As I was saying," Janis said tartly, "even if Meadow alibis him, on the other hand Thomas Seeker is a questionable character with priors. The way he turned on Meadow indicates serious mental instability. Since Lana provided him a good cash source if nothing else, he may have gotten angry when she decided she was done with her cancer charade. Enough evidence to hold him or not, he's the guy."

"He's the guy," Olivia echoed, except he wasn't. *I know he isn't, just like Cay said.*

* * *

Olivia drove to the constabulary with a bottle of water in the holder between the car seats. She found a parking place in front of the library. Before she could lock her car, Meadow, spotting her from the window, came outside and stood on the boardwalk, gesturing. "May I have a minute?"

Standing outside her car, Olivia took note of Meadow's full smile. She seemed none the worse for being tied and gagged a few days ago. "How are you doing?" Olivia asked just to make sure.

"I'm fine. Arnica works wonders for any soreness. But it isn't me that I want to talk about." Meadow's voice dropped as she whispered, "Sage and I wondered if you'd come over sometime, sooner rather than later? We have something to talk to you about."

"I could come by after dinner," Olivia said. "Anything I should prepare myself for?"

"It's not that kind of thing. We wanted your opinion on a project we've been considering, and you've become like family. If you don't have other plans, why don't you come for dinner? Six o'clock would be perfect."

"I'll bring a green salad. See you then." Olivia walked quickly away from Meadow with a distinct sense of foreboding. *If that wasn't a sign, then I don't know one. Tonight I will tell Sage about our bio mom when she's with Meadow. If only I hadn't taken so long to get to the truth.*

Once inside of the constabulary, Olivia greeted Antonia.

"Hey, good to see you," Olivia remarked, watching the girl's fingers typing rapidly on the computer keyboard.

"Just a minute, I'll be right with you," Antonia replied, eyes focused on her work.

She looks so efficient. Olivia paused to admire the young woman's desk. Next to her computer was a vase of yellow lilies. Next to the vase was a photo of Wilson Jones.

"That's a photo of Wilson Jones," Olivia commented.

"You're right. That's him," said Antonia, turning to look at Olivia. "We're back together now. He's living in my little cabin outside of town. I think we'll be married very soon."

"That sure happened fast."

"Well, kind of. I knew him long before I moved here."

"Remind me again?"

"We'd hung out here in Lily Rock before he did photography work for Lana. She wasn't his girlfriend or anything."

Maybe Wilson told Antonia that he wasn't Lana's boyfriend, but Sage says differently. At the very least those photos were evidence of them in bed together. "Wilson is quite the catch," Olivia assured the vulnerable girl. *And that's a big fat lie.*

"Oh, he'll make a wonderful husband. He's already booked reservations for our honeymoon in Cancun."

Before Olivia could ask for more details, Janis Jets came through the sliding glass doors from the back offices. She leaned over Antonia's desk. "Did you get the information on Thomas Seeker's previous arrests?"

"Just sent it over," replied Antonia.

"Come on back," Janis invited Olivia. "We can talk there. Seeker is right over there." She pointed to cell number one.

As Olivia walked closer to Seeker's cell she paused to look in. He sat in the corner of his bunk reading a magazine, looking as if he were waiting for his airline boarding number to be announced. A small table had been placed in the cell, with a bowl of candy and tissues.

Knowing Seeker could see but not hear her through the cell doors, she said with a whistle, "Wow, he's got it made."

"Antonia has taken quite a shine to our inmate," admitted Janis.

"Good thing she already has a boyfriend. I mean, fiancé."

"I think Thomas may be her backup plan, should Wilson fall through."

"She's not exactly picky for such a pretty girl."

"She does like unusual characters."

After Janis got them each a fresh bottle of water, Olivia related what she'd learned from Cayenne.

"She told me she knows who killed Lana and that the person needs to confess to heal everyone involved."

Janis's eyebrows shot up. "That sounds like a lot of hooey to me. I've heard of Two-Spirit people. I never put that together with our transgender community."

"I think that's the point. In our culture, you're either male or you're female. First Nations people see the situation differently. People go from one gender identity to the other more fluidly, and less of a big deal is made. Some take hormones and have surgery. Some do not. Everyone is different, and some Two-Spirits are considered deeply insightful to the point of being clairvoyant."

"Well, aren't you full of useless information," Janis replied dryly. "But that doesn't explain why Cayenne doesn't march right in here and tell me who killed Lana de Carlos. I suppose she thinks Seeker didn't do it."

When Olivia did not respond, Janis asked, "You think Cayenne doesn't need an alibi?"

"She doesn't have one. That's different than not needing one."

Janis Jets tapped her fingers on the table. "Maybe you accept Cayenne's airy-fairy ideas about Two-Spirit people, but I'm inclined toward the facts. I'll bring her in for an interview this afternoon, and we'll see what's what. I want to check her off my list of suspects, even though I'm sure the killer is Thomas Seeker."

Olivia felt her gut clench. "Do you want me around?"

"Actually, I want you to go. You're way too susceptible to Cayenne's spirit talk. And I don't need your influence right now. Go play your autoharp or whatever you call that ridiculous instrument and leave me to do what I do best."

* * *

Driving away from the constabulary, Olivia ran the conversation over in her head. *Janis may be right. I do lean into ideas that can't be proven but do have a possibility.*

Good ol' Janis. She wants to line up all the suspects and hand out citations and court dates. Even if a person wasn't the killer, Janis suspected they deserved punishment for something else once she found some evidence.

When Olivia reached home, she found Mayor Maguire waiting for her by the front door. With a rush of joy, she ran toward the dog, leaning down to give him a big hug. "M&M, you came to see me. Good boy!"

The dog smiled as if it were no big deal. He turned and moved around Olivia's legs, ending up by her right knee. They walked into the house together.

Once in the kitchen Olivia filled a bowl of fresh water for the dog, who lapped it up instantly. "It's not dinner time," she told him. "But how about a game with a snack?"

With dog bones in her pocket, Olivia and the mayor went outside to play fetch. Each time the dog returned the tennis ball, she handed him a small treat. "Gotta work for your fun sometimes," she explained to him.

As Mayor Maguire sprinted after the ball, Olivia looked over her shoulder. When she turned back around, Mayor Maguire had already dropped the ball at her feet.

"So you're home," came a familiar voice from the pathway.

Michael Bellemare stood several feet away, in his usual faded jeans and worn flannel shirt.

Olivia smiled at him and waved. *I'm going to act like the Wanda thing is perfectly okay with me.* "You and Wanda want to come over for a drink?" she asked. *Don't I sound nonchalant?* Since seeing them together, Olivia assumed she now had two neighbors instead of one.

A look of surprise came over Michael's face. "Wanda left a couple of days ago. She always heads out before Labor Day traffic."

Olivia felt confused. "I thought you were back together."

"We get together once a year. That doesn't mean we're back together. She's remarried and has a child in Chicago."

"I see," said Olivia.

"We always hike the week before Labor Day. It's kind of our thing since—"

"Your divorce?"

"Not exactly." Michael scratched the back of his head. "Do I still get the drink? I can explain more then."

"Of course." Olivia walked toward her house with Mayor Maguire's ball in her hand. "And you don't have to explain. I didn't mean to be nosy."

Five minutes later Michael Bellemare appeared at her back door.

She opened it wide for him. "Meet me on the deck. I'll bring a beer."

Olivia looked into the back of the refrigerator where she kept the beer for her guests. With a beer in one hand and a water in the other, she noticed Michael standing outside admiring the trees and the view of Lily Rock.

She handed him the bottle as they both stood in silence, looking into the grove beyond. Michael pulled a lighter from his pocket to spark the outdoor heater. "The evenings are getting cooler," he said, sitting on a deck chair next to Olivia.

Raising her bottle of water to tap his bottle of beer, she said, "I am looking forward to wearing sweaters again."

"You do look good in a sweater." Michael grinned, taking a long sip from his drink.

"Okay, that's enough about how I look. What have you been up to today?"

"Arlo wanted me to check on some of the electrical at the pub. It seems your gig is drawing a big crowd. Can't wait to hear you play . . . what is it? 'Oh Shenandoah'?"

A smile of surprise lit up Olivia's face. "You know I play that tune?"

"Sure. I know a couple of your songs. Saw them on the internet."

Olivia shook her head. *Someone told me that videos of my playing were online.*

"The songs are so old, no one ever worries about the copyright," she told Michael.

Setting his bottle down by the leg of the chair, Michael cleared his throat. "So, I want to tell you about Wanda. You had that one question you never asked the other day, remember? I'm assuming it was about her?"

"You don't have to tell me anything," she hastily added. "A lot of divorced folks get back together. I know because I work for attorneys who get the paperwork going. It's not exactly uncommon."

"We're not getting back together. We just get back together once a year; like I mentioned, a kind of reunion, but not really."

"Like that old movie?"

"No, not like that." Michael's voice dropped. "It's not a same time next year for sex deal." He cleared his throat. "Seven years ago, Wanda and I were married. She's a book editor. We lived together in a high-rise in Chicago with our son."

"Your son?" Olivia had not anticipated a child in the marriage.

"His name was Daniel."

She noted the past tense in his sentence. Her breath came slowly as she waited for Michael to continue.

"He was a lovely kid, and he died . . . from leukemia."

Michael wiped tears away with the back of his hand. "So every year, on Daniel's birthday week, Wanda and I go camping, you know, to celebrate his life and to talk about him. That's just what we do. No getting back together; that ship has sailed. Just remembering our son the best we can."

Without warning tears rolled down Olivia's face. *I feel his broken heart. Just like I miss Mom, he misses Daniel.* Without thinking, in a smooth movement, Olivia placed her water bottle on the deck, stood, and walked toward Michael, who remained seated, looking at her with surprise.

She didn't speak, but she did move his arms away from his lap as she got on her knees and wrapped her arms around his middle. She curled herself up to him, tucking her face into his soft flannel shirt, pulling closer to his body. Olivia took several deep breaths and then began to sob. He bent his head over hers as her chest heaved. They shared the same grief.

Michael made no attempt to stop her crying while he held Olivia close to his chest. She felt his breath sync with her, and then the wetness from his tears touched her cheek. They rocked their bodies together without saying a word.

Olivia rubbed her face against the flannel of his shirt to dry her cheeks. Her fingers curled into the soft fabric of his shirt. *I don't want to move.*

He held her, and then she felt him bend his head. His finger reached under her chin as he titled her face up to his. "You okay?" he asked quietly.

She nodded her head. "I don't have any words for your loss."

"You don't need to have any words. You were perfect. You are perfect."

He kissed her cheek and then stroked her hair. She savored the comfort of his body.

After several minutes, Olivia spoke. "My legs are falling asleep."

He released his arms as she stood from her knees, shaking one leg at a time.

"Thank you for telling me about Daniel and his mother. I think you're courageous," she said in a soft voice.

"I'm a big baby," Michael said. "I can't talk about Daniel without crying. Plus when I do tell people, I don't want to hear what they have to say. Nothing anyone can say helps, so I've stopped talking about him. That's why Wanda comes once a year, to relieve me of my own reserve."

Olivia stepped backward so that Michael could stand up. He stared down at her. "Not to change the subject, but now that we've hugged and cried together, when are we going on a proper date? That's all I think about, you know."

"But you know I'm leaving Lily Rock. Why start now with a proper date?"

"You'll most likely be leaving town tomorrow night after the concert, so I thought I'd better ask before you vanish like last time."

Before she could answer, a sharp yip came from the back door. "I think the mayor is calling," said Michael.

"Let's go inside and feed him. Then we can talk about our date," said Olivia with a smile. "I'm supposed to have dinner with Meadow and Sage tonight, but maybe after the concert you and I can grab a bite to eat?"

His happy grin made her heart leap.

By the time Mayor Maguire bent his head over his dinner bowl, Olivia and Michael had returned to their usual banter. "I don't want to eat at the pub," she told him. "It's our first date, and it would be weird with everyone looking on."

"How about this? I'm not in a hurry. You'll be tired from the gig anyway. Since I've waited over a year, how about we get the gig over with, and then you go down the hill back to Playa, and I'll meet you for dinner down there in a few days. Better choices for us and less company."

"But it will be a long way for you to get home."

"Yes, it will; I'll probably have to spend the night at your place. That would be my plan."

"I'll think about it," Olivia said, her cheeks flushing as she realized his full intention.

"You do that. Until then, I have to get going. Do you want me to show up tomorrow for your rehearsal? I can do last-minute sound checks, you know, like a roadie."

"Just what I need, an architect and builder turned roadie. That is so Lily Rock. Sure, you can come. I won't have time to talk, though."

"No worries. I'll be looking at you from the sound booth and that's all I need."

Olivia smiled and so did her heart.

20

WILDWOOD FLOWER

By the time evening rolled around, Olivia had gathered her leather tote and filled it with the paperwork she'd accumulated for Marla's estate. One file, dedicated to the DNA research, stood out from the others. Not so much because it was the thickest, but because the tattered edges showed considerable wear.

She'd spent hours looking through the information, waiting for an insight about how to tell Sage they had the same birth mother. Olivia had held the folder in her lap wondering, *When will I gather the courage to share all that's in this file . . .*

By the time the three women sat at the worn pine table in Meadow's kitchen, Olivia could barely look at the food on her plate. The knot in her stomach prevented her from swallowing. She fought back tears.

Meadow glanced past Olivia at the overfilled tote bag

resting next to her chair. "Did you bring some paperwork with you?" she asked innocently.

"I did," admitted Olivia.

"Something about the band?" asked Sage as she took a sip of wine.

"Not exactly. It's about Marla's estate and some DNA research." Olivia watched Meadow's face.

"Not more DNA research." Meadow sighed.

For a moment Olivia considered taking her folder home without further comment. What would be the harm? Sage didn't have to know about her birth mother, and neither did Meadow. Mona was dead. She was past suffering. This was the same argument she'd gone over and over in her head for the past several months.

"But you can't hold back the truth once you know it," Mona's voice said in Olivia's head.

"I'll get the paperwork and show you what I found," Olivia said quietly, ignoring the food on her plate. "I'm nervous about all of this and I won't be able to eat until I tell you everything."

Leaning over, she pulled out the thick manila folder from her worn shoulder bag. "I did some research when I found Marla's ancestry account on the library computer. Most of what I looked for was about the doc. But there was more." Olivia slid the papers out of her bag, handing one set to Sage and a duplicate to Meadow.

"I've been keeping this information to myself because I didn't know how to tell you both. I can't do it any longer. I want you to know I will do everything in my power to adjust Marla's estate to include Sage."

"Marla didn't put my name in the will, why would you want to change her wishes?" commented Sage, staring at the paper in her hands.

"As far as I can figure out, Marla knew she was ill and she wanted me to make things right, should she pass away. I think Marla knew she had enemies in town. Since I was a stranger to Lily Rock, she figured I would be less vulnerable and that eventually I'd sort out the mess and tell you."

Meadow leaned across the table to put her hand over Olivia's. "So let me understand. You think you have information that will alarm us?"

The tone in Meadow's voice surprised Olivia. Instead of sounding uncomfortable, Meadow sounded calm and very rational. Ditzy Meadow with the birdlike laughter had been pushed aside for the rational woman wearing the spotless denim jumper.

The woman looking at Olivia now was not the CBD herbalist, nor the Old Rocker, nor Mayor Maguire's handler. The Meadow before her, with her glasses freshly polished and the slight smile on her lips, was the one who had an advanced degree in library science and who had access to all of the town's public computers . . .

"You knew!" Olivia exclaimed, her cheeks flushed with amazement. "About Sage and her birth mother."

Sage chuckled. "Is that what you're trying to tell us, that we're half sisters?"

"Yes." Olivia's eyes filled with tears. "I've been trying to tell you for an entire year!"

"Do you want apple or peach pie, dear?" asked Meadow with a smile.

"I want to know what you know!" demanded Olivia.

Sage leaned over to pat Olivia's hand. "I know I'm your sister and that we have the same birth mother. Meadow has known for months. She looked up your search history at the library computer before you scooted out of town the last time.

Meadow is no slouch. She got into Marla's ancestry account and ran right home to tell me what she found."

"Everyone in Lily Rock knows," Meadow added with a big smile. "You both look so much alike no one was surprised. Such happy news. I just assumed you'd tell us when you were ready."

Olivia sighed with exasperation. "I'll take peach pie, thank you very much. You could have told me that you knew months ago!"

"Oh no, you needed to tell us, that's the best way. We don't rush things here in Lily Rock. We wait for the right time."

Olivia paused, remembering her conversation with Cayenne only days ago. *If the confession can be made from the heart by the one who committed the crime, then all of those hurt can be healed.*

Meadow slid a large piece of peach pie with a mound of vanilla bean ice cream in front of Olivia. Her stomach rumbled as she heaped her fork with crust and fruit. "I am feeling so much better," she said to both women, taking a large bite.

Everyone ate dessert without further discussion. Sage didn't ask any questions about Mona, nor did Meadow. They all smiled at each other across the table. When the dishes were being cleared, Meadow announced, "Since your dear mother is no longer with us, I have decided I will be mother to you both. When the holidays come around, you will be invited here to Lily Rock. I'll let you know the guest list so you can plan your gifts accordingly. We do appreciate a home-made item, so you can get started. Do you bead or knit?"

Olivia gulped back her quick reply, watching Sage grin. "I'm sure you can teach Olivia how to bead, Mother. She's dying to know!"

Olivia shot Sage the evil eye as both women burst into laughter.

"I don't understand what's so funny, but now that I have two daughters, I suppose they'll laugh at me behind my back as girls do. That's how families are."

"We'll finish clearing the table then, while you rest a bit," Sage told Meadow, signaling Olivia to follow her to the kitchen. When the swinging door closed behind them, Sage took the dessert dishes from Olivia's hand.

"Give me a hug," said Sage, tears glistening in her eyes.

The two women embraced, fitting easily into each other's arms.

When Sage pulled back, she added, "I want to hear about my . . . I mean our, mother after the concert. At least you can begin to tell me."

I thought I'd lose a sister but it turns out I gained a sister and Meadow as a mother.

"You will love Mona," Olivia told Sage, sniffing away her tears. "She thought about you every day."

* * *

"Check one, two, three," came the sound engineer's voice.

"Are you ready?" Arlo called from the hallway behind the bar.

Olivia had brushed her hair into a loose bun, pulling forward one wisp that dipped over her eye. Inserting another pin, she felt satisfied. *That should stay put.*

"Come on, Olivia," Arlo urged again.

Standing in the makeshift dressing room, Olivia took one last glance at herself. *Good choice on the dress.*

The lightweight fabric flowed around her body. The scalloped hem of the crocheted edge covered Olivia's legs to just below her knee. Her neckline plunged just enough to see the tops of her breasts. With a quick adjustment of the sleeveless top, she smiled at herself in the mirror. The overall effect was of natural elegance, except for the leather boots, which gave her an outdoorsy vibe.

One more thing. Olivia reached for a feather wrapped in tissue paper that she'd put in her tote the night before. She was only seven when she'd first played and sung for an audience. "Here's my crow's feather. When you wear this think of me, and remember all of us, those who sing from the heart," Mona had said.

Slipping the feather underneath the ribbon band, Olivia placed the wide-brimmed felt hat on her head. She tilted her head to the side and laughed. *Not exactly a Cinderella transformation, but it will get their attention.*

"Olivia!" shouted Arlo. He knocked from the hallway.

She opened the door to slide past Arlo and walk toward the small stage. A low whistle followed her. "Wow, you clean up fine," Arlo commented. She grinned. *Steady on. Smile. You're nearly to the stage.*

Unlike most performers Olivia rarely made a big entrance. Instead she walked around the bass player and the drummer to take up her autoharp in her arms before seating herself on the stool. With one leg crossed over the other, the folds of her dress rested against her slim legs. The strong beat of her heart gave her the courage to look out into the audience.

"And now I'd like to introduce my sister, Olivia Greer," came Sage's clear voice from the microphone. Sage's teaching experience made her the natural band spokesperson. She spoke slowly and clearly, glancing directly at Olivia.

Tucking the autoharp under her arm, Olivia walked to the microphone and gazed out at the crowd.

It did look as if all of Lily Rock had turned out for the

band's performance. She took her time catching the eyes of those she knew. Her gaze fell on Michael, who stood with his back against the wall. He gave her a quick thumbs-up, his eyes shining with anticipation.

In the front row Janis Jets sat with Antonia, who held Wilson's hand. Antonia's knuckles looked white under the shine of the spotlights. Next to Wilson was Seeker, a grim expression on his lips. *Meadow's alibi must have gotten him released from jail.* The seat next to him was empty.

Casting her eyes to the right then the left, Olivia noticed Cayenne and Meadow sitting together at the bar as Arlo poured drinks for them. Olivia's eyes rested on Cayenne's face, noting her dark eyes and high cheekbones. *Are you the only suspect left without an alibi to satisfy Janis Jets?*

Olivia cleared her throat, ready to begin her song. "Our first number will be a very old song that Sweet Four O'Clock has made their own. From the hills of Appalachia, the settlers and the Indigenous people sang this melody. My mother was from the Appalachian Cherokee Nation. She taught me the verses, and today I sing not just for you, but for my mother, and Sage's birth mother," Olivia paused to look over at Sage, whose eyes were shining, "and for all the other women who shared the melody before us. Here is a story about one wild and raging river that everyone called . . . Shenandoah."

Olivia made her way back to the wooden stool to the polite applause from the audience. She slipped her thumb over the strings to make sure that the tuning held. Then she nodded to the bass player, who began the melody.

By the time Olivia took the first breath to sing, the room grew quiet. Mesmerized by the unexpected clarity of her voice, everyone stared at her, breathing as one.

By the second chorus couples reached out to touch one another, their hands intertwining. Some eyes welled with tears, as a few people openly wept. *They're remembering. Remembering all the times they longed for love and for home.*

The crowd inhaled and exhaled together as Olivia sang the age-old words of the song. *This was supposed to be my goodbye to Lily Rock.* As the last note drifted away, the audience stood as one, cheering and applauding.

"Olivia Greer, everyone," shouted Sage into the microphone over the noise. She paused and then pulled her fiddle to her chin. Glancing at Olivia, Sage nodded, beginning the next tune.

Olivia slipped to the side, away from center stage to catch her breath. She stood in a shadow near the bar. Inhaling deeply, she listened to the band play a reel. *Is that Janis arguing with someone?*

Olivia looked over the room, her eyes locking on Janis, who poked Wilson Jones in the chest with her finger. She yelled something into Wilson's face. *I wish I could hear what she's saying.*

Before she could get closer, Olivia watched Jets poke Thomas Seeker in the shoulder. Thomas glared at Janis, turning his glance away from her piercing stare. He kept his focus toward the stage, tapping his foot to the fiddle tune.

Olivia slid back into the dark corner, waiting for the pause between songs when she would return to join the band. One more gulp of water and she stepped toward the platform, ready to perform the last two tunes.

"Hey, Olivia," shouted a man from the left side of the crowd. "Buy you a drink after the set?"

Olivia smiled as she took her seat on the stool. She took a moment to glance toward Janis Jets, who pointed at her, then back to herself, then to the bar. *I've been summoned.* She stepped toward Sage to whisper in her ear. "I have to do something, can I drop out of this one number?"

Sage nodded, starting up the next tune as Olivia slid away.

"What do you want?" she asked Jets. "I have a gig here."

"That's obvious, and you know what? You're pretty good."

"Thanks, but make it quick."

"Just want you to be the first to know, I got Lana's killer."

"Who is it?"

Janis shoved her hands in her pockets. "I don't exactly have the killer in custody, but I do know for certain who did it. Now if I can only get the confession, that would be perfect."

"I noticed you released Thomas Seeker. He's definitely not the one?"

"He has an alibi. We can thank Meadow for that," said Jets. "Like I told you, I could use a confession."

"Is the killer here, at the concert?"

"Of course. I wouldn't be telling you otherwise."

Olivia paused for a moment, wondering if she should tell Janis. She remembered Cayenne's words, *"Your part will become clear very soon."*

"I think I can help, if you want my help," Olivia offered.

"You? Miss Rocking the Boho Dress, all shiny and bright, with everyone in the house in love with you? I don't think so."

"I can help because I have a superpower, one that I haven't yet revealed, at least to you."

"Do you tell fortunes in that outfit or do card tricks?"

Olivia grinned at Janis. "No, I sing. And I know the song that will make the killer confess."

"How do you know that?"

"It's my superpower, didn't I just say? Be quiet and get your cuffs ready. I'm on next."

Olivia waited for Sage to finish the final fiddle notes before she stood up to the microphone. She pulled on the brim of her hat, shading her eyes before she lifted her head.

Speaking into the microphone, she said, "Our last song tonight comes from Appalachia, made famous by the Carter Family Band. We bring you 'Wildwood Flower.'"

Vibrant applause echoed through the pub. Olivia turned to the surprised band, who thought they would finish the set with another song they'd already rehearsed. "Go with me," she told them. "Key of G." The bass player nodded. They'd worked together long enough to give Olivia the freedom to improvise, trusting she had a plan.

She sat on her stool, pulling the instrument to her body, strumming the first chord as the rest of the band joined in. Sage bent forward, watching Olivia's fingers pluck at the strings. When Olivia changed chords, Sage began to fiddle quietly, as the rest of the band joined in.

Once they established their groove, Olivia began to sing, "I will twine, I will mingle my raven-black hair . . ."

As she sang, Olivia's voice lifted, filling the entire room with the sad lament about a woman who lost her one true love. The man had left her for another, and the woman wanted revenge. She wanted her old lover to suffer as she had suffered. But most of all, she wanted him to feel regret.

The crowd's attention, riveted on Olivia, made her face shine under the broad-brimmed felt hat. Her foot tapped on the top bar of the stool as she enveloped them into her story, her fingers flying over the autoharp strings.

As Olivia sang the third verse, a woman in the front row stood. She swayed to the music as if she were the only one in the room. The man next to her pulled on her hand, but she didn't sit down. Instead she yanked her hand away from him to move unsteadily toward the stage.

Now Antonia faced the audience, her eyes closed, her arms waving over her head. She cried, her sobs filling the air. Olivia watched the young woman carefully, taking a quick glance into the audience. Janis Jets stared and her jaw dropped in amazement.

Time to shift the music. Olivia replaced her words with a hum, bringing the music down a notch. She shifted her fingers into a slower rhythmic pattern. The band caught on and followed her, as everyone leaned forward, expecting the song to end.

Though the music got softer, Antonia seemed not to notice. Instead she danced more wildly, her arms waving frantically as if she needed attention.

Olivia blinked at Sage, followed by a thrust of her chin. The entire band stopped together to end the song, and the last note lingered in the silent room.

Only Antonia's sobs could be heard as she faced the audience, her face contorted in rage.

For an instant Olivia thought Antonia would step down into the arms of her boyfriend, but instead she watched in horror realizing that Antonia was not done.

Gripping the hem of her shirt with both hands, Antonia raised the fabric over her head, exposing her naked breasts to the entire audience.

"You see, Wilson?" she cried out. "I have great tits too. Better than Lana de Carlos, and they're real. I know you regret leaving me for her!"

Olivia looked toward Janis Jets with shocked amazement. *There it is, the confession you've been waiting for.* Janis strode to the stage. "Antonia Wazinski, I am arresting you for the murder of Lana de Carlos. You have the right to remain silent."

21

CALLING THE SHOTS

"Put that ridiculous autoharp down, for heaven's sake. We have a suspect to interview." Janis Jets looked grimly at Olivia.

"As you wish, Officer Jets," Olivia murmured under her breath.

"Grab Mike and meet me at the constabulary as soon as you peel yourself away from your fans," Jets directed, pointing toward the small crowd gathering near the bar.

I want to say hello to everyone first. Olivia stepped toward her group of fans with a smile. "Hello everyone, welcome to Lily Rock."

"Would you take a selfie with us?" asked a young man standing next to his girlfriend.

Seven selfies later, Olivia changed back into her jeans and shirt, pulling a jacket over her shoulders.

"You ready?" asked Michael, standing in the doorway. "Jets wants us back at the—"

"I know, the constabulary," muttered Olivia.

"Tired?" he asked, searching her face.

"Exhausted. Plus Meadow and I are having that open

house tomorrow for the entire town. I need to get some sleep before she arrives bright and early."

"Fear not," Michael smiled. "I've got your back. I'll help with setting up. You won't be stranded with Meadow all alone."

Olivia nodded to Michael as she gathered the rest of her clothing and her instrument.

"Let me drive," he offered, taking the autoharp from her arms. "I'll take care of your car. The least I can do, being your roadie and all."

She caught his eye in a silent thank you. *He really isn't like Don at all. I don't know why I thought that. Look how supportive— Uh oh, Olivia Greer. You know where this is heading.*

Michael took her elbow, guiding her out of the backstage area through the exit to the parking lot beyond.

* * *

When Olivia and Michael walked through the constabulary door, her cell phone rang. "We're here, Janis," she said.

"'Bout time too. I've got Miss Take Your Shirt Off in Public back in interview room one. The doors have been unlocked, just walk on back. Tell Mike to get behind the two-way mirror," Jets added. "You come with me in the interview room."

When Olivia explained Janis's instructions to Michael, his eyebrows raised in protest. "I want to be in the room with you two," he said firmly. Janis, standing in the hallway waiting for them, heard the last of his protest.

"I want a pony on my birthday. Not gonna happen. We need you behind the scenes just in case. Stop arguing, Belle-mare. And you, Ms. Meadowlark, follow me."

In interview room one, the suspect looked a lot worse for wear. She sat in a chair behind the large table looking small and forlorn.

"You want water or something?" Jets asked, eyeing her suspect.

"Or how about a cup of tea?" suggested Olivia. *I guess I'm the good cop.* Antonia barely nodded.

Olivia quickly returned with three mugs, all with teabag papers hanging over the side. "Chamomile," she told the women. "I'm embracing my inner Meadow." Olivia looked back and forth from Janis to Antonia. Since no one reached for their tea, she sat down to sip hers.

"I want a lawyer," demanded Antonia. "I want my phone call," she added, her elbows clamped tightly to her body, her eyes wide with fear.

"I want a pony on my birthday," added Olivia, imitating Jets's response to Michael.

Janis slid a phone across the table. "Make your call and make it quick."

"I don't know a lawyer," cried Antonia, her eyes filling with tears as she shifted from the one in charge to the hapless victim. "No one can help me."

"We will appoint a lawyer for you as soon as possible from the DA's office down the hill," said Janis matter-of-factly. "By the time we hear from them, you'll be here a couple of weeks. That works for me. I can go give out citations to tourists. And you, of course," Jets nodded to Antonia, "can chill in a cell."

"I want to go home," whined Antonia. "I don't need a lawyer."

"Can we get that in writing?" Janis leaned under the table. Yanking her briefcase up, she handed it to Olivia. "Since my assistant is otherwise occupied, maybe you can fill in as a temp," Janis muttered sarcastically. "Find the paper that relinquishes her rights in there. Make it snappy."

Olivia dug into the leather bag, coming up with a likely paper. "This the one?"

"First try, not bad. See me later and you may have a job waiting." Janis handed Antonia the paper and a pen. The policewoman sighed deeply, leaning back in her chair as she folded her arms in front of her chest. "Sign the paper," growled Jets.

Did she mean it that I might have a job at the constabulary?

Antonia began to scribble while Janis glared. Then without drawing attention to herself, Olivia slid Antonia's signed paper from her hand.

"You love Wilson, right? That's how all this started?" Olivia began, urging the young woman along.

"I did love Wilson so much! He was my sun and moon. That's why I moved to Lily Rock. He wanted to marry me. We had plans to start a family, two boys and two girls."

"But Wilson was already seeing someone else when you got to Lily Rock?"

"That slut! Lana de Carlos had no business stealing my man. She manipulated Wilson into thinking there would be money in it for him if he shot photos of her and posted them on the internet."

"Wilson was just taking photos?"

"That's what he told me. I believed him until I saw the pictures with Lana and Wilson. I'm not that stupid. The lens pointed right at her fake tits!"

Janis Jets spit out her tea. "Hold down the language, young lady; this is a police station."

Olivia did not bat an eyelash. "So when you saw the photos, you realized Wilson and Lana were a couple?"

"I'm not a fool," Antonia sat up, "despite appearances."

Olivia nodded. "How did you come across those photos?"

"I followed Lana's cancer story. Wilson posted on her website and social media accounts. Then I googled her name and discovered a second website with even more photos of Lana. They looked more . . ." Antonia's voice dropped as she glanced over to Janis for approval.

"Like porn, but not hardcore," she added. "On that site there were videos. It doesn't take a genius to realize who put up that second webpage. That creep up the hill. He did it."

"You mean Thomas Seeker?" asked Janis.

"That's the one, plus you should see those videos. Lana stood in the shower with Wilson, him running his hands over her naked body." Antonia looked over at Jets again and then added, "I knew for sure they were a couple when I saw that video!"

"So you plotted to kill Lana after you found the two websites."

"Don't be ridiculous. I confronted Wilson. He admitted that Lana's cancer journey was fake and that he went along to make more money. I tried to get him to take his share of the profit and leave her, regardless of whether she planned to keep going with her lie; he wasn't sure if she'd want to create a remission story. But he wasn't having any of it, and you know why? Lana had cast a spell over Wilson. He had no control."

"Or maybe Wilson had big dollar signs in his eyes," commented Janis dryly.

"Oh sure. He wanted to continue the story about her breasts, like creating a remission journey and then maybe her getting cancer again. And then they had this scene with the Please Fund Me page."

"Did Lana agree about continuing the cancer journey with a remission and relapse?" asked Olivia.

"No, she was done. That's when I knew I had the perfect plan." A smile crept over Antonia's lips. "I suggested he could just, you know, get rid of Lana and take all the money. We could pick up where we left off and tack on a honeymoon to Cancun thanks to Lana de Carlos." Antonia leaned over the table to whisper. "But what I really wanted was for Wilson to suffer, to regret what he'd done to me, like that song you were singing in the pub. That's why I planted those photos in your car. You'd think he killed Lana and chase him, which you did, by the way."

"So you wanted to be around to see your old lover regret his decision to leave you."

Antonia sighed deeply.

Olivia continued, "Is that why you showed up to help me the day we cleaned out Lana's stuff? Were you looking for more photos? Were you disappointed when you couldn't find them?"

"I didn't need any more photos!" Antonia hissed. "I wanted to collect more evidence that they were a couple—some DNA, for instance, from the sheets. You were too quick for me, plus the cops had taken most of that evidence when they checked the room the first time.

"But like I said, I'm not stupid. Once I walked into the room I knew Wilson and Lana smoked weed and did stuff. You could just tell, at least I could." Antonia reached for her tea with both hands, cradling the mug for support.

Some people like to revel in their misery. I would have run away so fast, but Antonia wanted to see all the ways Wilson cheated on her, including investigating the room where the couple made love.

"Let's get back to Wilson," said Jets. "Why didn't he kill Lana? Did he lack the guts, or was it because he found killing another human being reprehensible?"

"Or maybe Wilson really loved Lana," added Olivia.

"No!" shouted Antonia. "You're both wrong! Wilson stayed with Lana not out of love, but because she was a cash cow."

"You two could have gotten back together once Lana left."

"I didn't want to get back together with that swine. I wanted him to pay!" *I'll have to find out later why she spent so much time with him then, even saying they were engaged.* "Plus Lana thought she'd come back from vacation, reunite with her followers, and be pregnant. How could I stand by and let that woman live my dream?"

The corners of Antonia's mouth tightened. "What actually happened is that Wilson refused to confront Lana, so I had to do it for him.

"I went to her house, and who was at the front door but the pervert—that Seeker character. So I waited in the grove until he was done, and then the weed guy showed up to give her the weekly supply, so I waited some more. Finally, I trapped Lana at the front door. She must have thought the pervert or the weed guy had returned, so she opened the door. Boy, was she surprised!"

"And you told her about Wilson being your one true love?"

"Yes." Antonia teared up. "And I got real close to her. She moved outside to back me up. While she was yelling, I pulled my scarf off my neck to dab at my tears. Then lickety-split I flung the scarf over her neck, turned her right around, and yanked real hard until she stopped struggling."

Olivia stared at the young woman and shook her head. *She shows no sign of remorse.*

Janis reached across the table for Antonia's scarf. "Since you've confessed, you won't mind me borrowing this scarf and this mug to check for DNA, would you?"

Antonia's jaw dropped. "I washed the scarf," she whined.

"But there are fibers from the scarf embedded in the flesh around Lana's neck," explained Jets matter-of-factly. "They're already in evidence." Balling the scarf in her hand, Jets pointed to Olivia. "Grab the evidence bags in my briefcase, would you?"

Olivia handed them over, then Jets bagged the scarf and the tea mug.

The officer stood up. "Hey, Mike, you can come in now? I need some help getting the wildwood flower to her cell." Jets opened the door and walked into the hall.

Olivia took the moment alone with Antonia to ask one more question. "Why did you leave the photos in my car?"

Eager to explain, Antonia answered, "Jets didn't even suspect Wilson for days, and I was getting impatient. So I dropped the sexy photos in your car. Wilson is such a fool. He was waiting for Lana to join him at the hot springs while I was wringing her neck and the police sat on their hands."

Olivia could hear Michael and Janis talking in low voices in the hall.

Antonia licked her dry lips. "I had a beautiful plan for Wilson's arrest, you know. Once I got this job, I had a front row seat. From the desk I could listen in on Janis's conversations to be a part of the investigation. Then I led Janis to think Wilson was her man by keeping you on the trail with the photos. That took some thinking."

"What made you think Seeker took the more intimate photos and videos?"

Antonia's eyes filled with tears. "I suspected that Seeker guy was the one who put up the other Lana de Carlos website. I mean, who else could get that close to her? So I confronted him. I got Seeker to sell me his pictures. It took some persuasion. He was more than willing to hand them over when I traded him for a photoshoot with me."

Ick. Antonia has a gift of using people via their most vulnerable spots. Redirecting the conversation, Olivia asked, "So you wanted me to pursue Wilson and to convince Janis he was the killer?"

"I led you to him, didn't I? But when the county sheriff brought him back to Lily Rock, I had to amp up my plan. So I deliberately walked by his cell every chance I got just to make him see what he was missing. When he couldn't stand it any longer, when he begged me to come closer, I even pretended to love him again."

Olivia's eyebrows raised.

"I thought he was going to prison. You had him in jail. I saw a bright and sunny future for myself. After Wilson's conviction I planned to send him letters. He'd be in prison regretting losing me while I lived my best life. He'd know what he missed and he'd be so very, very sorry. I could have written a book and sold it about him and the fake influencer."

"But you underestimated Janis and her investigation," Olivia interrupted. "She knew Wilson wasn't guilty as soon as her people interviewed the staff at the spa. Wilson was easily recognizable by the staff. He'd been sunning and swimming with Lana every weekend for a year."

Olivia felt no empathy for the crying girl. "You really had me believing that you two were a couple. I mean, the way you hung out with him in the cell and sat with him at the concert."

"I was waiting for him to regret what he'd done, only he never did. He was sad that Lana died, which made me furious."

At that moment Janis and Michael entered the room together. The girl began to struggle as Michael grabbed one arm and Janis the other.

"You really should call a lawyer," Janis admonished, moving Antonia around the desk and into the hallway.

"Meet me in the truck," Michael called over his shoulder. "I'll give you a ride home."

Olivia nodded. Tears rose in her eyes. *Love isn't always kind. Sometimes it can turn quite ugly.*

* * *

Olivia slept in late the next morning. By ten o'clock, the sun streamed from her window, making her blink in the glare.

"M&M," she mumbled, reaching her hand over the covers. She felt his soft fur under her fingertips. Then with a huff, he rolled over for a belly scratch. She happily complied.

"When did you show up?" she mumbled to the dog.

"About an hour ago," a familiar male voice replied.

Olivia sat up, startled at the voice.

"Want some coffee before you get out of bed?" From across the room Michael looked at her with a friendly smile. He added, "I didn't want to wake you until the last minute, but Meadow will be here within the hour to set up for the open house. You remember agreeing to that, right?"

Olivia reached her arm out from the covers, taking hold of the much-needed wake-up brew offered by Michael. "I nearly forgot! The entire town will be here in a few hours."

Olivia sat up, her back against the headboard. Before she could ask how Michael got into her house, M&M rolled into Olivia's body to lie next to her, his head on her lap.

"This is cozy," Olivia remarked. "How did you get in my house, by the way?"

"I spent the night." He smiled at her. "Not like I wanted to, but the great room sofa is very comfortable." Michael yawned. "For one night, at least," he added with a wink.

"You didn't go home?"

"It was four in the morning by the time we got back from the constabulary. I was a bit concerned about you being alone, so I just stayed. Turns out you sleep like a baby. Good to know for the future."

We have a future?

"Antonia's story kind of scared me, when it comes to love."

He shook his head. "I'm all in. If you want more time to figure things out, that's okay with me. Plus now you don't have to leave Lily Rock. Sage told me that you finally woke up—you know about the sister thing."

Olivia felt surprise. "You knew we were sisters?"

"Oh hell, sweetheart, everyone in Lily Rock knew. You and Sage could be twins. You look the same, walk the same, are both musical. Only you would be the one to think it was a big secret. On the hill, we know stuff."

"I thought I was the only one who knew and that Sage would be angry because I withheld telling her for so long!" exclaimed Olivia.

"You underestimate Sage's feelings for you. Anyway, now that everyone realizes that you know, there's nothing for you to run away from. You can stay here."

"I can think of two reasons to leave. One is you. The other is a job. Marla's estate is costing me more money in attorney's fees right now. When it's settled things might change, but not for a while."

"I am a big problem," Michael admitted, completely ignoring the job part. "Just give in and we'll work it out. I can be your right-hand man, personal assistant, and companion. All in this fine form of a human being." He grinned as he swept his hand over his torso.

"What about your work?"

"Architecture travels. I can plan my work way ahead to coordinate with your touring."

"You certainly have it all figured out, at least in your mind," said Olivia dryly.

Taking another sip of coffee, she sat back in the nest of pillows behind her back. *I don't even feel like running anymore.*

"I found a renter for the house," she commented. She watched as Michael's jaw tightened. "She has a job in town. Her recommendations were stellar. I think she'll be a good fit for the house. You'll like her too. Since you are such close neighbors, it's important to me that you two get along."

A vein throbbed in his forehead. He cleared his throat. "You're teasing me, right? You didn't get a new tenant, did you?"

"I did get a new tenant."

He looked down at his hands, apparently trying to hide his disappointment. *I've gone too far.*

"You kind of get ahead of yourself and start making plans for my life. You know that, right?" she added gently.

Now a small smile returned to his lips. "So you *are* testing me. That's what you're doing? With the tenant stuff, that's all made up—"

"Actually, it isn't made up. I do have a new tenant." Olivia waited just long enough to keep him off balance. She knew the future of their relationship depended upon Michael Belle-mare not calling all of the shots.

With a sigh, Olivia relented. "And the new tenant would be Sage. She's moving in before Halloween. At least that's what she told Meadow last night at dinner."

"Sage is my new neighbor," Michael stated.

"She is and she will be the co-owner of the property.

Papers are being drawn up right now and things will be official in a couple of weeks. We have to file with the county."

Relief spread over Michael's face. "You're staying too. I heard the co-owner part."

Placing the mug on her bedside table, Olivia slipped her legs over the side of the bed, bare feet dangling. "I'll stay here in the smaller bedroom suite, and Sage is taking the larger suite. We'll live here together."

"Good plan. I can build out back, you know, make a studio for the band."

"Just a minute," she told him firmly. "No more plans from you. I'm leading this rodeo, and I can't believe I just said rodeo."

Michael held his finger in the air. "If I'm not mistaken, I just heard Meadow drive over the gravel with her truck. Arlo and Cay will arrive very soon with the food. Maybe you'd best get ready for your open house. I'll go upstairs and direct people, but only if it's okay with you, of course."

"Throwing parties has never been my forte. Remember, I've always been the one in the band, the one who sits backstage until it's time to go on."

* * *

As voices filled the downstairs, Olivia closed the door to her room to get ready for the open house. She took a long shower, washing away the fatigue from the day and night before.

By the time she opened the door, she recognized familiar voices. "Hey, Cay, bring the keg," shouted Arlo.

"Don't forget the Brussels sprouts," Meadow added. "Put them over there on the table. And I've already set up a microphone for Olivia to greet everyone."

"Olivia, are you ready for your party?" Michael called from upstairs.

I am ready.

As soon as she made her way into the great room, Sage placed a bottle of seltzer water in her hand. "For you, honey. By the way, Meadow mentioned that you wanted to say a few words to start up the party."

Olivia looked around the room crowded with her friends from Lily Rock. She took a sip of seltzer and then walked to the microphone. With a deep breath she began to speak.

"I want to thank everyone for coming today to this long overdue open house. But before we begin, I'd like to say a few words about my friend, Marla." Olivia smiled at the faces staring back at her.

"*Our* friend, Marla Osbourne," she restated, emphasizing the plural. "Without Marla I wouldn't have met any of you. Without Marla we wouldn't have this one-of-a-kind house to appreciate. But more importantly, without Marla, I'd still be an outsider."

She raised her bottle of seltzer water. "To Marla!"

"To Marla," they repeated together.

Olivia took a sip, her eyes searching the room. She found him in the back.

As people turned to each other to talk, she raised her glass over her head, smiling at him.

Michael raised his glass from the back of the room mouthing, "To us."

To us, and to coming home.

ACKNOWLEDGMENTS

Special thanks to my husband who listens to every word of every book read aloud. He comments when we walk our dogs in the morning and his insights give me inspiration to complicate the lives of all of my characters in the most intriguing ways.

To my daughter Emily who holds a vision for me and my books that I can't quite grasp myself, but every once in a while, I get a glimpse.

To Minnie and Adam Westie, my spiritual companions who happen to be dogs. They don't like Mayor Maguire but they don't hate him either.

To Christie Stratos who keeps better track of my characters than I do, and who holds me to an exacting standard of thinking, writing, and creating.

To Kate Tilton who unabashedly showed me the path

forward, using her magical spreadsheet, into the world of connecting with like-minded readers.

ABOUT THE AUTHOR

Born and raised in Los Angeles, Bonnie Hardy is a former teacher, choir director, and preacher. She lives with her husband and two dogs in Southern California.

Bonnie has published in *Christian Century*, *Presence: an International Journal for Spiritual Direction*, and with Pilgrim Press.

When not planting flowers and baking cookies, she can be found at her computer plotting her next Lily Rock mystery.

You can follow Bonnie at
bonniehardywrites.com
and on Instagram @bonniehardywrites.

facebook.com/bonniehardywrites

instagram.com/bonniehardywrites

goodreads.com/bonniehardy

bookbub.com/authors/bonnie-hardy

amazon.com/author/bonniehardy

Made in the USA
Las Vegas, NV
20 September 2021